# Reconquest: Mother Earth

## Carl Alves

End of Days Publishing
Copyright © 2014 Carl Alves
ISBN: 9798474951256

Cover art and design by Kealan Patrick Burke

Created in the United States of America
Worldwide Rights

All rights reserved. No part of this book may be reproduced, scanned, or distributed in any form, including digital, electronic, or mechanical, to include photocopying, recording, or by any information storage and retrieval system, without the prior written consent of the author, except for brief quotes used in reviews.

This book is a work of fiction. All characters, names, places, and incidents are products of the author's imagination or are used fictitiously. Any resemblance to any actual persons, living or dead, events or locales, is entirely coincidental.

# DEDICATION

*Reconquest: Mother Earth* is dedicated to my two supercool sons, Max and Alex, and my wife, Michelle, without whom this wouldn't be possible.

# ACKNOWLEDGEMENT

I would like to thank the folks at Montag Press, in particular Mara Hodges, who made this novel better in many ways, and Charlie Franco, for breathing life into this novel. Special thanks to Jamison Rock and Daniel Korzen for their technical expertise in military matters. I would like to thank the great people in the horror writing community, in particular Brett J Talley, Benjamin Kane Ethridge, and Tim Marquitz for their sage advice. An extra special thanks to the men and women who serve our country in the military, and a shout out to the Navy SEALs, who are real life superheroes.

## Chapter I

Charles Amato stared at the enclosed area. His three years of Navy SEAL training and ops could hardly prepare him for what he was witnessing.

Charles closed his eyes and shook his head. When he opened them, the impossible scene had not changed. He fought his instincts to run away. He had to take responsibility and do something.

Clutching his gun, he did not take it out. The threat wasn't immediate, and he did not want to appear hostile to the alien life forms fenced inside the motor pool storing military vehicles.

The alien nearest him was a large, stocky light-blue skinned creature whose spiky head looked oddly small in comparison to its tall, wide frame, which was over three meters in height. Its long tongue darted in and out from its sharp teeth. Four short and stocky legs supported the alien's hairless body. Its four spindly arms, each with six thin fingers, shot out in all directions.

The alien looked like it was jumping rope as it bobbed its head and shifted its weight to each of its four feet. It gazed at Charles but did not move toward him.

The second alien had a tall, angular body with a dark brown face and wide, oval eyes that looked almost human. Its pupils were the size of a quarter. Wiry tendrils just below its nose had the appearance of a long mustache except that the tendrils shifted and moved like appendages. Short, matted hair covered its head. Its mouth was located just above its neck. Two sets of

1

short, mosquito-like wings from its back flapped continuously, creating a buzzing sound.

The second alien stood on an open-air vehicle that resembled a train, except that it hovered in the air and was not supported by tracks. A trail of smoke emanated from the rear of the vehicle. The alien's upper torso stuck out, and it drove in a circle, not paying any attention to Amato.

Charles slowly stepped backward, hardly believing what he was seeing. Perhaps this was a hologram created by a computer wiz on a SEAL team, but these creatures occupied physical space and had mass.

Mentally retracing his tracks, he had returned from the base's infirmary after receiving treatment on his sprained ankle. He had injured it on a jump during HALO training when he had been trying a maneuver while falling through the air.

After getting his ankle evaluated and rewrapped, his mind had been locked in on rest and relaxation during the upcoming weekend until he had encountered this situation. First, he had heard a buzzing sound. Then, he had spotted the vehicle moving, before getting a full view of the two aliens.

Other than the sprained ankle, Charles felt fine. He was not sick, hallucinating, or delirious.

He considered his options. If they were hostile, he did not want to attract their attention. Although he was armed, he had no idea of their capabilities and did not want to find out.

He looked around but could not see anyone nearby. He felt alone and isolated, wishing there was an officer to advise him.

The two aliens continued to ignore him. How the hell did they get here? Not just to the planet Earth, but within the Navy

SEAL base on Coronado Island. They did not have a ship adequate for transport from a location thousands or millions of miles away. What did they want? They were not wearing any suits, which meant they were capable of breathing the Earth's air. They probably came from an environment similar to this one. What did it all mean? Were these two a precursor of what was to come, or had they arrived here accidentally?

The light blue alien chirped something incomprehensible. The second more human-looking alien did not reply. It tilted its head back and forth in a swaying motion. He wanted to call out and announce his presence, but the words stuck in his throat.

Charles had to do something. He was not a helpless civilian. He was a member of the most elite naval special warfare unit on the planet. It was time for him to get past his fear and act.

The second alien drove its hover-train towards the edge of the fence. The alien shook violently and screeched as its tendrils grabbed the fence.

The light blue alien began to jump up and down on its four legs and shrieked in unison with the other alien.

"What the hell?" Charles shook his head. He had to get help.

***

Navy SEAL Ensign Peter Estabrook sat behind his desk listening to the sob story of First Class SEAL trainee Pappalardo.

He had no time for this nonsense. Not everybody was cut out to be in the SEALs. Peter had discovered that firsthand when more than three quarters of his training class dropped out.

They only wanted the very best, and not everybody could cut it. He had known many good men who did not make it through training, but to whine and complain on your way out like Pappalardo was pathetic. According to Pappalardo, it was everybody else's fault but his own.

"The instructors aren't giving me a fair shake, sir," Pappalardo said. "I mean I could do this stuff. They just aren't being fair."

Peter tried to hold back his anger. He felt like grabbing the kid by his throat. If Pappalardo couldn't make it through this stage of the training, there was no way he would make it through Hell Week, where many strong men folded under the pressure.

"I can assure you that none of the trainers have treated you unfairly," Peter said. "We only accept the best and don't make apologies for our high standards. I am sure that there are other careers within the US Navy that would be more suitable for you."

"Hey, I can be a SEAL, sir," insisted Pappalardo. "I'm better than a lot of these other guys. They ain't got nothin' on me."

Peter gritted his teeth. "You have some kind of nerve, Pappalardo. You come into my office making all kinds of demands. I was trying to let you off easy, but you want to push it. Do you have any idea of what it means to be a SEAL? Do you?"

Pappalardo stammered but did not reply.

"Let me tell you, son, I have served as a Navy SEAL in two wars and more combat missions than I can remember. It means sitting in a lake for hours hoping you don't get discovered, waiting to ambush your enemy. It means diving off of a plane four miles up in the air and trying to land on a moving target. It means going into enemy territory in the middle of a firefight and rescuing a POW. Do you have any idea what it would be to have an Al Qaeda officer interrogate you? You make me sick. Do the right thing and drop out, because I can assure you that things will get worse, and you'll experience hell unlike anything you've ever known. I'll start the paperwork to get you transferred. Go pack your bags."

Pappalardo started to argue, but Peter ushered him out of his office. He shut the door and returned to his desk.

Thinking of Pappalardo made his stomach turn. Being treated like dirt was the norm in the Navy SEAL program. That had been going on since JFK had first commissioned the teams. It was necessary because battlefield conditions were worse than training conditions. In his day, nobody complained to the officers unless they lost a limb.

A knock on the door caused Peter to groan. If that was Pappalardo again, he was going to strangle the kid.

"Come in."

First Class Torpedoman Charles Amato stood at the door. His face was flushed, and he was perspiring heavily. He shook as he spoke. "Sir, I have a situation that requires your immediate attention."

Peter sighed. "What's the problem?"

"Sir, I need you to come with me immediately." Amato's voice wavered.

Peter's face tightened. "Gain control of yourself. What's the problem?"

"Sir, I can't even begin to describe what I witnessed by the vehicle storage area. Please follow me."

"This better be good," Peter said.

"Sir, this is a matter of national security."

Peter put on a light jacket and walked out of the building. His senses were immediately alerted to a change in the air as they walked through the base. It was nothing tangible. It felt like the onset of a major storm, except that the skies were cloudless, and it was a perfectly sunny day. The base looked like any ordinary college campuses, save for the drab buildings and lack of color.

Amato breathed heavily as they walked. He had known Charles Amato for three years and had always found the kid to be mentally and emotionally stable. He had seen Amato perform quite admirably in training when they went to Nova Scotia in the depths of the Canadian winter.

An eerie buzzing noise grew louder. "What's that?"

Amato had a tremor in his voice. "You'll see."

They turned around the bend and approached the motor pool. When he first saw them, Peter was too stunned to speak. It took him a minute to finally say, "What the hell is this?"

"Sir, I have no idea. My guess is that they are alien life forms."

*Alien life forms.* The words hung in the air as if frozen by liquid nitrogen. *Of course, they're alien life forms, dummy*, Peter felt like saying. *Do they look like they came from the San Diego Zoo?*

"This is insane," Peter muttered. The air around him seemed to tighten.

"I agree, sir." Amato approached the fence and looked closely at the alien on top of the vehicle. "They don't seem to be trying to communicate with us?"

Peter stood next to Amato as the two aliens chirped. The large, squatty alien with the eight limbs had a shrill, high-pitched voice, while the alien with the tendrils that resembled a mustache spoke in a flat, monotone voice.

"Maybe they don't know how to communicate with us," Peter replied in a low voice. "Perhaps they're as confused about the situation as we are."

The large, light blue alien jumped up and down on its many legs. The earth shook underneath it. It tilted its spiky head and issued a loud cry as its tongue swirled in the air. It then looked at the alien in the vehicle, who appeared to be nodding.

After observing for some time, Peter asked, "Amato, have you tried to initiate contact with the alien subjects?"

Amato shook his head. "I didn't know what to do, sir, so I observed their actions, much like we are doing now. Instead of trying to initiate communication, I went to find you. Should I have tried to talk to them?"

Peter shook his head. "What you did was fine." Peter stepped forward. "I am Ensign Peter Estabrook of the United States Navy. You have landed in Coronado, California at a US naval facility. We would like to help you in any way possible, but we need to know your intentions."

Still inside of his vehicle, the smaller alien approached the fence. He spoke something incomprehensible as his mustache flailed wildly.

"I guess we don't speak the same language," Peter said.

"So, what do you think they want?"

Peter's face tightened. "How should I know? I'm as lost as you are." He continued to watch in lurid fascination. "You know what I've been wondering since I got here?"

"What's that, sir?"

"Why are these two alien creatures staying within the fence? It should not be difficult to leave, especially for the one in the vehicle."

Amato frowned. "I don't know, sir. Perhaps they feel the barrier is more impenetrable than it actually is."

"If I landed on a foreign planet and found myself in a cage or an enclosed area, I would try to find a way out. Thus far, these two haven't shown any inclination to escape.

"Well, we can't stand here all day waiting for something to happen. This is going to be big, Amato. Real big."

Peter took out his cell phone and called Lieutenant Mitch Grace. He had more confidence in Mitch than any man alive, but what would Mitch do when he saw these aliens?

*\*\**

Mitch Grace worked the grill in his kitchen like a seasoned professional, whipping up hash browns, sausage, and eggs on his cast-iron skillet. Normally he would not cook such an elaborate breakfast, but this morning he was not dining alone.

The scent wafted through the small apartment. Wearing her powder blue bathrobe, Deborah kissed him lightly on the back of his neck. Her long brown hair was still damp from taking a shower. "What did I do to deserve you, Mr. Grace?" She peeked over his shoulder. "You're too good to me."

"That's Lieutenant Grace to you. I'd like to refute your statement, but as the forefather of our great nation once said, I cannot tell a lie." He turned and gave her a kiss.

"Smells great."

"I'm using a special recipe I learned when I was out in Guam, lots of exotic spices. In a few minutes this bountiful feast will be all yours. Well, yours and mine." Mitch lowered the flame on the burner and began setting the table. "In that case, you'll get nothing. This was a test and you failed miserably."

"What are you going to do, take a stripe away from me?"

"I just might," Mitch replied. "I know people in the Navy."

"Fortunately, the rest of the Navy doesn't take the SEALs seriously. We think you're a bunch of yahoos."

They sat down to eat on the cozy wooden kitchen table. Mitch savored every bite, much better than anything he had eaten in Afghanistan. It felt strange being home after completing his second tour of duty. He had arrived in San Diego last night. Deborah had picked him up at the airport. They spent so much time away from each other, it was hardly ideal for a successful relationship. Deborah, a naval intelligence officer, had recently spent time in the Persian Gulf. Besides being his significant other, her high level of clearance in the navy allowed her to be privy to his missions.

Their time apart had been torture. In the middle of the war zone, no matter how tough things got, thinking of Deborah always pulled him through.

Upon his return, all Mitch wanted was a good meal and a good bottle of wine. He and Deborah had gone out to eat at one of their favorite restaurants in Little Italy. It felt so good to be back home, certainly better than wearing heavy gear in sweltering heat.

As they were doing dishes, he said, "Maybe we should do it. You know, tie the knot, make it official. I wouldn't make you change your name if you didn't want to."

Deborah put down the wet dishrag. "We've been down this road before. What kind of marriage can we have if each of us is going to be in Timbuktu for God knows how long? You know I love you. I absolutely do, but being in a relationship with you is trying. There are nights when I can't sleep because I'm worried sick that some terrorist is going to ignite a bomb and kill you."

Deborah had been married and divorced once. Her ex-husband was a car salesman who had not been able to handle her being away so often, finding solace with another woman. She had explained to Mitch that she had been young and naïve, thinking her ex-husband would love her enough to stick with her even when her schedule got difficult. To her credit, she made the divorce quick and painless, and moved on with her life.

"If that happened would you be any less heartbroken if we weren't married?"

"No." Deborah closed her eyes. "But my idea of getting married would mean to raise a family and have a house with a white picket fence. When I made my career choice, I knew that would be difficult. I've already tried once unsuccessfully. If we're going to be married, I don't want to be away from you for so long."

"Then I'll quit."

"I don't want you to quit. You're the best of the best. It would be selfish for me to let you quit just so that I could have you at home. What you do is more valuable than anything you could do in the private sector or in another branch of the military."

"And all this time I thought you hated us SEALs. What did you say the first time we met? All we do is smash and bash everything in front of us?"

Deborah smiled. "But you do it so well."

"Maybe I don't have to quit. I just finished my second tour. They won't send me back again unless I petition for a third tour, not to mention the war efforts are winding down. I could become a full-time instructor. If now isn't a good time to get married, then when is?"

Deborah shook her head. "I don't know."

Mitch sensed he had struck a nerve. "You have to concede that the timing is good."

"You know the statistics. Most SEAL marriages don't last more than a few years."

"We'll make it work. I love you."

"Yeah, but who knows what the future will bring?" Deborah asked.

Mitch gestured wildly with his hands. "We'll deal with the future later. Let's deal with the here and now. So, are we going to do this?"

"Maybe."

"Maybe? I just argued a great case, counselor, and all you could give me is a maybe."

Deborah asked questions about the logistics of a wedding, and Mitch had an answer for each of her concerns.

"So, is this a proposal?"

Mitch pulled out a one carat diamond ring from his pants pocket. Just then his phone rang. Only important calls came in on this cell phone.

Mitch felt torn between love and duty. He searched Deborah's eyes.

"Answer it," she said after the second ring.

He answered. For nearly a minute he did not say anything. "Okay…Can you tell me what it is? It's happening right now…I'll be there." Mitch frowned and turned to Deborah. "This isn't happening the way I planned it."

She chuckled. "Does it ever? So, what's the emergency?"

Mitch shrugged. "I don't know. It was Peter Estabrook. He said that it was an extreme emergency involving national security. Whatever's going on has to be huge. Estabrook sounded…scared."

"Huh. That's not reassuring."

Deborah's cell phone rang, and she answered. After thirty seconds she hung up. "Well, it looks like whatever this emergency is, I'm involved too."

"Let's go to the base. I'll drive." He put the diamond ring back in his pocket. It would have to wait.

After putting on their uniforms, Mitch and Deborah hardly spoke on the drive to the naval base. Estabrook had not given much detail on the phone, which meant the situation was grave.

He put on a news station. The governor of California was giving a speech on his plan to fix California's economy.

As they pulled into the base, he asked Deborah, "Are you ready for this?"

"I certainly hope so."

## Chapter II

Mitch's eyes went wide as he drove through the entrance and spotted armed guards scattered throughout the naval base. Peter Estabrook was waiting for him. After exiting the car, he and Deborah separated. She had her own briefings to attend.

Mitch followed Estabrook to the motor pool. As they walked, Estabrook briefed him.

Mitch's jaw dropped. "Holy mother of God." It was one thing to hear about the two creatures, and it was an entirely different thing to witness them. Despite himself, he shivered. Real live aliens, here on the base. This wasn't a Hollywood movie set or some elaborate hoax; this was the real deal.

When Mitch reached the metal chain-link fence, the shorter, more human-looking alien with the wild mustache flew its hover vehicle toward him, stopping near Mitch as it reached the outer edge of the fence. An acrid smell emanated from the vehicle, causing Mitch to cough. He backed away and continued to cough until he was able to breathe regularly again. Mitch stared at the fenced-in area. Not sure if it was a visual trick, it seemed darker inside of the fence than outside.

The alien's tendrils gripped the fence. Its entire body shook as it shouted at Mitch. While he maintained his position, the alien continued shouting until it appeared to tire out. Too bad he couldn't communicate with it.

Estabrook continued briefing him, but Mitch had tuned him out as soon as he saw the aliens. He mentioned something about a meeting being held shortly to deal with the situation. They had already been in contact with senior military officials. For now, Mitch had no interest in doing anything other than staring at the aliens.

The second alien approached him. Its eight appendages appeared more like four arms and four legs than spider legs. It was more than double the size of the first alien.

"What are we going to do with you?" Mitch asked.

The mustached alien bobbed its head, its wings continuing to beat. It had to have a more advanced bio-system than a hummingbird, which had to feed constantly in order to maintain its energy as it flapped its wings.

Estabrook tugged at his arm. "Lieutenant Grace, we're meeting in two minutes regarding the visitation." Mitch nodded. He told a guard, "If anything happens, let me know right away."

"Yes, sir."

"What kind of shit did we step into, Pete?" Mitch asked.

"I really don't know, sir. But I think this will be the day that changes everything."

"You might be right."

Upon entering the Quarter Deck, they made a pit stop at the weapons locker, where they each took pistols, just in case. They entered a large conference room. Sitting inside were a number of people including his almost fiancée Deborah. Bewildered expressions and nervous murmurs permeated the room.

"Lieutenant Grace, you are the most senior officer here," Estabrook said. "Would you like to take the lead?"

Mitch nodded. "Ensign Estabrook, please brief everybody in the room regarding the events that led to the discovery of the two alien subjects." When he was finished, Mitch thanked him.

"Ensign Gomez, can you tell us about the chain of communication regarding today's events?"

Marisol Gomez, a public affairs officer, nodded. "The chain of command has been followed for this incident. All of the official people, up to and including POTUS, have been made aware of the extraterrestrial presence. An effort has been made to conceal any such knowledge from the press. Admiral Wilson and the Secretary of State are en route to the base."

Mitch breathed deeply. It would not be long before higher authority figures arrived. Until then he had to make sure nothing bad happened, which was like saying he had to plug a hole in a dam with a cork. "So, what do we know about our friends?"

"They seem to be able to survive in our atmosphere," Deborah said.

Mitch nodded. "True. However, I noticed the color of the air is darker in their immediate vicinity. It's also more difficult to breathe."

"You get close enough to those buggers, and you start choking," Estabrook said.

"It's possible they're emitting a harmful vapor when they breathe," speculated Sam Mapp, a resident scientist. "We inhale oxygen and exhale carbon dioxide. Perhaps when they are respiring our atmosphere, they are emitting another gaseous combination. Another possibility is that hovercraft the one alien had and vapor it was emitting, possibly modifying the surrounding atmosphere. I would like to analyze the air inside the fence."

"We'll arrange that," Mitch said. "But first we have to estimate the threat level of the visitors. What about transportation? I'm not an aviation expert, but it would seem impossible that they could make a journey requiring light years on the small alien's buggy. Any guesses?"

"Perhaps they have some sort of beaming mechanism they use for long distance transport," Lori Patton, a communications officer, said.

"Sort of like in one of those sci-fi television shows," Mitch mused.

"Anything is possible," Patton agreed.

"Pete, I want a complete check along the perimeter to see if we can find a device they might use for transportation. What about talking to them?"

"We have attempted several forms of communication," Mapp said. "We tried a variety of frequencies and signals consisting of mathematical formulas and logic quotients that NASA has used on satellites and unmanned probes in case the vessel comes in contact with an alien life form. Thus far the visitors have not responded."

"I don't know that I want to talk to them," Estabrook said. "I have a bad feeling about these two. Especially the little one."

Deborah frowned. "You know nothing about them. They may be here to help us."

"Maybe, but I would still rather see them gone. You only saw the video footage. Up close, it's a whole different story."

"How could you say you would like to see them gone," Mapp protested. "We have an incredible, once in a lifetime opportunity to learn by studying these beings."

17

Mitch held up his hand. "I understand your scientific interests, but right now, our primary concern is security. In what ways can they harm us? Do they pose a threat? We need data to analyze on these creatures to determine this threat level. That's what I want you to focus on."

"Well, they seem harmless enough," Mapp said. "They're staying inside the fence. If they were looking to harm us, they would have escaped by now."

Mitch sat back in his chair. "I've been thinking about that. The natural response for a person in that situation would be find a way out. Certainly, if they are capable of something as sophisticated as deep space travel, then jumping the fence should be no problem. Yet they stay there, walking around, circling the perimeter. Any theories?"

"Maybe they're afraid of us," Deborah offered.

Mitch looked into her deep brown eyes before responding. He was glad to have her here, not just because of his personal feelings for her. Deborah had great intuition and remarkable intelligence. Still, in this case, he disagreed with her. "I don't think so. The little one went right up to the fence and stared at me. That hardly seems like something it would do if it were afraid. It's something else."

"Like what?" Deborah asked.

Mitch pursed his lips. "I don't know. Maybe they can't. I'm not talking physically. The larger alien looks like it could rip apart the fence with its limbs. Maybe they aren't allowed to, and they're waiting for us to open the gate for them."

This opened a number of debates. Mitch excused himself. There was an urgent phone call waiting for him from General McDermott.

"Lieutenant Grace, I understand you have a very serious situation on your hands, one involving two extraterrestrial beings." McDermott's voice carried an authoritative tone. Without having met the man, Mitch could picture him in his mind: sharp features, eagle eyes, penetrating stare. He had met more than his share during his time in the service.

Mitch looked into the room for Deborah. She was engaged in a heated exchange with Peter Estabrook. "You understand that correctly, sir."

"I will be leaving momentarily to join the party. What I am about to tell you is highly confidential. Do you understand that, Lieutenant Grace?"

"Yes, General. I understand."

"Good. This isn't the first time that we've been visited," said General McDermott. "I don't know for certain if these are related to the previous alien visitations, but I'm guessing they are. If so, they are extremely dangerous. Before the situation gets out of hand, you must exterminate the two aliens."

Mitch's heart was racing. He closed his eyes and tried to regulate his breathing. "You want me to kill them."

McDermott's voice began to take on a desperate quality. "You heard me right, Lieutenant. You don't want to play games with these boys. I know them all too well. They can do serious damage to the good citizens of this country. Before anything like that happens, you have to kill them."

Mitch shook his head in disbelief. "I'm sorry, sir, but I can't do that in good conscience. The two aliens have shown no hostility."

"Grace, there is no discussion here. This is an order."

"All I know about you is the voice on the phone. I don't know who you are, or if you have the authority to make that call. If you want me to take that action, then I need to hear it from one of my commanding officers."

"Fine, Grace. Go ahead and play the good soldier. Who's your CO?"

Mitch gave him his chain of command in the proper order.

"You'll be getting that call soon enough." A click sounded on the other end.

Mitch rubbed his eyes before returning to the conference room. In a matter of hours his whole life had been turned upside down. He thought he had been prepared for every eventuality. Now he was having doubts.

When he returned to the room, he addressed everybody. "Any decisions that are going to be made regarding our two friends will be out of our hands soon. The best thing to do is to sit tight and wait."

Deborah gazed at him. She seemed to be picking up on his apprehension. "What was that all about?"

Mitch smiled. "Just a concerned general. Nothing to worry about."

"So, we're not going to do anything?" Estabrook asked.

"Not unless or until they force us to take action," Mitch answered. "Until then we wait for the reinforcements to arrive."

Estabrook shook his head and turned around on his swivel chair. Mitch knew that inaction did not sit well with Estabrook. If he had received the call from the general, Mitch had no doubt he would have followed those orders.

Mitch was no pacifist. He had inflicted many casualties on various missions. Among the SEAL teams he commanded, he was known for having no fear and taking it to the enemy with ruthless aggression, but he wasn't about to start an intergalactic war without having a damned good reason.

After more debating, the conversations came to a halt when Charles Amato entered the room. "Sir, we have company."

## Chapter III

Mitch took a deep breath as he followed Amato out of the conference room. He was in a no-win situation. Since he was only temporarily in charge, whatever actions he took would be heavily scrutinized. He did not know how to deal with aliens. Up until an hour ago, he did not believe they existed.

Wearing his naval uniform with his tightly cropped brown hair, Amato was stone-faced as they left the building. Mitch coughed as soon as he stepped outside. The atmosphere had changed. The air was both darker and denser.

As they walked past the training facility and firing ranges, Mitch said in-between coughs, "So tell me about the visitor, Amato."

"This one's very different from the first two, sir."

Mitch waited for him to elaborate. "How different? Size, color, appearance, smell? Give me some specifics."

"Physically this one is smaller than the others, and it is different in the aspects that you mentioned, sir. But it's more than just that."

Extracting information from Amato was like pulling weeds. "Be specific."

"This one actually talks, sir."

Mitch raised his brows.

"I guess the other two speak in their own language, but the new alien can communicate in English."

"Hmm. Did you speak to it?"

"Briefly, sir. I think it was trying to gain information from me. I told it that I would be right back. I couldn't get myself to talk to the alien."

"That's all right, Amato. If it's any consolation, I'm not sure what I'm going to say to it. So, how did it get here?"

"I don't know, sir."

"What do you mean, you don't know?"

"From one moment to the next it just appeared, sir."

"It materialized out of thin air?"

"That's affirmative, sir."

As they rounded a corner, Mitch spotted a small, floating fur ball behind the fence. His heart beat rapidly and sweat dripped from his forehead. He could hardly believe that he was about to speak with an extra-terrestrial being.

Mitch had never seen anything so peculiar as this third alien. Even the first two looked normal in comparison. It was less than three feet in height and was suspended in the air. It did not have wings but kept itself afloat. It had two narrow, raccoon eyes that were deep black with white circles around them. Dark gray fur covered its body from head to toe. Mitch had a hard time discerning its facial features, which were masked by fur. It had four short limbs with long, razor-sharp claws attached to them.

Mitch jumped back when it moved like a lightning bolt from one side of the motor pool to the other. It moved so quickly that it seemed to disappear from its original spot and reappear in its new location.

Mitch stood at the fence, not sure of what he should say or do.

"Greetings, my friend from Earth." The alien spoke in a low and monotonous tone as if it were concentrating on getting every word right.

"Hello, I am Lieutenant Mitch Grace of the naval branch of the military of the United States of America of the planet Earth." Mitch felt foolish going through this lengthy introduction. He figured the alien had knowledge of the planet. The fact that it knew the language was proof enough. "As a representative of both my country and my planet, I welcome you."

The alien tilted its head slightly. "Thank you for your welcome. My name would be imperceptible to your tongue so I will not burden you with trying to remember it. My position is that of the Minister of Science of the Acantalinia System. I come as a representative, the first of my kind to visit your fine planet."

Mitch paused. General McDermott had told him about alien visitations in the past, and that these current visitors were likely linked to the previous ones. If McDermott was right, then the Minister of Science lied. "What brings you to my planet?"

"As part of my responsibilities as the Minister of Science, I travel to uncharted galaxies to begin the process of incorporation into the intergalactic community. It has been decided by the governing council that it is time for the planet Earth to join our community. I am here as an emissary of a world more vast than you can imagine."

Mitch felt small and inadequate. "There are representatives of my government who would be more appropriate for you to speak with, but until those individuals arrive, I am the senior most representative of my government's military forces."

"Lieutenant Mitch Grace, there is much about the universe that you need to learn. I would like to share this information with you, Lieutenant Mitch Grace. In turn there is much that I would like to ask you."

*Minister of Science.* If this alien truly held this position then its objectives should include exploration and learning, not war and colonization. Still, Mitch felt uneasy because of its peculiar voice and appearance. "I will help you in whatever manner I can."

"That is the spirit of cooperation, Lieutenant Mitch Grace. Please allow me to leave this barrier, so that we can talk up close."

Mitch stroked his chin. "I can hear you just fine where you are."

"You live on a primitive planet. There is much that your people can learn in areas such as space travel, mathematics, medicine, and transportation. I have studied your planet for some time and although you have made great strides in technological advancements over the last two hundred of your Earth years, you remain far behind."

"I like my planet the way it is."

"You should. However, improvements can be made. If you would let me out of this cage and invite me to speak with you, then you will be positively enlightened. I would like to be inside of one of your buildings."

Mitch hesitated. The Minister of Science was not in a cage. The vehicle storage area was fenced in, but there was nothing covering the top. Based on the way the Minister bolted from one place to another, it should have no problem getting out, so why was it asking to be let out? "Why are you asking for my permission? You could escape at your own will."

The Minister's facial expression become softer, but Mitch could not tell if it was a smile or an expression of anger. "I would not go somewhere that I am not wanted. I can only help you if you want help."

Mitch frowned. That sounded like an evasive answer, something a politician might say. "I really am not a person of great importance. You should be speaking to a more suitable representative of my nation. If you wait here, I will go back and make phone calls to see if I can find someone more appropriate."

"I would like to speak with you, Lieutenant Mitch Grace. You have well above average intelligence, and it is you that I choose to give my message."

"With all due respect, I am not worthy of this information."

Mitch's head turned in a zigzag motion as the Minister of Science shot like a projectile across the vehicle storage area. The alien moved with frightening velocity, but Mitch could not determine its source of propulsion.

For the first time since they had been talking, Mitch noticed the original alien visitors. Initially, they had been moving around and making considerable noise. Since the Minister of Science arrived, they had been sitting silently on the ground.

The Minister stopped moving. "Please return quickly, Lieutenant Mitch Grace."

As Mitch walked away, he tried not to show his fear. Although the aliens had not made any overtly hostile moves, he feared what they were capable of doing.

Before leaving, Mitch gathered Charles Amato and the other SEALs guarding the vehicle storage area. He spoke in hushed tones. "Listen to me. Under no circumstances whatsoever are you to let out the aliens."

"But, sir, there is nothing preventing them from leaving," Amato said. "They can just lift the latch and pull the gate open or climb out."

"I understand that. Just follow these instructions. I want absolutely no deviations. Do you understand?"

"Yes, sir," they collectively responded.

"The Minister of Science, the small alien that hovers in the air, may try to engage you in conversation and ask you to let him out, but you are not to do so. If anything unusual, and I realize this entire ordeal is beyond unusual, but if anything odd happens, contact me immediately."

Mitch could hardly explain his own actions. He was operating on gut instinct. He returned to the building where he and the other officers had been meeting. Thoughts buzzed in his head. Amato had told him earlier the Minister of Science had just appeared. *But how?* Extraterrestrials landing on this planet should require elaborate space vessels. These three apparently teleported.

When he entered the Quarter Deck, Deborah was walking toward him. Without thinking, he hugged and kissed her. He knew this type of behavior would be highly frowned upon, even reprimanded, but he didn't care. He felt this horrible foreboding and wanted Deborah to make sure she knew how he felt about her. She always made him feel better, despite the circumstances.

"What's going on, Mitch?"

He told her about his conversation with the Minister of Science and his concerns about the alien asking to leave the cage.

"So, what are we going to do? You know the general I was talking to on the phone?"

Deborah nodded.

"He wants me to kill the aliens."

"What?"

Mitch grinned. "And you think I'm paranoid."

"Why is it that you men are so distrustful of these aliens? Estabrook sounded like he wanted to kill them, too. You guys watch too many movies. I'm sure not all aliens have the intention of taking over our planet."

"But what if this one does?" Mitch asked.

"So, you think we should kill the rest of them?"

"No, but I think we should be prepared. I'm going to tell Estabrook to get some high-powered weaponry, just in case."

Deborah followed Mitch into the elevator. Neither spoke. Inside of the conference room small groups had converged with scientists on one side, public relations and communications people huddled in another group, and intelligence officers off to another corner. Estabrook and the SEALs stood front and center. Mitch could tell by the perpetual scowl that he wore, that Estrabrook wanted to be in the middle of the action.

"Pete, come with me for a second." Mitch briefed him on the arrival of the third alien. "I think we should be prepared in case of hostile actions by the extraterrestrials. I want you to gather men and heavy artillery. Get grenades, rocket launchers, automatic weapons. If something happens, on my order, I want you to launch a counter assault. Hopefully it won't come down to that. But, just in case…"

Estabrook nodded. "We'll be ready."

"Good."

Once he returned to the conference room, he resumed the meeting. Sam Mapp asked to be given the opportunity to talk to the Minister of Science. Mitch saw a crazy gleam in his eye, and he would bet that Mapp would give his first born just to talk to the alien. Mitch denied his request. He could picture Mapp letting the Minister out.

Mitch fielded questions while watching the clock. Each tick brought him closer to the freedom from making decisions. He only hoped his superiors had the wisdom to make sound judgments.

Mitch had an ominous feeling when he received a call on the radio. Under the current circumstances, any call would either be bad news or additional complications.

Mitch recognized the panicked voice of First Class Torpedoman Charles Amato. Loud roars sounded in the background. "Sir, we have a critical situation at ground zero."

"What's going on, Amato?"

"A new batch of aliens have appeared and are still materializing. They're overrunning us. We're trying to hold them back, but there are too many and they're too powerful. Holy shit!" What sounded like an airplane roared on the radio, followed by machine gun fire in the background. "This situation is out of control."

"Are they attacking?" Mitch thumped his foot furiously.

"What the hell…aahh."

That was the last he heard from Amato.

Mitch yelled, "We need reinforcements immediately! We are under attack."

Mitch ran out of the room, pulling out the service pistol he had taken from the weapons locker in the Quarter Deck. Based on what he heard, it would do little good. He called Estabrook on the radio as he ran down the stairs. "Pete, whatever you got, we need it now."

"What's the situation?" Estabrook asked.

"The aliens are attacking."

"Okay, we're coming. Try to hold them off."

"My understanding is that there are many more now."

"Oh, Christ," said Estabrook. "All right, we'll be there."

By the time he finished talking to Estabrook, he was outside. A mammoth winged creature flew overhead. It was dark blue and had two sets of wings. Mitch ducked as it shot out streaming blue jets from its eyes. The shot obliterated a parked military vehicle.

Mitch ran toward the motor pool. Before he got there, the blue alien with four arms and four legs was hovering over a guard whose face was covered with blood. The alien hammered its fists into the defenseless man. Mitch fired several shots from his pistol. The first shot hit the alien in the shoulder, causing it to turn around. The next shot hit it in the throat and the final two went into the alien's head. It fell to the ground.

Mitch ran toward what he believed was the source of the alien entrance onto the planet. Acrid smoke and the heat of flames covered the air. Nearby, a shed was on fire. Two more dark blue, winged aliens flew past him like fighter jets.

He stopped in revulsion at the sight of a giant slug, twelve feet in length with light green skin, which had the overall appearance of a mass of fatty tissue, swallowing a soldier whole. The man's entire upper torso was inside the slug. His legs, which were immobile, hung outside.

Mitch was going to shoot but decided against it. The man was certainly already dead, and he did not have the time or the bullets to waste.

Near the storage area, a number of SEALs and other Navy personnel were engaged in a firefight with the aliens. The humans were losing badly.

A winged alien deftly avoided machine gun fire and picked up a soldier with its talons. Mitch watched in horror as it tore the man's head off. The head dropped to the street and rolled along the asphalt.

Not far away, a Jeep was driving with two men in the back firing machine guns. A dark blue winged alien soared from above with high speed and shot out a blast from its eyes. The Jeep exploded upon impact, killing its passengers.

Mitch cried out. His morning had started off so well. He was finally going to propose to Deborah, and now this.

He continued moving, his head clouded with confusion. What could he do to counter this massacre?

When he finally reached the fenced in area, it was as if the gates of hell were opening. Every few seconds, a new alien appeared at the opposite end of the fence. They were coming from a milky, semi-translucent square about ten feet in height and twelve feet in length. Different species of aliens appeared, all looking capable of inflicting considerable damage. Some aliens came out in land or air vehicles. Others flew or traveled on foot. One alien had the appearance of a moving plant. Its skin was the color of grass and it appeared to have a long stem with tendrils that swirled in the air.

A group of aliens working in concert overtook three soldiers firing machine guns. He still had not seen Estabrook and his men. What difference would it make? They wouldn't be able to stop the aliens. They had to regroup.

The best thing that Mitch could do was contact others in the Navy and other branches of the military so they could mobilize against the aliens.

An alien with the appearance of an armor-plated elephant without a trunk charged at Mitch. It was bronze and had massive, hoofed feet. It gave a deafening roar.

"Christ almighty," Mitch muttered. It would trample him if he did not do something soon. He took a shot at the elephantine alien, but the bullet bounced off. He turned and ran as fast as he could, hoping he could outrun the large predator.

The elephant alien emitted another loud roar. The ground trembled as the creature followed him. He glanced back. It was going to overtake him. As he turned to make a final effort to evade it, he collided with one of the alien's large legs. Time slowed as he spiraled in the air. He did a seven hundred twenty-degree rotation. Chaos surrounded him in every direction. He had no control over his body as he tumbled to the ground.

Mitch landed on his hip with a crunching thud. He let out a cry of agony as searing pain crippled his body. His instinct was to get up and move out of the alien's path, but he could not move.

He screamed. He saw what was about to happen but was powerless to stop it. His entire body lifted off of the ground as the alien's massive leg connected with the surface. One more step and it would crush him. Desperately, he tried to turn his body, but could not evade the armor-plated ET. Its hoofed foot connected full force with his shoulders and the back of his head. Spinning all around him. His face slammed against the asphalt. Gravel filled his mouth. His eyes closed as darkness enveloped him.

## Part 2
## Chapter IV
## Five Years Later

Mitch opened his eyes and let out a low groan. He closed them quickly, the brightly lit room scalding his eyes, and released another groan. He tried to move his hand, but it would not respond.

Mitch opened his left eyelid slowly. He tried to look around but did not have the strength to move his head more than a few centimeters.

His lower lip trembled involuntarily. Where was he? He felt pain, soreness, and intense sluggishness. Every time he attempted to move, his slow mind and weak body thwarted him.

He slightly curled his fingers. It was not much, but it was more than he could do a few minutes ago. He made a great deal of effort to elevate his head, but still could not.

For now, he gave up trying to move. He was expending too much effort and not getting results. Instead, he stared at the white ceiling.

Half-formed memories flooded Mitch's head. What had happened?

*Mitch was back in the naval base in Kuwait. He had been called in by his commander — he couldn't remember the man's name. His commander told Mitch that they needed to overtake and control the Dartayun Dam, a major hydroelectric source an hour northeast of Baghdad. Intel indicated that Fedayeen and Baathist loyalists were going to bomb the dam and flood Baghdad downstream.*

34

*This would be a joint mission between Mitch's SEAL team and a squad of Polish Grom commandos. Prior to the strike, Mitch and his team tried to simulate scenarios that could happen when they tried to overtake the Dartayun Dam.*

*Two nights before the mission, Mitch met with the Polish squad leader. They split the teams up and located several key locations within the structure to hit first. Mitch did not like the idea of collaborating with the Polish commandos. He was unfamiliar with their tactics, and familiarity was one of the things that made his team excel. In addition, Mitch had latitude in his missions to employ whatever tactics necessary to accomplish his goals. If their methods did not mesh with that of the Grom team, then this could lead to trouble.*

*The night before striking the dam, Mitch felt the normal tightening in his stomach he got before a major operation. He hardly slept that evening, going over all eventualities, even though he knew that once the action started, anything was possible.*

*They set into action the following evening. It was a clear, moonless night, too quiet for Mitch's liking.*

*Four Pave Low special-operations helicopters took off from the base in Kuwait. It took five hours to reach their destination. On the way to the dam, each helicopter had to be fueled in midair by a KC-130 tanker.*

*The beginning of the mission turned out to be dicey. The helicopters had to hover over the dam while weaving through a maze of high-powered lines. When the choppers established their position, the SEALs and Groms rappelled down thick ropes and onto the upper level of the dam with extreme stealth. Speed was of the essence.*

*Mitch was the first one down, setting the pace for the others. He hit the ground and sprinted with his machine gun held at chest level.*

*He had the layout of the dam memorized and knew precisely where to go. At the end of the walkway, he reached the power plant control room and found an alien with blue skin and eight limbs screaming at the top of its lungs.*

*Mitch shook his head violently. Alien creatures in Iraq? That made no sense.*

*He broke through the door. Inside were two dam operators. He yelled surrender in Arabic repeatedly with his machine gun raised and aimed at them. He scanned the room and found no alien creatures, but of course there wouldn't be any.*

*The two dam operators jumped out of their chairs. It was times like these that Mitch had a hard time telling apart the good guys from the bad guys. These Iraqis were two frightened men caught in the wrong place at the wrong time. Being a combat veteran, Mitch knew that warfare was not all black and white. Although these two control room operators were not likely to fight back, Mitch had to be wary. The bad guys did not always wear black hats. However, if he saw the blue alien, he would shoot it on sight.*

*Two more SEALs entered the room. They apprehended and tied up the operators. Mitch got on his radio and contacted other team members. Within minutes, they had seized control of the dam without a single bullet being fired. Within the hour, they also took an adjacent power station and several buildings within the complex, without using any gunfire. The only injury occurred when a Grom commando was hurt while rappelling from the helicopter.*

*The job was not done. They searched each building until dawn looking for explosives and potential saboteurs. Although he had reviewed the blueprint of the dam, he did not realize just how massive a structure it was until he was inside. Methodically, the SEALs and Groms searched, but did not find anything.*

*When they were done, day was breaking in Iraq. Mitch conferred with Deborah about what he was going to do next. No wait. That was impossible. He had never worked with Deborah on any mission, let alone one in Iraq during the war.*

*Since there had been no resistance, Mitch decided to free the dam operators and let them continue their work. This was not part of his original plan, but as was often the case, he had to adjust as he went along.*

*Even though the raid had been successful, the danger was not over. The threat of the Fedayeen loyalists overtaking the dam and flooding Baghdad was very real. Mitch was not about to let his guard down. For the next six days, his team patrolled the dam and the surrounding area until the regular armed forces could arrive to relieve them.*

Mitch opened his eyes and looked around this strange room that he now found himself in. He was sure he was no longer in Baghdad. He had returned from combat. He knew this because he had been with Deborah. He had proposed to her.

Mitch tried to stretch his mind and remember something, anything, about what had happened to him.

Mitch continued to try to piece back his memory, but found it taxing. Before long, he fell asleep.

Many hours later, he awoke with a fit. He clenched his hand into a loose fist. When he tried to elevate himself, his arms shook. He looked around the sterile room and knew he couldn't be in a military hospital, or for that matter any hospital he had ever seen.

Nearby him on a table was an emerald green box that had all kinds of buttons and switches. The inscription on the machine had characters, which he presumed to be numbers and letters that were unlike any human language he had ever seen. He expected to be hooked up to IV tubes, but instead he had super thin tendrils that resembled the roots of a plant that fed from the machine into various parts of his body. The whole thing looked freaky, but he did not have the strength to remove it.

He floated in and out of sleep over the next several hours. He would wake up only briefly before fatigue overwhelmed him. He felt like a baby, not having enough energy to sustain wakefulness for any significant period of time.

He jumped back in his bed in fright. His head snapped forward. He tried to scream but could only groan. He closed his eyes and opened them once more, hoping this nightmarish vision would leave.

His heart beat like a jackhammer. He was not imagining things. A gigantic alien life form hovered over him. Its skin was light green, and its torso was long and lean.

Mitch's entire body shook as he tried to cower away from it. *Alien beings.* He vaguely remembered encountering them before.

He desperately wanted to get out of the bed but was powerless to do so. He clutched the metal railings.

"Relax, Mitch Grace." The alien's soft voice reminded him of wine being poured into a glass.

The soothing voice did little to lessen his anxiety. He had to escape, but his muscles would not cooperate with the pleas from his brain.

He couldn't let the alien get to him. "P-pl-please."

"Be at ease, Mitch Grace." The alien lowered his head. "I am here to help you."

"Help," he cried out, even though he doubted there was anyone who could save him from this creature.

The alien drew back its head. "You have been through a difficult ordeal. For a great quantity of time, you have been in a sleeping state. Comatose, I believe is the correct word. But now you are coherent. This provides me great joy, Mitch Grace."

Mitch closed his eyes. He still felt weak. Maybe he had been in a bad accident and was unconscious and dreaming in a hospital bed. He opened his eyes and turned his head in revulsion when he still saw the alien.

"Please, Mitch Grace, be still. I have read about the effects of your condition. It is likely that you are feeling disorientation. Your memory must be lacking." The alien tilted its head. "Yes, poor memory and damaged body, I would surmise."

Mitch felt terrible sadness. What if he was dead? He felt like crying, but no tears would come.

The alien spoke to him in its soothing voice. "This must be difficult for you. I have little comprehension of these feelings, but I will help you. You must trust in me."

He was not sure if he should believe the alien. If he was dreaming, then it did not matter. He would play along. Maybe he could learn something. "What ha-happened?"

The alien shook his head. "I have no details of the sustaining of your injury. You were hurt, badly hurt. Trauma to the brain, edema. You have been comatose, and I have been your caretaker...doctor would be your equivalent word."

*Mitch closed his eyes and moaned as images flashed in his head. The phone call, an alert to danger, then a fence. Inside were two aliens who looked very different than the one in front of him. He tried to concentrate on his memories. A third alien, much smaller than the others, appeared. There had been something sinister about the small alien. Then there were explosions and people being torn apart.*

"How did I...get hurt?"

The alien shook its head back and forth. "I wish I could answer your question in a satisfactory manner, but I do not have this data. It was a bad time. Many humans were killed. You were caught in the war."

The word made Mitch cringe. "War?"

"Yes. It was bloody and brutal. So many dead."

Mitch closed his eyes and buried his head in his pillow.

"I should not speak of these things. After your ordeal, you should not be subjected to this."

Mitch ground his teeth. "Tell me."

"You must rest first. It is too soon. No, no. I will tell you everything, but you must rest. As your doctor, I deem it your medicine."

"Please."

"Rest now. In time. When you wake up, I will be here."

Mitch became drowsy. He closed his eyes and, within seconds, was asleep.

***

Mitch woke up convinced that he had the strangest dream of his life. He froze when his hands touched the metal rails surrounding his bed and he saw the root-like tendrils attached to his body. He slowly raised his head, saw the alien, and felt like crying. It was no dream.

"You have risen out of your sleep, Mitch Grace."

Mitch regarded the creature. Judging by the alien's sharp facial features and lack of mammary glands, he assumed the alien was male. He almost looked like a praying mantis. His thin legs looked like they could snap with ease. His hands were dainty, and he had the longest fingers Mitch had ever seen. His mouth and nose were like slits. Long, oval eyes with black pupils occupied much of his face.

"This has to be a dream," Mitch muttered.

"I understand your emotions." When the alien spoke, he sounded like he was singing. "I have done much reading on humans who wake from a coma."

"Coma?"

"Yes, my research indicates that is the appropriate term for your prior state. When humans revive from comas, they feel denial. They find it hard to accept that what they have gone through has truly taken place. Earlier you experienced anger and depression. Classic symptoms as such. Very much like the textbook indicated."

Tears welled in his eyes. His mind was slowly accepting that he was really talking to an alien. "How long have I been in a coma?"

"Let me do some quick conversions." The alien had a distant look. "Approximately five of your Earth years have passed since you have been comatose."

Mitch let out a low shriek. "Five years? Five fucking years!"

"Yes. For my species that is a brief period, but for humans it is considerable. Your average lifespan is roughly one fifth of the average lifespan of my species, so I understand your trauma."

Mitch was mortified. He wanted to fall back into a coma. "I can't believe it."

"The pleasant news is that you are alive." The alien's voice rose. "If I were to find the truth inside, I did not think that you would ever wake. I estimated your probability of survival to be 3.87%. That you are alive is a signal of your resiliency. You have made all my efforts worthwhile, Mitch Grace. Truly remarkable. I am glad that I convinced them not to discard you."

"What?"

The alien's long fingers touched his face. "I should have omitted that part. I must remember the fragility of your brain caused by edema. My sorry to you."

"Explain, please." Mitch felt nauseous.

"When I arrived on the first day, I saw death and destruction. The human dead were being discarded. I examined you and found you to be alive. They were going to disintegrate your body, but I pleaded with the Chief Medic to allow me to nurture you back to health. He told me that it was wasteful of time. I let the Chief Medic know that I have come to this planet to cure and would leave if not allowed to achieve the goals I set. You became my patient.

"Let me introduce myself. I know that you are known as Mitch Grace, which I uncovered from the metallic piece that you had on your person. You would have difficulty pronouncing my name, so I will shorten it to Sarm for your ease of calling."

"This is crazy," Mitch said.

"I fail to see why you would question the sanity of the situation."

Mitch was not sure how much more he wanted to learn. Five years had passed. From the sound of it, things had not gone well. "What happened since then?"

Sarm's smile faded. He looked down at Mitch with his big, black eyes. "I should not increase your burden at this pivotal moment in your recovery."

"Tell me. Please." Mitch reached out and touched Sarm's slender green arm. It felt leathery, and he quickly recoiled his hand.

"I am afraid your species did not fare well. It should not come with surprise. The technology from this planet is primitive. The humans never had a chance, although your people fought with valor."

Mitch's lips began to tremble as tears gathered in his eyes.

The alien was unusually quiet.

"Tell me what happened. All of it."

"I will tell you everything in time. I can see that your face grows tired. For now, I will share the summary of events. The armies of your planet united from what I have learned from your history in an unprecedented fashion. While they were planning a defense, they were overrun. The Minister of Science's forces destroyed your armies before they could fight back. It was a sad outcome, but it was filled with inevitability."

"You fucking bastards." Mitch shouted through gritted teeth.

"In approximately one half of one Earth year, the human population was one tenth of what it had been, and there was no resistance left. Your governments and fighting machines had been mostly destroyed. Many remaining people had been taken by the Minister and his forces. Most humans have become a source of free labor. I am afraid that your species no longer has control of this planet. I feel sorrow for your plight."

Mitch shook the railings on his bed with what little strength he had left. "Why? How could they do this?"

Sarm shifted his long fingers in an interlocking motion. "Why does anything like this happen? The Minister of Science wanted your planet and had the ability to take it. It is unfortunate, but Earth is not the first planet to experience involuntary occupation."

"Christ have mercy."

"Ah Christ. If my memory is correct, He would be a major deity of your planet. I have read your Bible."

Mitch rolled his eyes. "That's wonderful."

"I try to read as much of your planet's literature as possible. I have read many of your famous historical documents as well as classical writing. One can learn a great deal about a species by reading their literature."

"I don't care about that. Who's in control of the planet now?"

"Technically a council rules, but the true reality indicates the Minister of Science makes all of the vital decisions."

Feeling compelled to act, Mitch struggled to prop himself up. His arms felt like rubber.

Sarm reached out, but Mitch shrank back. "I only mean to help you, Mitch."

"I don't need your fucking help." Spit flew from Mitch's mouth. "I don't need your sympathy. I don't need anything from your kind."

Sarm backed away. "I understand your anger. To wake up after a five-year coma and find out that your species has been significantly reduced and are now subservient can be devastating to the psyche. I understand that you do not trust me since I belong to the group that bears this responsibility."

"You don't understand anything."

"Not true. My home planet has been under hostile occupation since the time of my youth. I know your hurt. I have also done research to know the theory of what you are feeling in your awakening. True, the theoretical can never match the reality."

"What do you want from me?" Mitch asked.

"Allow my assistance in your recovery. I cannot atone for the evils that were done to your people, but I can help you."

Reluctantly, Mitch extended his hand and touched Sarm's leathery skin. The alien pulled him up with ease. Mitch looked at Sarm wide-eyed, misjudging the alien's strength because of its thin frame. With his free hand, Sarm lifted the pillow and propped it under Mitch's head.

Mitch nodded, but could not bring himself to express gratitude. Sarm was one of them, one of the beings who stole his planet.

"I will give you honesty in our dealings. Your path of recovery will be difficult. A successful recovery will require exertion of the mind and body, but you have shown fortitude in coming out of your comatose state. Therefore, I have the belief that you will overcome this current shortcoming in your physical condition."

"Why bother?" Mitch closed his eyes. "What do I have to look forward to? Becoming a slave to this alien domination?"

"Life is worth living. There is an entire universe out there of which you lack knowledge. Many, many wonders that continue to fascinate. It is why I am here, to continue to learn and develop."

"I don't give a shit about the rest of the universe. I care about my own planet. I want it back."

"I fear you ask for something far more difficult to obtain than your rehabilitation."

Mitch struggled to get out of the bed, but Sarm eased him back into a reclining position. Heavy fatigue fell on him like a rain cloud as he closed his eyes.

"Pleasant dreams, Mitch Grace."

He allowed the blackness to overcome him and fell into deep sleep.

## Chapter V

"One foot in front of the other," Sarm said. "That is the way it must be done. Slowly and easily, you will make it."

Mitch grunted, sweat dripping from his body as he gripped onto a metal railing. He wore a light blue hospital gown that Sarm must have pilfered from a hospital. He trembled from exertion. "I can't do it."

"You can. I would not tell you if I did not think you were able."

On the first day of Mitch's awakening, Sarm had tried to engage him in conversation, but Mitch had been reclusive. It had been hard for him to accept that he had been in a coma while his world had been taken over, and now his only companion was a tall, slender green alien. Sarm had left him alone, only returning to check Mitch's vitals, and perform other medical tasks.

On the second day, Sarm had attempted to make him walk, but still angry and bitter, Mitch had refused to cooperate. Sarm would not relent, and by the third day, Mitch agreed to try. Now, he regretted that decision.

The alien had started off by swinging Mitch's legs across the bed. Effortlessly, he lifted Mitch, but his legs were unsteady, and he fell. After giving him a minute to recover, Sarm once more lifted him to his feet. He howled in pain, his legs shaking, but Sarm held him steadily. Mitch asked the alien to let him down, but Sarm would not let go.

Sarm then asked him to step forward.

"Just leave me alone," Mitch said.

"It is for your own good that I am doing this. What you require is...perseverance. That is the word."

"I can't do it." The floor was covered with Mitch's sweat. "Maybe tomorrow."

"Let us not put off for tomorrow that of which has the possibility of being done today. You have shown sufficient resiliency by surviving your most trying ordeal. If you are the one to do that, then you can do this. You must persevere, Mitch. Show me of what your species is capable."

A cold glint surfaced in Mitch's blue eyes. His face tightened. He grunted as he moved his left foot forward.

"Superb," Sarm shouted. "That is the action that I wanted."

Mitch closed his eyes and took a long breath. That last step had been excruciating.

"The next one will be done with more ease."

Mitch cursed loudly as he moved his left leg forward.

"That is the way. You have made it far. Now is not the time to halt."

"Bring me back to the bed," Mitch said.

Sarm shook his head. "You have not walked enough to complete my satisfaction."

"Screw you."

"Curious expression. I will have to look for it in your literature. More effort, please."

Mitch did not want to continue, but Sarm would not relent. The sterile, white walls provided him no inspiration. He stared at the curious looking alien. Although he did not care for Sarm since he was one of them, he sensed that the alien was genuinely trying to help him. He took a deep breath and continued walking.

Mitch took four tedious steps, and Sarm clapped his hands. He motioned for Mitch to continue. He took two more steps. Sarm nodded. After four more steps, Sarm gathered him in his arms. "I knew you had the fortitude inside to ensure the completion of the task."

Reluctantly Mitch thanked the alien. Without his help, Mitch would never have been able to start walking.

Sarm had explained to him how difficult his recovery would be. "Indeed. My research indicates that many of your basic functions will now become laborious. In addition, you will need to be retrained in some of your formerly routine tasks such as eating and dressing."

"I don't think so, pal."

"Denial, a classic symptom."

"Go to hell."

"Verbal abuse, another classic symptom."

Mitch wished he had a real doctor. Sarm had told him that Mitch was his first human patient. Most human physicians were located in mines and slave farms to attend to ill and injured workers. Sarm's own planet had been occupied since his youth, and he had studied to be a healer to leave his planet.

"So how did you come to my planet, anyway?"

"Although Earth has not been part of the intergalactic community, it has been studied from afar, and has been visited in secrecy. I believe there was an unintentional landing in your town of Roswell. Much data had been accumulated."

"You mean those stories of alien landings in Roswell were true."

"Indeed, they were," Sarm said.

This sparked Mitch's memory. He had been inside of a building with other people. Deborah...she had been there. A military person told him that this wasn't the first time that extraterrestrial beings had been on the planet. The man had told him to kill the aliens. Mitch sunk back into his pillow and closed his eyes. Why hadn't he listened?

Sarm peered down at Mitch. "Your face has the appearance of trouble." He grabbed Mitch's wrist and felt for a pulse. "Heartbeat is regular. What ails you?"

Drowning in despair, Mitch said nothing. He had the opportunity to end this disaster before it started and chose not to. He was responsible for the deaths of millions.

Mitch shook his head.

"Of what was I speaking? Yes, I was informed of the habitation of Earth. I was curious to interact with a new species, so I told my contact that I was interested. At the appropriate time I was to dial my locater to a set of coordinates to teleport to Earth."

"You don't need a big spaceship for travel?"

"Oh no," Sarm replied. "That would be inefficient. Teleportation is the preferred method of intergalactic travel. It must be well-coordinated from a location in a nearby solar system, or the effects can be disastrous, but I had confidence in those coordinating the journey and thus I made an agreement." Sarm's voice grew quiet. "I was not knowing that the planet would be under hostile occupation. When I arrived, many had already died. It was most fortuitous that I found you when I did, prior to your discarding."

"Thanks for picking me up out of the trash."

"It was my pleasure."

"Why didn't you think this would be a hostile takeover?"

"I had not a reason for such a thought, but I arrived to a war zone."

Mitch pursed his lips. "You said that you had to arrange for teleportation from a nearby solar system and it had to be coordinated. There was a large invasion force. How did that take place?"

"Undoubtedly the Minister of Science engaged in a large coordination effort. The undertaking must have been vast and costly, but well worth his investment."

"If you came to be a healer, then why aren't you doing that?" Mitch could not get his mind off his conversation with the general and the devastating results of his inaction.

"It is true that my hope was to deal with humans on a medical basis, but unfortunately that was not the assignment dealt for me. Instead, I study your planet's ecosystems and its various inhabitants. I study plants, trees, fish, insects, animals, but very little human interaction I fear."

"Why don't you leave?" Mitch asked, not really interested, just making conversation.

"The true answer is that you are the reason."

Mitch's brow furrowed as he regarded the alien.

"I made it my mission to see that you would survive, although I had calculated your survival probability to be small. I came here to further life, and you provided me opportunity. I could not leave while you were clinging for your existence. Now that you are awake, it has all been made worthwhile."

Mitch bit back tears. Perhaps he had misjudged Sarm. "You spent a long time on this planet just to see this through."

Sarm tilted his head back. "Five of your Earth years is a small piece of time for me. I am still young in my lifespan. The typical lifespan of my species is nearly five hundred of your Earth years."

Mitch was not prone to displaying emotions. It was not that he was stoic; he was just so in control of himself that they never showed. Now he could not control himself. All choked up, he barely managed, "Thanks."

"I did not hear you. Your vocal cords seem to be constricted. Let me perform an examination upon you."

Mitch raised his hand. "I just wanted to thank you for not leaving me."

"That is unnecessary. To not perform these duties would be a denial of who I am. Now it is time for nourishment. You will enjoy what I have prepared for you. It is a meal consisting of vegetables of my own gardening."

Sarm carried him in his arms like a small child to the dining area. Surprisingly, the food was very tasty. By the end of the meal, Mitch could barely keep his eyes open.

When Sarm insisted that he needed to rest, Mitch wasn't about to argue. As the alien gathered him in his arms and explained how tomorrow would involve rigorous therapy, and how Sarm would be strict in his ways, Mitch was half-asleep.

He planted Mitch on his bed. "Rest easy, Mitch."

## Chapter VI

Mitch continued to put one foot in front of the other. A few feet away, Sarm shouted encouragement. Learning how to walk again was one of the most difficult ordeals of his life.

As Mitch continued to exert himself, his mind wandered to the Middle East. For a moment, he was back in Iraq. With clarity, he remembered one of his missions. Mitch's SEAL team was given the task of capturing offshore Iraqi oil terminals. During the previous Gulf War, the Iraqis had attempted to blow up these terminals, which made it imperative for his team to seize them. Destroying the terminals would badly pollute the Persian Gulf and delay the cleanup and reconstruction activities. Winning the war was a foregone conclusion. Winning the peace would be a greater challenge.

The mission had been a joint effort between his SEAL team and the Polish Groms. The sound of helicopters and high-speed boats operating blitzed the calm night air as they made their way to the target.

Operating with quickness and surgical precision, the enemy did not have a chance to react. In less than one hour, naval boat crews had taken command of Iraq's two major offshore oil terminals in the Northern Persian Gulf, along with two valve stations, a pipeline, and an onshore pumping station. Mitch's team then began the process of clearing a path for the warships and cargo vessels that would be accessing the Persian Gulf into Iraq.

Mitch had thirty total hours of sleep during the next eight days. This was one of the most critical operations of the war and there was no time for it. Luckily, Mitch operated well without sleep.

He led a small flotilla of high-speed Mark five boats and rigid hulled inflatable vessels through the narrow Khawr Az Zubayr waterway, which connected Umm Qasr, the only deep-water port in Iraq, to the Persian Gulf.

Clearing the waterway proved to be far more difficult than capturing the oil terminals. On the second day, the team found three vessels filled with mines. Mitch and his SEALs were on edge at all times since some of these ships had Italian Mantra mines, which could sink American and British warships traveling through the region.

The Khawr Az Zubayr waterway was a graveyard of sunken and abandoned vessels. Over the next eight days, Mitch's team searched through eighty-seven ships. The tides rose and fell, and in the process exposed dangerous shoals. On the fourth day, gale force winds exceeding fifty-five knots hammered Mitch's fleet. Visibility was either limited or non-existent. To make matters worse, Iraqi death squads opened fire on the fleet. On more than one occasion, Mitch thought for sure they wouldn't make it out of this alive, and that he would never see Deborah again. He prayed silently to make it through. Not especially religious in his upbringing, Mitch found himself turning to God more frequently in these trying times.

Mitch asked the men to hold on until the storm cleared. He had been through similar rough times and had always managed to find a way through it, but for many of the men on his team, this was their first war. He would find out what kind of character and mental fortitude they had. A day later, his prayers were answered when the storm passed. Rejuvenated, his SEAL team was ready to meet the attack of their enemies and complete their mission.

They fought off the death squads in a hellacious firefight, then cleared the aquatic graveyard of mines. He counted his blessings that he had only lost two men in the fight.

Up ahead of him, Mitch sought his destination, the door leading to the outside world. He wanted desperately to make it out of there on his own two feet. It would be a major victory in his recovery.

Mitch held Sarm's arm as he slowly walked across the room that had been his home during his five year coma. Each day, he walked more and more. He still needed Sarm's assistance for longer distances, but he could now get from one side of the room to the other on his own.

He felt clammy yet still surged with adrenaline as he thought about the outside world. Would it be like he last remembered it, or had things changed drastically?

"You are doing super. Keep going, Mitch."

Mitch nodded. If nothing else, Sarm was encouraging. He never failed to complement Mitch when he showed progress or encourage him when he struggled. From time to time, he lashed out at the alien in anger, but that never deterred Sarm.

He walked out of the room and down a long corridor as Sarm supported him. He reflected back on his intense SEAL training and sighed. His body had deteriorated badly since then, his muscles atrophied, fat where muscle used to be.

They rounded the corner at the end of the hallway and walked into an open area that had tall, three-legged chairs. They looked like they were designed for giants. Blue, thorny plants Mitch had never seen before lined the floor. A large window that looked tinted stood at the far end of the room.

Now that he could see the outside, he walked with renewed vigor. Sarm, standing at his side with what passed for a smile on his alien face, hardly assisted him.

Mitch passed a series of blue plants that swayed in a mesmerizing pattern. He watched them, entranced.

"They are mahalias. These creatures are not native to your planet."

"Creatures?" Mitch's brow furrowed. "They look like plants."

"They have an appearance similar to Earth plants, but they are not. They will eventually leave their glass casing and walk outside on their own."

"These plants are going to walk away?" Mitch asked. "That's crazy."

"I enjoy nurturing mahalias and then watching them move onward."

Mitch turned his attention away from the mahalias and focused once more on the door. Beyond it he would see the sun's rays, breathe the air, and feel the afternoon breeze.

He walked past the mahalias and grasped the door handle. He gasped when he first saw the outside and the dark, blue air in the sky. He could feel its increased density. He trembled as he regarded Sarm. "What's going on here?"

"The atmosphere has adapted to its new inhabitants. The evolution has completed."

"But inside, the air isn't like that." Mitch's eyes were pleading with Sarm, as if he could do something to change what had occurred.

"I had it filtered to match the molecular composition of the Earth prior to the occupation in order to have assistance in your healing process."

After turning away from Sarm, Mitch began coughing. He grabbed his knees and could not stop.

"Take deep breaths, Mitch. Your lungs will find acclimation to the environment. Your grandest barrier is that of the mind, seeing what appears to be a foreign atmosphere."

Mitch held his head low. "I remember it starting to change when the aliens arrived. I felt it. The air was tangibly different."

Most of Mitch's long-term memory had come back to him. He was cognizant of his family and his life as a youth, going to college and joining the SEALs. He remembered how he met Deborah, and what they enjoyed doing. He even recollected most of what happened on the fateful day of the alien invasion. The only things that completely escaped him were the events immediately preceding his blackout.

Mitch used the principles of underwater diving to help himself breathe normally. As part of his underwater training with the SEALs, his instructors had taught him to inhale a deep breath through his nose and lungs from his diaphragm to increase the capacity of his lungs, exhale the breath of air until he could no longer breathe out, then inhale one last deep breath of air through his nose and lungs before going into the water.

He looked out and recognized that he was in LaJolla, a suburb of San Diego, but this was different than the Southern

California he was used to. Gone were the loud noises, traffic, and people. Also gone was the smog in the horizon. The land surrounding the building was filled with a sprawling flora of dazzling colors. The plants and shrubs were much larger than before. To his left were trees the size of tall buildings. On one bush, lavender star-shaped fruits as big as a pumpkin grew.

Mitch jumped at the sight of an engorged, massive centipede near his feet.

Sarm put his hand on Mitch's shoulder. "No need to have worry. It will not harm you. They clean the soil and increase its fertility."

A vessel flew across the horizon. He stared as it zoomed away.

"Follow me, Mitch." Sarm led him to a large house composed of yellow, nearly transparent material. "This is the location in which I perform most of my studies. When not attending to your needs during your sleep, this was my most common location."

Mitch's brow furrowed. "What's inside?"

"You shall see."

They entered what looked like a mini-wildlife preserve. Inside were many plants, most not recognizable. A winged creature with skin that resembled black rubber flew past them. It let out a high-pitched shriek. Nearby, a brown alien with a long feathery tail flew at an excruciatingly slow pace, like a turtle crawling.

"Why is it flying so slow?" Mitch asked.

Sarm chuckled. "Your eyes are mistaking you. It is not flying. It is floating. Its native atmosphere is less dense, and it can float in this more buoyant atmosphere."

Enclosed in big and small cages were a variety of animals, including frogs, lizards, cats, and monkeys. Scattered among them were cages with alien creatures. Mitch kept away from these.

An enormous aquarium stood at the far end of the room. A creature with dozens of small tentacles was attached to the wall. A translucent fish swam past it. Mitch was in awe when he saw the translucent fish pass right through a large rock. Meanwhile, a bigger fish with layers of teeth swallowed a half-dozen goldfish.

"What's this all about?" Mitch asked.

"This is my research facility."

"What do you do here?"

"Study how Earth species and foreign species react to the changing atmosphere."

"What has your research shown?"

Sarm hesitated. "The majority of Earth dwellers have responded well to this change in environment. Most animal and plant species have adapted. There are exceptions. A number of species of birds are near extinction as well as larger mammals such as bears and elephants. My understanding is that effort has been expended to prevent extinction."

"That's ridiculous. Like it's not bad enough that you killed off the people, now you have to kill the other planetary life as well."

"Although I do not support the Minister of Science and the governing council, I would not think it their intention to kill off species with poor adaptive capabilities."

"How benevolent of them. What have you people done to Mother Earth?"

"Very curious," Sarm said. "Why would use the female sex to describe your planet?"

Mitch shrugged. "It's an old term. The Earth nurtures and feeds all life just as a human mother cares for her children. Mother Earth is all knowing, alive, sacred." Mitch stooped over and peered at what he thought was a hamster inside of a large cage on the floor. Something odd about the hamster caught his attention. He looked closely. Its fur was evaporating, and its body slowly began to thin out and elongate. Its legs and arms retracted inside of its body.

"What the hell's going on here?" Mitch asked. "What kind of freak experiments have you been trying?"

"I am not performing any experiments of a peculiar nature."

"Then what's this hamster doing?"

"It is not a hamster. Please observe."

Mitch glanced at the creature. Scales now replaced its fur. The body had become even longer and thinner, and its face had shrunk. A long tongue slithered out of its mouth. Mitch watched in lurid fascination as the hamster took the appearance of a snake.

"What the hell is that?"

"That is a satchmore," replied Sarm, "a very unusual creature from the Metelkesian Galaxy. It has little intelligence but has the ultimate in adaptive capabilities. It can take the appearance of beings it encounters. I allow it to roam, and then find out what it meets."

"Can it look like a person?"

"No. Humans are too large in size for satchmores. Delightful little creatures."

"If you say so."

After Sarm finished the tour of his research facility, Mitch followed him outside. For a while, he gazed out in the distance. For better or for worse, this was his new world. He desperately longed for his old one but knew he would never see it again.

***

Mitch howled in pain as Sarm stretched his back muscles.

Sarm regarded Mitch, who was breathing heavily. "Would you like to stop?"

Mitch grunted. "No. Let's keep going."

"I have noticed that your attitude toward rehabilitation has undergone a distinct transformation. You no longer display reluctance and anger."

"That's because at first I wanted to slip back into a coma. Now, I've resigned myself to the way things are, and I'm going to make it work. Before the attack, I was in an elite group of my country's military called the Navy SEALs."

"Yes. I have read about them."

"Well, in order to pass the training, I had to go through something called Hell Week. I had four hours of sleep in five days. They put us through every imaginable hell. At the end of the week, I was wading through a quarter mile of frigid water. I kept thinking that I wasn't going to make it. I seriously contemplated going back to the shore and ringing the brass bell three times."

"What does that signify?" Sarm asked.

"If you ring the brass bell three times, that means you quit, so I reached deep down and said to myself, 'They're going to have to drag my body out of this cold water before I quit.' If I can handle Hell Week, then I can handle a little rehab."

"That is the attitude I like."

Mitch continued stretching. Now that he had gotten over his distrust of the alien, he grew curious about what Sarm had done to keep him alive. While they stretched, he learned that Sarm had provided him with nourishment by those crazy looking root things, which turned out to be a living organism. Sarm had gone through a litany of actions to bring him back to health using electrical and vibrational stimulus for his muscles and joints, playing music from a radio, and talking to him on a regular basis. When Mitch had shown no sign of recovery, Sarm performed rubbing and massaging exercises on his muscles, applying hot and cold sources to various parts of his body, pinching him at strategic points, and finally placing odors under his nose and bitter items on his tongue.

"And all of that didn't work, I'm guessing."

"No," Sarm said. "You woke up in a time period far longer than what was described to be normal. Most humans in a coma state stay there for a period of two weeks to three months. Your case was extraordinary in many ways."

Mitch smiled. "I was just trying to be difficult."

They continued stretching until Mitch was too fatigued to continue. He was stiff and sore, but clearly feeling better. He no longer needed Sarm's assistance to move around. He had never been dependent upon anyone in his life other than his SEAL team members, and he did not want to start now.

"You will be pleasantly surprised at the change in your diet tonight," Sarm said.

"Oh yeah, how's that?"

"I was able to capture a rabbit outside."

"You ever have rabbit stew?" Mitch asked.

Sarm shook his head.

"Then tonight will be a first for you."

Sarm helped Mitch gather vegetables from his garden. Mitch concocted an impromptu stew, not sure what would work and what wouldn't since many of the ingredients were completely foreign to him. He had no potatoes but used a root that had the flavor of yams.

Mitch cooked the stew over a fire with a pot Sarm provided. They spent the evening eating his tasty concoction and exchanging stories about each other's culture.

## Chapter VII

Panting and nearly out of breath, Mitch turned the corner of the high school track. His legs felt rubbery on the asphalt. Instead of letting fatigue overcome him and slowing down toward the finish line, he kicked into an extra gear and sprinted toward Sarm, passing the alien in full stride.

The alien clicked the stopwatch and sauntered toward him with his tall insect legs. "One minute and forty-four seconds. It is your fastest time yet." Mitch bent over and clutched his legs. "Next time I would like to see you achieve a time of a minute and thirty seconds."

Mitch looked up and nodded. "I just want to improve. Every day I want to get faster and stronger."

"To improve your condition, you must set measurable goals and take steps to reach them. That is the way. Now you must stretch."

"You're the stretching Nazi," Mitch said. "You're worse than my old track coach."

"I have learned of your physiology, and stretching is of essence, especially due to the inactivity of your limbs and muscles during your comatose stage. There are no fast answers, Mitch. Slow and steady is the way."

Sarm made him undergo a rigorous stretching routine that included his arms, his legs, his back, even muscles Mitch didn't know existed.

They were at an abandoned high school near Sarm's research facility. It held an open field and a weight room. In addition, it was secluded. After a month, Mitch was used to being around Sarm, but was not ready to deal with other aliens.

Every day, Sarm made him work out until he was completely spent, but he never complained. In fact, he did more than Sarm required. His goal was to get back to his old level of physical conditioning.

Mitch felt discouraged the first time he had lifted weights. Sarm wanted to start him off slowly, but when he told Mitch to bench press a forty-five-pound Olympic bar with ten-pound weights on each side, Mitch scoffed at him. He insisted they start with forty-five-pound plates on each side and felt humbled when he could not lift it. He kept lowering weights until he reached the weight Sarm had originally put on the bar. That was all he could lift.

He worked on different muscle groups doing bicep curls, squats, and leg extensions using little weight. As disenchanted as he had been with his lack of strength, he was pleased that since then he had doubled the weight he could lift.

The alien amazed him with his strength and agility. When they jogged together, Sarm had to slow down for him to catch up. He was also astonished at Sarm's wealth of knowledge, especially about the history of the United States and the planet Earth.

After they finished stretching, Sarm said, "Darkness is coming in our direction. We must be in the return path home."

"Why do you do that?" Mitch asked.

"Do what?"

"You speak in such a peculiar manner. Your English is fluent. You have a very good command of the language and don't even speak with a noticeable accent. You have a large vocabulary, better than most native speakers, but you say so many things incorrectly. You don't use the words properly in a sentence."

Sarm rubbed his head. "That is the result of my learning method of your language."

"How did you learn English, anyway?"

"Prior to my arrival, I purchased language modules at an intergalactic fair. Not knowing with which to familiarize myself, I was told that the most beneficial languages to have knowledge of were English, Spanish, German and Mandarin."

Mitch raised his eyebrows. "You know four Earth languages? That's impressive."

"Languages come to me with ease. I have fluency in thirty-two languages. It has proved to be useful, since as I told you prior, I have led a mostly nomadic life, having lived on various planets."

Later that evening, when they were sitting by a fire outside and Sarm was reading yet another book, Mitch said, "You're something else. I've never met anyone who reads as much as you."

Sarm was a voracious reader. He read nearly a book a day along with the medical journals and textbooks he was constantly scouring over.

"There can be no greater pleasure than the pursuit of knowledge. I need to constantly feed my mind."

This gathering of new information never seemed to end. At night, he would ask Mitch questions about how humans lived prior to the invasion, the United States government, and events around the world. When Mitch began to tire of these questions, he kept in mind that Sarm never tired in helping him.

"I lack a colloquial knowledge of your language. You are the only human with whom I have had conversation. I met a human female, but she only spoke Portuguese."

"Well, when you say things improperly, I'll tell you the correct sequence of words to use in the situation."

Sarm's face formed what Mitch had recognized as a smile. "That would be a prime idea. Perhaps before long, I will be like a native Earth speaker."

"It would be a good idea, not a prime idea."

Sarm held up a long, thin finger. "Indeed, it would be."

***

Mitch shoveled dirt on top of a tree that he and Sarm had just planted. They had planted common trees such as elm, pine, and oak along with alien ones Mitch had never seen before. As his physical rehab progressed, he also felt the need for intellectual stimulation, so he volunteered to help Sarm with his research.

Mitch planted his shovel into the ground.

"Are you ready for some rehabilitation today?" Sarm asked.

"No," Mitch said. "I have something else in mind. We need some R and R."

Sarm shook his head. "What is R and R?"

"In the military, it's an acronym for rest and relaxation. After a tough assignment you need time off to regroup."

"Interesting. What would you like to do for your R and R?"

"There's a private beach I used to go to around here. I'd like to do some surfing."

Sarm frowned. "Gliding on top of the water on a board composed of fiberglass and polyurethane. I understand it was a popular recreational activity among your people. The thought of it terrifies me."

"Why?" Mitch asked.

"I can't swim. Submerging myself in water is the one of the most horrid possibilities that I can imagine."

Mitch furrowed his brow. "Don't you have water on your planet?"

Sarm nodded. "But transportation is done on large, sturdy vessels, not these narrow boards. Most species in the universe, unless they are aquatic creatures, avoid water entirely. Humans are unusual in that regard."

Mitch rubbed his chin. That gave him a distinct advantage over the invaders of the planet.

Mitch patted the alien's shoulder. "Well, my friend, you're in luck today. In my old life as a SEAL, I practically lived in the water. I've put my trust in you; now it's your turn to put your trust in me. I won't let you drown."

"But we lack the appropriate equipment."

"There's a surf shop by the beach, if it's still standing."

Since Sarm was not capable of fitting in a conventional automobile, they took his low, shiny-black flying craft. It was unlike anything Mitch had ever seen. He had flown helicopters and planes, but nothing with this type of technology. Mitch asked the alien if he could teach him how to fly it, and Sarm said they could start that afternoon.

They landed the vessel on the shore of Black Beach, which once upon a time before the aliens invaded it had the distinction of being the largest nude beach in the United States. They walked around for a half hour before Mitch finally found the surf shop among the obliterated stores. Much of it was in rubble, and they had to dig their way through. Fortunately, the merchandise was still in good shape, and they each took a surfboard.

Mitch struggled to swim offshore a few hundred feet. Like Sarm had said, he would have to relearn even the simplest of functions. He had once been a proficient surfer and now could hardly get started. Once on the board, waves knocked him down repeatedly. The surf was rougher than he remembered, presumably due to the change in the environment.

Mitch couldn't stop laughing when Sarm tried to surf. He had a hard time coaxing the alien to get into the water, promising to be near him at all times. Sarm kept getting knocked over by the waves. Good balance was not one of his many physical attributes, and his large feet weren't conducive to staying on the board for long. Mitch attempted to teach him, but it became apparent that surfing was beyond the alien's capabilities.

Afterward, they sat on the beach watching the waves pound the shoreline. Sarm sat on his board since the sand irritated his skin.

"I fail to see why surfing is something one would do for rest and relaxation."

"It's a chance to get away from everything. For instance, I didn't think once about how that son of a bitch Minister of Science took over my planet."

Sarm nodded. "It is likely that you will never overcome your animosity. If I were on my home planet, those feelings would still be harboring inside me."

"What you mean to say is that you would still be harboring those feelings. Tell me more about the Minister of Science."

Sarm stood and leaned on his surfboard, explaining that while still important, the Minister held a minor position in the intergalactic council. His objective was to further the understanding of science and technology in the overall flow of the universe, whatever that meant. Although this position normally went to academics, he got the appointment through family connections. His father had once been the Lead Minister of the Governing Council, a high-ranking position. The only thing that held him from attaining higher ranks was his poor relationships with those at the very top levels of intergalactic politics.

Apparently, there were no rules to prevent him from conquering a planet, especially a small, distant unimportant one like Earth, as long as he wasn't building an empire. Mitch took exception to this description.

"How did it go down, Sarm?"

"I do not know how things were pulled toward the planet's center of gravity from a position in the atmosphere." Sarm's eyes narrowed.

"It's an expression. What transpired during the invasion?"

"Going down means transpiring. I must make a mental note of this."

Sarm explained how the military forces of the United States of America attempted to fight back, engaging in ground and air strikes using planes, tanks, and missiles. Their attack centered on the entry point onto the planet, the Coronado naval base. The alien entry point was a chance occurrence and could easily have been another location. The aliens used locators for teleportation, which eliminated dangerous entry points.

The human weapons were primitive in comparison to the alien ones. The more destructive ones, like nuclear weapons, weren't feasible due to the fallout. The Minister of Science had been prepared for battle, understood the humans' weapons and methods, and took decisive measures. With great sorrow, Sarm told him the humans had no chance, even though they had banded together in unprecedented fashion.

Representatives of nations across the planet met at the UN building in New York, ratifying an agreement to fight together. One day after this historic agreement, the Minister began a relentless attack, annihilating humans by the millions. Entire cities burnt to the ground. The aliens stalked and killed the population.

Sarm had not been there at the beginning, having been enlisted to treat the wounded among the invading forces. Fortunately, the humans had not wounded or killed enough invaders to make a difference, since the Minister of Science brought in reinforcement mercenaries to fight against the humans.

Mitch gritted his teeth. "But what was his motive for taking over the planet?"

"He wants to rule his own world. His position of Minister of Science is a minor one. He sees himself as a conqueror. Earth was an easy target. Here, no one will challenge his sovereignty. He has complete dominion. Currently, there is little more than a small security group on the planet. The mercenaries hired for the invasion have left. Naturally, he intends to keep his costs low in his operations, and with the human forces defeated, there is no reason for them to remain. What are left on the planet are primarily merchants, miners, and those involved in the slave trade, a rather unsavory group if you ask me. He has named Mogenheim as the chief marshal of the planet, an individual known for his ruthless domination of natives."

It was all about a hunger for power. Hatred began to smolder inside of Mitch. He so wanted to destroy the Minister of Science. That immediate distrust he had felt when he had first encountered the alien had been justified. It also told him to trust his instincts. If he ever encountered the Minister again, he vowed that the alien bastard would not get the better of him.

*** 

Nearly four months after Mitch woke from his coma, he was nearing his previous strength and fitness levels. Sarm never relented in his rehabilitation efforts. On this occasion, he strapped a harness around Mitch and attached it to a cart. Sarm sat on the cart while Mitch wheeled him around La Jolla.

Mitch carried him without complaint up hills, across streets, and through parking lots. Judging by the freshly paved roads,

72

Mitch surmised that the aliens had performed reconstruction after the invasion. After an hour, he began to struggle. He only stopped to drink water despite his aching muscles. He became tired of Sarm's encouragement and cursed at the alien, who never took offense when Mitch yelled at him, which only further infuriated Mitch.

By the time they reached home, Mitch felt invigorated as he reflected on how weak he had been, and how far he had come. The first steps were the most difficult ones.

Sitting on the grass outside of the research facility, Sarm brought him a fruity concoction loaded with nutrients. When he first tried it, he had nearly vomited and could not finish the drink, prompting Sarm to mix it with blended fruits to give it a more appealing taste.

After drinking it, he handed the glass back to Sarm. "It feels good to be strong again. I felt so worthless before. Now I feel like I can conquer the world."

"I would like you to be stronger, faster, and have greater agility than you had previously," Sarm said. "There should be no limitations to your recovery."

Mitch nodded. "It's been enjoyable helping you with your research, but eventually I have to move on."

Each day he planted new trees and plants, worked the field in front of the research area, and collected data from test subjects. In addition, he had become proficient at flying Sarm's aircraft. His ability to fly planes and helicopters made him a quick study.

"Your company is always welcome."

Mitch shrugged. "It doesn't seem like I have a place in this world anymore. I used to feel so full of purpose. Now…"

"You will find your place in Santanovia," Sarm said, referring to the alien term for the planet Earth. "I was once like you until I discovered my purpose."

"So, you came out here all by yourself. Is there a Mrs. Sarm out on some planet?"

Sarm let out a shrill noise that Mitch recognized as laughter. "No, there is not. My species operates in a different manner than Homo Sapiens. The role of the male is to impregnate and start the procreation process. After that, there is little interaction with the female, who raises the offspring."

"And you don't have any interaction with your father?"

Sarm shook his head. "Upon reaching my adulthood, I developed a strong relationship with my father. We communicate frequently."

"Hmm, interesting. So, you just knock 'em up and leave, but then you develop a relationship with your offspring later in life?"

"That is correct."

"That's weird."

"When you have been to as many solar systems as I have, you come to the realization that there is no such thing as normal. The variations among species are vast and a single pattern of behavior does not emerge."

"You mean to say, there is no single pattern of behavior. I think you're missing the boat, Sarm. Just look around you. You have an incredible ability and instinct to nurture. You would make a great father."

74

Sarm looked as if he were contemplating Mitch's words, but did not respond.

"So, you have lots of offspring out there?" Mitch asked.

"Only four. Did you go through the human ritual of marriage?"

Mitch shook his head. "The day this all started I proposed to my sweetheart, Deborah. She never had the chance to answer my proposal. I last saw her when I left the building after finding out that the aliens were attacking. I keep tossing it around in my head. My guess is that she left the building shortly after me. She must have with all hell breaking loose outside. And if she did...You're the expert in probability, Sarm. What chance did she have of surviving that day?"

Sarm looked away. He finally admitted the odds of her survival were highly improbable. Ever the optimist, he pointed out that Mitch's survival was also highly improbable.

Mitch narrowed his eyes. "If I ever get another chance at the Minister of Science, one of us is going to die."

"The Minister is a formidable opponent."

"As am I."

Later that evening they were roasting a pheasant over an open fire. Mitch asked the alien. "So, don't you ever feel there's something missing in your life? Don't you feel empty without a female companion?"

"No," replied Sarm. "I have many family and friends. Your tradition of having a wife seems a burden."

Mitch sighed. "God, I miss Deborah."

"There is always hope. I could have easily dismissed you due to your low probability of survival, but I did not give up hope and neither should you."

Mitch nodded. "I won't."

There wasn't a day that passed by that Mitch didn't think about Deborah. He knew the chances of ever seeing her were slim, but as long as there was that tiny bit of hope, he would not let that flame extinguish, and it would continue to burn brightly in his heart.

## Chapter VIII

Sarm shouted encouragement as Mitch continued to do reps on the bench press. He then assisted Mitch in putting the bar back following his bench presses.

That was the most weight he had ever lifted, even before the coma. When they first started, Mitch did not envision that in only six months he would have come this far using Sarm's unconventional techniques. Considering he had never had a human patient, Sarm certainly knew what he was doing.

As they walked back to the research center, Mitch said, "That formula you gave Radley seems to be working. She was breathing better this morning."

"The German Shepherd's lungs had contracted. The response from their species to the atmospheric change has been gradual in nature. The formula I used had crushed roots from my home planet that we give to infants who have difficulty breathing. It was a...hunch." Sarm smiled. Mitch had just taught him the word a few days ago. "I will give it to the other canines in the facility," Sarm said. "We will closely monitor their breathing. If this goes well, I will report my findings."

Radley seemed to be behaving like a normal, healthy dog, even giving Mitch and Sarm more enthusiastic affection than usual.

The research facility resembled a large green house. The material used for construction was clear like glass but far sturdier. It had sliding solar panels that looked like they could have come from a science fiction movie. Mitch enjoyed being able to see Sarm perform his research inside while Mitch tended to chores outside. Not to mention it gave the facility a vibrant, airy feeling even when they were stuck inside for hours.

Even if Sarm's treatment on Radley worked, the logistical issues surrounding providing this treatment would make this a difficult problem to solve. Of course, the Minister of Science only cared about making the planet more hospitable for aliens. He didn't give a damn about the death of native creatures, especially humans. If not for using them as slave labor, he would probably have ordered the eradication of the human species.

Once they returned, Mitch began working the fields. He had never farmed prior to this but found it enjoyable.

After an hour, Mitch took a break. "Did you get that fertilizer you wanted to test?"

"I have not. I am glad that you remind me. I will get it."

Mitch watched Sarm enter his craft and depart before going back to work. He was at peace working the fields. As he was tilling soil and planting seeds, he came to the conclusion that it wasn't enough to survive in this new world. He was going to need to reclaim it.

\*\*\*

Mitch propped up his feet as he read an old Time magazine detailing the war in Iraq. It seemed so distant, a lifetime away. Loud footsteps startled him. He reached for his handgun, the one he had taken from an abandoned gun store, and was surprised to find Sarm, since the alien normally moved quietly.

Sarm waved his arms frantically. "What did I do? I was so foolish. Oh stupid, stupid Sarm. I have made a tragic mistake."

Radley seemed to match Sarm's mood as she paced around the room, growling and barking. Sarm and Mitch had grown close to their pet over the last few months.

Mitch grabbed his arm. "Just calm down."

"No. I could not have been more stupid."

"Tell me what happened, Sarm. Whatever it is, we'll figure it out."

"I went to get the fertilizer from a mikanian distributor," Sarm said, referring to a red-faced alien with large bulging eyes. "I was explaining to him the various projects that I was working on, including your successful rehabilitation. I should have kept quiet, but I am very proud of your progress, and had to share it. The mikanian told me that it was most fortunate that you had recuperated since there is a shortage of humans to work a mine in Mexico. Since I am not a licensed slave-owner, I could not claim that I own you. A bounty hunter is coming to pick you up. I tried to help you and now look at what I have done!"

Mitch sat down. "It's okay, Sarm."

"No, it is not. I have ruined everything," Sarm lamented.

"Actually, this is what I need. You've done all you can for me. Physically, I've never been stronger. I can't stay here forever. I've stayed this long because I'm afraid of entering a world that's nothing like I remembered. I've been stalling and procrastinating, keeping myself busy by assisting you, but this isn't my place. My place is among my people. I may not like what my world has become, but sooner or later, I have to join the rest of humanity. I just needed a kick in the ass to realize it."

Sarm expressed many concerns about his departure, but Mitch insisted it was for the best.

They immediately began packing. Sarm gathered dried meats and assorted fruits from his garden. Meanwhile, in a large duffel bag, Mitch packed clothes he had acquired from an abandoned department store. Next to his clothes, Sarm placed a solar powered e-reader. Mitch eyed the alien curiously.

"You will need books to keep your mind sharp."

"If you say so." Mitch gathered his assortment of weapons. He had a knife with a long blade, a Swiss Army knife, a handgun, and a rifle, all scavenged from different places. He would have preferred a machine gun.

Sarm put together a makeshift emergency medical kit, composed of bandages, ointments, and an assortment of herbs and pills, many of which he had made himself.

"Can I have your road atlas?" Mitch asked.

"Of course." Sarm put the atlas in the duffel bag.

"I guess I'll take the car," Mitch said, referring to a Ford pickup truck that they used for hauling items.

"That would not be prudent. Humans traveling along your old roads are apt to be captured and sold into slavery. Second, although in this area repairs have been made, much of your highway infrastructure was destroyed. No, road travel would not be wise."

Mitch raised his hands. "Then what am I going to do?"

Sarm offered his aircraft, but Mitch was reluctant to leave him without transportation. His alien friend managed to persuade him to take the vessel.

Mitch resumed packing. He and Sarm loaded the craft with the items he had packed. In another couple minutes, he was almost ready to leave with just a few small items remaining. He took a final look at his old home. In a strange way, he felt attachment to it.

Sarm gave him a pouch with several discs made of a thin alloy that was used as currency by the planet's new settlers. Mitch started to protest, but his alien friend would not hear it. "The cards have monetary credits and could be used for the purchase of goods. It should be sufficient for any immediate needs, and it will not be traced back to me."

Mitch nodded.

Sarm opened the rear hatch of the craft. "It is powered by a self-rechargeable fuel cell that is charged by the vibrational properties of the vessel. There is no way to refill it. The current cell should last a long while." He walked toward a shed that he had built and pulled out another cell that was slightly larger than a brick, but much denser. "When the first cell expires, replace it with this one. When this gauge has reached the bottom, that is the indication to replace it. You should not require a replacement for at least a year, depending upon the distance of your travels."

Mitch took the spare cell and placed it carefully in a secure spot.

They walked back toward the house to get the rest of Mitch's belongings.

"It will be safest to travel in the evening. If you encounter trouble, recall the evasive maneuvers I taught you. The craft is very nimble. Stay clear of the salenkos." Sarm was referring to the winged blue aliens that Mitch saw on the first day of the invasion. He knew how deadly they could be. "If unprovoked, they should not attack you."

"I'll try to avoid trouble. Believe me."

"I have heard of human settlements, but I have no knowledge of their location. That may be your best option."

Mitch nodded. "I'll be on the lookout."

Sarm lowered his head and touched it with his thin fingers. "I wish this did not have to occur so soon."

"It's okay. You've done all that you can. I'm ready."

"I wish there was more I can do."

"No, Sarm. You've done everything and more. I just want to thank you. I want to thank you for everything. I could never have made it this far without you. And I want to tell you that I am sorry."

"Sorry?"

"You have been nothing but good to me, and I have been unfair to you. From the very beginning I treated you poorly, yet you never once let that stop you from helping me. I resented you because you were one of them, one of the aliens that stole my planet, stole my life from me. But you were never that. You came into an undesirable situation and have done some real good here. You breathed life back into me. Besides the rehab, you helped me mentally and emotionally. I appreciate everything you've done for me and I'll never forget it. You have been more than just my physician or my physical therapist, you have been my friend."

"Friend?"

"Yes, Sarm. You have been a good friend to me even when I haven't been one to you."

"I want to thank you, Mitch Grace, for being my first human friend."

Mitch grasped Sarm's slender arm, pulled the alien closer to him, and hugged him. Sarm tapped him on the head in a strange show of affection.

Sarm's face turned pale. There was a rumbling in the distance. "Oh no! Not yet!"

Mitch gritted his teeth. "Shit."

"You have to leave now," Sarm said.

"No," Mitch said. "It will look like you let me get away. I can't let you take the fall for that. We'll make it look like I escaped." Sarm was about to argue, but Mitch cut him off. "There's no time. Just brace yourself."

Without any further instruction, Mitch dragged Sarm toward him by his thin arm and elbowed the alien to his head. Mitch didn't use his fists, wanting to bruise Sarm, not hurt him. It didn't look convincing enough, so Mitch elbowed him in the forehead again. A third elbow did the trick, busting open Sarm's head. The alien's blood flowed down his face.

"You okay?" Mitch asked.

Sarm waved his hand. "Just go."

The alien was approaching quickly in his vehicle. Beige in color, it looked like an oversized dune buggy, and drove toward them at high speeds. Mitch wouldn't have enough time to make it to Sarm's vessel. Instead, he ran back toward the house, a plan formulating in his head.

He crouched to keep himself hidden as the alien exited the vehicle. It had green skin and two heads with faces that resembled a turtle. It lowered itself and appeared to be speaking to Sarm. Mitch could not tell what Sarm was saying. All he could hear was a low moan from the alien.

As the bounty hunter moved toward the house, holding what looked like a pistol in his hand, Mitch ran toward the rear exit. He waited until he heard the opening of the door, and then edged his way around the side of the house, trying not to make any noise as he crept through the tall grass. The grass swayed back and forth with the strong wind.

Mitch jumped at the sound of something fast approaching, but it was only Radley. Mitch gestured for the dog to sit, and Radley obeyed. He kept moving alongside the house until he got to the front. He made eye contact with Sarm, who was still lying on the ground. Sarm pointed toward the vessel and motioned him to make a run for it.

Mitch took off. The sound of running must have alerted the bounty hunter as he exited the house and ran toward Mitch. A pop was followed by a whoosh in the air. Mitch ducked, sure the alien had shot at him, but no bullets came in his direction. He turned to find what looked like a grappling hook coming at him. There was not enough time to elude it, and it latched onto Mitch's shirt.

"What the hell." Instead of grappling hooks, this was something else altogether. It was a yellow and furry creature, eating away at his shirt and trying to sink into his skin.

Mitch pulled at the thing furiously as it attempted to burrow into his skin. Meanwhile, the bounty hunter was pulling Mitch toward him using the metallic wire attached to the creature.

Mitch dug in his heels, trying to prevent himself from being pulled toward the slaver. He screeched as the yellow creature bit his skin.

Out of nowhere, Radley jumped on top of the two-headed alien and knocked him to the ground. This was the opening Mitch needed. He grabbed the furry yellow creature and ripped it off his chest. A chunk of his flesh came with it. Its jaws were snapping at him. He tossed the thing to the side and ran for Sarm's vessel, blood flowing down his chest, not looking back. He ran into the opening of the vessel and manually closed the hatch, not waiting for the vessel's slower hydraulic system.

A quick look outside showed the bounty hunter still fighting off Radley. Sarm was now on his feet, apparently trying to keep Radley at bay. Mitch worked the controls, started the vessel, took one look back at the bounty hunter running at him, and ascended with a lurch. He did not know where he was going; only that he was embarking on the next chapter of his life.

## Chapter IX

As Mitch's vessel soared through the air, he studied the craft's controls. Although he had flown it before, this was his first solo flight. Sarm had previously labeled the buttons and controls in English. He had also drawn a layout of the cabin and labeled it for Mitch.

Once he reached one thousand feet, he put the vessel on autopilot. The sky was clear and free of traffic. He went to the cabinet with the first aid kit and began cleaning and bandaging his chest. It was a minor wound, nothing that would set him back. Fortunately, he was well-schooled in dealing with wounds.

He studied the three-dimensional radar system that constantly scanned and visually displayed a hundred-mile radius. A communications link was next to it, but he did not plan on using the comm system. He intended on following Sarm's advice to keep himself inconspicuous.

He wandered around the spacious cabin, glancing at the monitor to make sure that nothing entered his airspace. The ceiling was five meters high and ten meters long. The interior was light gray and sterile-looking. It was as fast as a fighter plane, but Mitch was cruising at a low velocity.

He removed the autopilot as he crossed Southern California, not far from the Nevada border. He contemplated his destination. Should he stay in the United States? He wanted to find other people, but where? Maybe there were people hiding from the aliens in a secluded mountainous area, but people tended to congregate in cities.

He was close to Los Angeles, Phoenix, Las Vegas, and San Francisco. He ruled out San Diego — too many bad memories from Coronado. He could fly somewhere remote like Northern Canada. Having done SEAL training there, he could survive, but he felt a need to be around people.

On the radar screen, three oncoming aircraft were eighty miles away from his current position. As he got closer and the resolution improved, he realized that they were not vessels, but salenkos flying in a pattern. He descended and landed on the open desert to avoid the blue, winged creatures. Sarm had told him that the salenkos would not bother with him if they were not threatened, but he did not want to take a chance.

He pulled out a bottle of water and the road atlas. He needed a plan. Now that he was out of imminent danger, he did not want to fly aimlessly.

Mitch kept changing his mind between a city and a rural destination. He decided on Las Vegas. He and his SEAL buddies frequently went to Sin City to blow off steam. He was not much of a gambler, but he always had a good time.

Mitch went back inside of the cabin to escape the heat. It had to be at least a hundred degrees Fahrenheit. Checking the radar screen, he could no longer see the salenkos.

He lay on the oversized cot in the back and quickly fell asleep. He jolted awake an hour later. He had been having a nightmare.

It was back on the day of the invasion. He observed himself speak to the Minister of Science. He urged himself to pull out his pistol and kill the Minister. As much as he pleaded, his body would not listen. Deborah came out to help him, and the Minister ripped her body apart with his sharp claws.

He woke up breathing heavily, trying to piece together the part of his memory that was still missing, the part directly preceding his blackout. After a few minutes, he gave up. Whatever happened was in the past, and there was nothing he could do about it.

When Mitch resumed his flight, there was heavy air traffic. He felt paranoid that another craft would pull him over and search the vessel, even though he realized there was no way they would know a human was commandeering it.

It did not take him long to reach Las Vegas. It was eerie to find nobody walking the streets of Las Vegas Boulevard and no cars on the Strip. He smiled when he saw the "Welcome to Fabulous Las Vegas" sign. Although slightly faded, the sign was still in good shape.

He descended and landed his craft in the empty parking lot of the Mandalay Bay. After turning off the power, he looked around warily. It was too damn quiet. Vegas was never this quiet. The town never slept, always filled with hustle and commotion.

He stepped out of the aircraft with his duffel bag. He wanted his weapons close at hand. After putting the handgun in a holster, he locked the vessel. Moving cautiously out of the parking lot, he gripped his gun at the sound of rustling in front of him. He loosened his grip when he realized it was just three iguanas passing by him.

He walked into the lobby of the Mandalay Bay. Although still elegant and mostly intact, it was empty.

"Hello," he called out. There was no answer. "Anyone here?" He walked behind the counter. Most of the computers remained. One of the drawers had a key in it. He turned the key and opened the drawer. Inside, the contents appeared to have been ransacked. Only a few loose pieces of hotel stationary remained.

He checked the other drawers. They were similarly trashed, and the cash registers were empty. He couldn't imagine the old currency was still worth anything.

He walked past the lobby into the once bustling casino floor. Amazingly, the lights and slots were still on.

Mitch found a slot machine ticket voucher on the floor. He picked it up and placed it into a slot machine. He pulled the lever, and it began to spin. "How about that?" he muttered. It came up with a cherry, a blank space, and a single bar. Apparently, his luck at gambling still hadn't changed.

He left the casino floor and entered the Red Square restaurant, which was also empty. Wine bottles were stacked from floor to ceiling. He helped himself to a bottle and put it in his duffel bag.

He rode the elevators to different floors but could not find anybody.

An hour after he entered the casino, he stepped out into the hot desert sun as a snake slithered past. It looked as if the desert critters had reclaimed this territory.

He turned south and did not encounter anybody at the Luxor or the Excalibur. The New York, New York was similarly deserted. Gritting his teeth, he crossed the street. Normally crossing Las Vegas Boulevard was perilous because of the traffic, but now the streets were empty. Vegas had turned into a ghost town.

He walked south toward the MGM Grand. He stopped suddenly, his heart beating fast at the sound of music.

Mitch quickened his pace. A man wearing black pants, cowboy boots and a cowboy hat stood at the front entrance. He wore a large smile.

"Welcome, my friend," the man said, "to Sam and Ron's Casino. I don't reckon I've seen you 'round these parts before."

"I'm new here."

The man extended his hand, and Mitch shook it. "Since you're a newcomer, the first ten dollars in chips are on the house." The man handed Mitch ten chips.

"Chips?" Mitch frowned.

"Of course. You can use them for food and beverage, or you can use them for any of our parlor games. What's your game?"

"Game?" Mitch asked. He felt like he had just entered Bizarro land.

"Are you a blackjack man? Perhaps you enjoy craps or baccarat. We run poker tournaments most nights. There's a poker game going on right now, if I reckon correctly.

Mitch peeked inside but could not see anything. He did not know whether or not he should take this silly looking man seriously. Could they really be running a casino in this post-apocalyptic world?

"Perhaps ladies are your fancy. We got blondes, brunettes, red heads, Orientals, whatever you like. You can watch them, and if you want some company later, we can provide that as long as you have some good old American cash."

Mitch shook his head in disbelief. It seemed so wrong. They should be trying to survive, trying to find a way to get back at the aliens, anything but this.

"Don't say much, do ya, partner?" the man said.

"I guess I'll look inside." Mitch had to investigate.

Mitch stepped inside the casino. His first impression was that this was a crazed recreation of the Old West. Near the entrance, an older man played the piano. He could not recognize the tune, but it sounded like something from a Western movie.

The MGM Grand was cavernous to say the least, at times the biggest casino on the Las Vegas strip, but in its reincarnation as Sam and Ron's Casino, the owners had curtained most of it off.

A half-dozen blackjack tables, several craps tables and three poker tables occupied the front of the casino. Further behind, slot machines chimed. A number of older ladies were pulling the arms of the slot machines. Mitch chuckled. He thought he was going to crack.

Mitch took a seat at the bar.

The bartender, another fixture of the Old West, was cleaning a glass. "What can I do ya for?"

Mitch shot him a sideways glance. "I'll have a beer. What do you have on tap?"

"We have Iron Horse, Kid Lightning, Rock Head, and Sarmon's."

None of these names meant anything to Mitch. He supposed that the brewing companies he remembered no longer existed. "I guess I'll take a Rock Head."

"Good choice." The bartender poured the beer from the tap and gave it to Mitch. "That will be two bits."

It seemed preposterous that they were still using the old currency. Mitch took a gulp of beer and cringed. It tasted harsh. He had tasted quality homemade beer, but whoever had brewed this either had no idea what they were doing or lacked proper ingredients. If this was a good choice, he could only imagine what the others tasted like.

One of the poker players pounded his fist onto the table and glared at another player. An argument ensued although he could not hear what they were saying.

The piano player stopped playing and left. A stereo blared "Welcome to the Jungle". A heavyset man wearing a suit with black, slicked back hair stood on the stage and spoke in a hoarse voice. "And now for your afternoon pleasure, give a big round of applause to the gorgeous ladies of Sam and Ron's Casino. Welcome Ginger Lynn."

The spectators gave catcalls. Mitch sat detached, observing the crowd.

A tall, slim brunette with long legs stepped from behind a curtain. She was wearing cowboy boots, a thong, and slim straps that barely covered her breasts. She gyrated to the music, performing a striptease. Her face looked worn, as if she had been through tough times. Mitch took a sip of his beer and once more cringed. He supposed that everyone who lived through the invasion had been through tough times.

The men watched her like rabid animals. Something in their eyes disturbed Mitch. Hopefully this casino had adequate security in case they got out of control.

Did the casino patrons do this all day or was this a reprieve from their daily grind? Did this mean they had begun recreating their fractured society? This casino was obviously a business endeavor.

Ginger continued dancing into the next song. He was halfway through his beer and doubted he could finish the rest.

The patrons switched their attention from the stripper to the two men at the poker table who had been arguing earlier. Their dispute intensified. The man with the thick brown mustache and scar on his cheek stood face to face, jawing with the man dressed in the sharp blue sport coat and tie. It would only be a matter of time before this came to blows.

The man in the sport coat shoved the other man, who tripped over his chair and fell to the floor, his hands breaking the fall. The sport coat guy grinned triumphantly and picked up the chips lying on the table.

The music stopped playing and Ginger finished her routine. The man with the brown mustache pulled out a gun.

Suddenly the other's grin dropped, and his eyes went wide. "Please don't shoot me." He dropped the chips he had picked up.

"You cheatin' son of a bitch. Nobody cheats Luther and gets away with it."

"Please don't. My daughter's waiting for me."

"You should have thought about that before you cheated." Luther put the gun to the man's head.

Mitch moved quietly from the bar. With all eyes on these two men, nobody paid him any attention. Pulling out his Ruger, he walked behind Luther. He pointed it at the back of Luther's head. "Put the gun down."

Still pointing his gun, Luther turned and glared at Mitch, telling him that it wasn't any of his business, insisting that the other man cheated him.

"In my past life I was a Navy SEAL. I have killed before. I can and will kill you, so don't try me." Before, he would never have mentioned this, but the government had collapsed years ago, so he figured protecting his identity no longer mattered.

Luther's hands shook harder. He put the gun on the table.

Mitch motioned to the poker dealer. "Pick it up."

The dealer cautiously lifted the by its handle.

"Sit down, both of you."

Luther and the man in the sport jacket sat. Mitch circled the table, shaking his head. All eyes were on him despite the presence of a naked woman onstage. "Have you people lost your mind? Five short years ago, our planet was taken over by aliens. And here you are gambling, watching a striptease, like nothing happened." He turned to Luther. "And what the hell is your problem? You would kill someone for such a stupid reason."

"He was cheating."

Mitch shook his head. "Billions of people were killed in the alien invasion. Most of our population has been wiped out. Each of you has had family members and loved ones killed by those bastards. How can we beat the aliens if we're killing each other?"

The poker dealer, still holding the gun, spoke in a soft tone. "Um, we lost that war long ago."

Mitch glared at him. "We lost only if we accept defeat. If we keep fighting, they haven't won. We have to stick together if we want to reclaim Mother Earth."

Mitch paused. He did not plan on sermonizing, but murmurs of agreement ascended from the crowd. Murmurs turned into shouts. Not a big talker, he had nothing left to say. He sat at the bar and finished his bitter beer.

The mood at Sam and Ron's Casino became much lighter after Mitch's impromptu speech. He sat at the bar, trying to avoid attention. The dispute between the two poker players ended when they shook hands.

"Do you mind if I sit next to you?"

Mitch turned and gazed at the stripper, Ginger Lynn.

"Sure," he said, not wanting to be rude.

Ginger ordered a gin and tonic. "What you did was amazing."

Mitch shrugged.

She put her hand on his shoulder. "Don't be so modest. I've seen plenty of arguments over card games here. Most of them wind up with one or both people in their graves. Sometimes innocent bystanders get caught in the middle. I've never seen someone talk them down like that. Look at Luther and Greg now. They look like life-long friends. What you said was God's honest truth, but you said it from the heart, and that's why everyone listened."

Mitch thought stopping two guys from blowing their brains out was no big deal, in this crazy place, but Ginger insisted otherwise, arguing that New Las Vegas wasn't so bad. There were about a dozen operable casinos. She offered to take him on a tour.

Mitch put down his beer. He could not get over its unpleasant taste. "Sure."

Ginger grabbed his hand and led him outside, where the brightness hurt his eyes.

"The casinos all have new names," Ginger began. "Treasure Island is now El Terrible's. The Venetian is Hotel Paradise. There's a bunch of other ones."

As they walked down the Strip, Mitch wondered aloud what they did for food. Ginger explained that farmers from California supplied them with meat, fruit, and vegetables, usually twice a week. Amazingly, they still used American dollars for transactions, even though the currency was useless to the aliens. That was one thing Vegas had no shortage of—cash. For more essential goods like food, they operated on the barter system.

They walked past the Planet Hollywood Casino, which had been leveled. Mitch stared, wide-eyed. "What the hell happened here?"

Ginger had a distant look on her face. "It got hit during the attack. I was dancing at my old club. The whole place started to shake, knocking me off the stage. The Stratosphere was taken out too, but most of the Strip was spared."

Mitch looked into the horizon and could not see the tall tower. "I noticed you're still using electricity. Where do you get it from?"

Ginger didn't know, but suggested that Sam, the owner of Sam and Ron's Casino might have the answer.

They trekked past where the Stratosphere had stood, before turning back.

They went inside of The Decadent Dream, formerly known as The Flamingo, to get water. Mitch purchased some local bottled water and hoped for the best.

The Decadent Dream was crawling with unsavory-looking prostitutes. The vast majority of them were older and looked worn out. Mitch thought it might be a good idea for them to start looking for another occupation. They fawned over him like he was a fresh slab of meat from the butcher's shop. He politely declined their propositions and asked Ginger if they could leave.

Halfway on their walk back, Mitch finished his bottle of water. He wished that he had gotten another. It was sizzling hot, and he knew from his days with the SEALs how important it was to remain hydrated.

Ginger was a real talker. She told him everything about her life including seedy details he would rather not know. Her real name was Elizabeth McNeice. She moved to Vegas when she was twenty-three. Prior to that, she had been living in Los Angeles where her acting career was going nowhere. As a child, she had appeared in commercials and sit-coms. Her parents had divorced when she was young, and her mother's life consisted of binge drinking and parties that never ended. Ginger spent most nights by herself in their house in Marina Del Rey.

When she was fifteen, her mother died of a cocaine overdose inside of the house of a well-known movie producer. Afterward, Ginger lived with her father in Orange County, but he let her do whatever she wanted, which involved a great deal of drinking and drug use. Ginger hit bottom when she began working as a prostitute on Hollywood and Vine, and knew she had to leave.

She thought that she could find success as a performer in Las Vegas. She had been taking dancing lessons since the age of three. From right out of the womb her mother had been determined to turn her into a famous child actor.

Unfortunately, all Ginger found were closed doors. She worked numerous jobs including waiting tables and dealing cards. Desperate for a performing job, she became a stripper at a club off the Vegas Strip. At first, she thought this would only be temporary until she could find a legitimate dancing job, but after a while she lost interest in pursuing other opportunities.

"So why would you still want to be an exotic dancer with everything that's happened? It seems so trivial."

Ginger shrugged. "I had been doing it for a while and I'm good at it. When I found out that Sam and Ron were going to run a casino and they needed dancers, I said why not. What else am I going to do?"

Mitch took a deep breath but did not reply.

"So, you plan on continuing this?"

"Sure, unless I get a better offer."

She smiled at Mitch, and he looked away. Whatever she was looking for, he doubted he could give it to her.

"What about you?" Ginger asked. "What's your story? What are you looking for?"

"I was in a coma for five years and have been awake for about six months. Right now, I'm trying to figure out where my place is.  You folks here are the first people I've seen since I went under."

Ginger frowned.  "And you don't like what you see."

"It's just that this is very different than what I was anticipating.  I'm not sure what I thought I'd see, but it sure as hell wasn't this."

When they returned to Sam and Ron's Casino, the mood was friendlier, less sinister, more human.  Gone were the untrusting looks.  The people no longer seemed like they would slash each other's throats at a moment's notice.

Ginger led him behind the stage.  Expensive paintings and sculptures, undoubtedly pillaged from casinos, adorned the back offices.  The desks had computers and other furnishings that reminded him of a typical office.

A man was typing a memo and drinking coffee.  When he saw them, he stood up with a big smile on his face.  "Well, look who it is, the man of the hour."

"Sam, this is Mitch Grace.  He's new in town."

"Mitch Grace, welcome to New Las Vegas."  Sam extended his hand, and Mitch shook it.  "I'd like to thank you whole-heartedly for what you did earlier.  You diffused a tense situation.  Last thing I need is another person getting killed. Bad for business."

Mitch raised his brows.  "This happens often?"

Sam looked away.  "I wouldn't exactly say often.  It happens from time to time."

Mitch shook his head and sighed.  "I can't believe it.  This is ridiculous."

"I don't disagree," Sam said. "But it's the way things are. People are demoralized and sometimes they lash out in bad ways. Enough of that. I'd like to show you my thanks by inviting you to dinner. I'm sure you could use a nice hot meal."

Mitch's initial instinct was to say no. He did not want to get further immersed in this town, but he had nowhere else to go. "Sure. Why not?"

"Very well, you and Ginger can come up to my suite at let's say eight tonight, and my old lady will cook you a meal that's to die for."

With a couple of hours to kill before dinner, Mitch and Ginger went back to the lounge where a mediocre singer was crooning Frank Sinatra songs while Ginger smoked a strongly scented cigarette. She now wore a flowery dress, contrasting greatly with the outfit Mitch had initially seen her wear.

"So, Mitch, do you have a place to stay tonight?"

Mitch pulled away, avoiding the smoke. "I was going to stay inside my aircraft."

"Don't be silly. Stay in my suite. I'm sure it's a lot more comfortable."

"Look, Ginger, I don't think that's a good idea. I was engaged before my coma. Although that was five and a half years ago, to me it's only six months. And I don't..."

Ginger put her cigarette down and put her hand on his. "I'm sorry. I didn't mean to give you the wrong impression. I don't want you to stay so that we could get it on or anything. I have an extra Queen-sized bed and I thought you would be more comfortable. We don't have to do anything you don't want to do."

Mitch felt bad for inferring that she wanted to sleep with him. He did not want to appear rude, so he accepted her offer.

She planted a kiss on his cheek. "In that case, let's get your stuff."

Ginger wanted to accompany him, but he told her he would rather go alone. He slowly walked up Las Vegas Boulevard. As he crossed the street, he had to jump back to avoid two racing motorcycles.

After putting a change of clothes in his duffel bag, he decided against bringing toiletries because they were probably abundant in the casino's hotel.

When he returned to Sam and Ron's Casino, Ginger was waiting for him at their table. "I thought you weren't going to return."

"Don't I look like the honest type?" Mitch asked.

"Most guys I meet these days aren't far removed from pond scum. Not you, Mitch. You're altogether different from any guy I have ever met."

"That's good, I guess."

By the time they reached Sam's suite on the twelfth floor, Mitch was convinced he knew everything about Ginger's life from the time she was in diapers to present day.

Sam was dressed casually in shorts and a tee shirt. He introduced his significant other, Pamela, who appeared more suited dancing alongside Ginger than cooking dinner. She wore a very short red skirt and a red shirt with sequins. Within minutes, Mitch could tell that Pamela was fun to be around, but not bright.

"Wait 'til you taste the meal that Pamela whipped up."

"Where did you cook this?"

"We have a huge gas grill on the balcony," Sam replied.

They ate in the dining area of the suite. For his own personal usage, Sam had selected the largest suite in the hotel. It looked more like an apartment. Mitch was pleasantly surprised that Sam's boast was correct. He was guilty of stereotyping, thinking that since Pamela looked like a Playboy Bunny, she would not be able to cook a decent meal. They ate a terrific meal of pork chops, baked potatoes, Cesar salad and fresh bread. Everything tasted very fresh. Mitch surmised that the food was sourced from a local grower. There was a distinct lack of anything pre-packaged with loads of preservatives.

Mitch waited until after dinner to ask Sam a multitude of questions. "So why did you remake the casinos here in Vegas?"

"I guess this doesn't seem appropriate to you?" Sam asked.

"Not really."

Sam smiled. "This is what we know. I've been in the gaming business most of my life. I used to be a pit boss at the old MGM Grand. I lost my wife and daughter in the invasion. I wasn't sure what to do. Some folks and I wondered whether we should stick around. When we decided to stay, it was only natural that we went back to doing what we know. My partner Ron used to work in casino security. We decided to start this new place. Everything was already set up, so the conversion was a cakewalk."

"There should be more on people's minds than gambling," Mitch said.

"People need a break from reality. That's what Vegas has always been about. It's a fantasy, a place where people's dreams come true."

After dinner, Sam brought out a bottle of pre-invasion Scotch. He offered Mitch a cigar, which he gladly accepted. Mitch was enjoying this night more than he thought.

Mitch had been contemplating this for a while, so he figured now was a good opportunity to ask, "What do you use for electricity?"

"For a while we were using the old system, but it fell into disrepair. So instead of re-inventing the wheel, we decided to tap into the aliens' power source. They have power stations near the Hoover Dam, and we're borrowing a little, free of charge. I figure that's the least they could do. 'Course they don't know it."

Mitch grinned. It wasn't much, but they were sticking it to the aliens.

"Why do you still use American dollars since they have no value to the aliens?"

Ginger, Pamela, and Sam all laughed.

"That's all right with us," Pamela said. "Because we don't want to have anything to do with them."

"We'd be more than happy if we had no interaction with them at all," Sam said in a low tone. "Unfortunately, they make their presence felt."

Mitch asked what he meant by this, but Sam was evasive.

At midnight, Mitch said his goodbyes. Although he was tired, he could have stayed longer, but Sam had a casino to run and he did not want to impose on his generosity.

Before going to her suite, Ginger wanted a nightcap. They went to the lobby, but before she could get her drink, gunfire came from outside. Mitch pulled out his Ruger and ran out of the casino.

Another shot sounded, followed by a scream. He proceeded cautiously.

A kid who looked no older than sixteen staggered up Las Vegas Boulevard. The kid's blood flowed onto the street.

Mitch abandoned caution and ran toward him. Before he got there, the kid fell face first into the asphalt.

Mitch carried him off the road. Ginger held the kid's hand. He was wearing a black Tap Out tee shirt. He had a diamond stud earring in one ear and a nose ring to complement it. He groaned loudly and began to breathe heavily, his shirt soaked in blood.

"What can we do?" Ginger asked.

His body went limp. Mitch felt for a pulse. "Nothing. He's dead."

Although he had never met the kid, Mitch wanted to cry but no tears would come. Ginger sobbed softly. All of the good feelings that he had developed after meeting Sam Arcuri and his Playboy Bunny girlfriend were gone. What was going on in this town was not right.

## Chapter X

Mitch and Ron Ezrin, the other proprietor of the casino, buried Andy McCoy's body in the desert not far from the Strip. He had three bullet wounds, one of which pierced his liver. A teary-eyed Ginger accompanied them. The kid had no family, all of them having died in the alien invasion. He did odd jobs for some of the casino owners, including Sam and Ron.

They returned to the casino at four in the morning. Although fatigued, Mitch still wasn't sleepy. He had experienced the loss of colleagues, but this death deeply disturbed him. How could people kill each other at a time like this? In New Las Vegas, apparently it wasn't uncommon.

As they were taking the elevator to Ginger's suite, she sighed. "Every week or two, you see or hear about someone going down. Usually by gunshot or knife wounds. The problem is we don't have any law around here no more. Sometimes the folks get riled up, and you get some vigilante justice, but I'm not so sure that's such a good thing."

"Wonderful. So, this is basically an outlaw Wild West town."

Ginger turned away. "You might say that."

"I don't understand why you don't organize better. How can you have a society without laws and a police force?"

Ginger tried to change the subject to some popular culture topics from before the invasion, but Mitch wasn't interested, and his concentration waned. As they both got ready to sleep, he discovered the stage wasn't the only place that Ginger felt comfortable walking around without clothing.

He was staring at the Las Vegas skyline when she came from behind and began massaging his back and neck.

"You're all tense," Ginger said.

Mitch smelled her perfume. It smelled like an expensive one, probably pilfered from one of the casino stores. He closed his eyes as her hands sunk into his skin. It felt good. She pressed close against him. He could feel her breath on his neck. "You know, there's plenty of room in my bed for you. I wouldn't mind sharing it with you."

Mitch turned and opened his eyes. She was now wearing a robe. "Ginger, this has nothing to do with you, believe me. You've been nice to me, and I appreciate it. You're a beautiful woman. Although it was almost six years ago since I last saw my fiancée Deborah, it seems like yesterday. I don't know whether she's alive or dead. She was with me at the time, so she was probably killed in the attack." Mitch paused and took a breath. "But since I woke up, I haven't stopped thinking about her. Every day, her memories linger in my head."

Ginger put her finger to his lips. Tears had formed in her eyes. "Don't say any more. I don't know what it's like, since I never felt like that about someone, but I can tell you truly love her. Maybe someday you might feel that for me, but I'm willing to wait. I've never met a guy like you. If I had met someone like you when I was younger, things may have been different. You don't have to worry about me. I won't come on to you again."

Mitch smiled. "Thanks, Ginger."

When Mitch's head touched the pillow, he had no problem finding sleep.

***

Mitch woke to the smell of sausage and pancakes. He propped himself up as Ginger put two trays on a table in the living room.

The food smelled great. Before he even inquired, Elizabeth told him that the kitchen downstairs made food for her upon request. Amazingly, the hotel still offered many of the same services the old MGM Grand used to offer, minus the extravagant stuff.

Mitch's stomach growled. He put on a pair of shorts and joined Ginger at the table.

After they finished eating, they took an elevator downstairs, bringing their trays along with them. When they reached the lobby, people were gambling, drinking at the bar, smoking, and having a good time. It was as if the death of Andy McCoy meant nothing to them.

He was greeted with a half hug by Sam Arcuri. "Hey, Mitch, just wanted to give you a heartfelt thanks for helping bury the kid. I wish you didn't have to witness that. There is an ugly side of this town. And believe me, I know it's not perfect, but I firmly believe that the idea of New Las Vegas is worth pursuing."

Sam gave Mitch a card good for free food and beverage while at the casino. Mitch thanked him. Sam was a good man, just a bit misguided.

Mitch was sitting at the bar drinking iced tea when Ginger sidled up next to him. "I'm on in fifteen minutes. Are you going to see the show?"

Mitch grinned. "I think I'll pass. I pretty much saw it all yesterday."

"I wouldn't be so sure about that," Ginger said. "I like to throw in new moves to get the crowd going."

"I have little doubt that you'll thrill them."

Ginger kissed him on the cheek. "Have fun. Meet me back here."

Mitch explored the town. These folks had no direction in life without the roots of their old society. He vowed that he would not wind up like them.

He met up with Ginger before nightfall. They sat at the table drinking beer in front of the stage where a magician was performing. This cat was nowhere near the caliber of the old performers like Siegfried and Roy.

The magician stopped when a piercing siren sounded in the casino. Mitch looked around and found a mixture of alarm and fear on the patrons' faces as they gathered their chips and belongings.

Sam Arcuri ran onto the stage, knocking over the magician. The magician's parrot began squawking, then flew away.

"What the hell's going on here?" Mitch muttered.

Sam grabbed the microphone. "A sweeper has been spotted just north of Las Vegas Boulevard. I repeat, a sweeper has been spotted and is coming in our direction. We at Sam and Ron's Casino take every precaution to ensure the safety of our patrons. We would like everyone to move to a shelter located in the basement until the threat is over. There is enough room for everyone. Thank you for your cooperation."

"My husband's out there!" a woman shouted. "I heard him calling me."

Sam raised his hand. "Ma'am, please do not leave the casino. Thus far, none of the sweepers have gone inside the buildings. I can't guarantee your safety once you leave."

"But he's calling for me. He was at the Decadent Dream earlier. He must have come over here to get me."

Mitch couldn't hear anything above the noise in the casino. He wasn't sure if the woman was really hearing her husband or if she was crazy.

The patrons and employees followed Ron Ezrin to the shelter.

Mitch demanded to know what was going on, so Ginger and Sam enlightened him to their alien problem. The sweepers would go through the streets, and capture people walking by, wrapping them up in a web or cocoon. Sam assured him that they would be safe if they stayed inside. They had never bothered entering one of the casinos before, since people could always be found roaming the street. The Vegas residents tried to fight them at first, but quickly realized they were overmatched and now just went into hiding.

Mitch slammed his fist on the table. "I can't accept that. This is no way to live. Damn it, we can't let these aliens roll over us."

"Mitch, there's nothing we can do," Sam said. "It's about survival. You were in a coma for the worst part of it. Things are getting better. Are they perfect? Absolutely not, but it's much better than it used to be. Everybody around here lost loved ones, but we're the lucky ones because we're still here."

"You call yourself lucky. This isn't any kind of life. This country was built on freedom. It's something I fought and killed for. We don't have any freedom. We can't even walk the streets without the possibility of sweepers getting us."

Ginger put her hand on Mitch's shoulder. "Maybe things will change, but for right now, this is how it is. You have to let it go, Mitch."

Mitch bit his lip. "So now what? We just wait it out."

"All of the casinos have employees stationed on and off the Strip looking for the sweepers and other aliens. We're in constant communication, so we'll know when the sweepers are gone, just like we knew they were here."

Mitch propped his chin on his left fist. The people abducted by the sweepers would probably be used as slave labor in mines, just as he had been slated for prior to his escape.

Mitch turned when a yell came from beyond the gambling parlor. He looked up and found the woman whose husband was missing running toward them.

Sam's eyes narrowed. "What are you doing here? You should be downstairs."

"I have to find my husband," she screamed. "He's out there."

Ginger grabbed the woman's arms. "Look, I haven't heard anybody calling from outside. I'm sure he's safe inside one of the casinos. Going out there ain't going to help anyone."

"Listen, ma'am," Sam said. "I'll get in radio contact with the folks at the Decadent Dream, and they can check and see if he's there. In the meantime, just stay put."

The woman had a far-away look. For a moment, he contemplated physically subduing her, but it wasn't his place. If she had a loved one out there, then it was her right to do what she could to help him.

The woman broke free from Ginger. "I have to find him." She ran off screaming.

"Oh boy." Sam whistled. "This isn't good."

Ginger shook her head. "This woman's not a local. Otherwise, she would know better."

The three looked at each other, not saying a word. A loud scream came from outside. Mitch pulled out his Ruger and ran toward the casino exit. He still had his knife sheathed.

"What are you doing, Mitch?" Ginger asked.

He ignored her. Outside, dusk was settling. He glanced to the left and saw nothing. He turned right and spotted what only could be a sweeper, causing his stomach to churn.

It looked like a monstrous insect, at least two meters in height and three meters in length. It was covered by a shiny, black metallic shell. Its head turned in all directions. It had two pairs of large pincers and six legs, four in the back and two in the front. Its underbelly had a compartment-like structure where it held its victims, two of which were wrapped in a sticky, yellow substance.

A scream coming from the woman who had run out of the casino took Mitch's attention off the sweeper. The sweeper approached her. She was partially covered by the same sticky, yellow substance that had enveloped the other victims.

With resolute determination, Mitch walked out onto the street. Sam and Ginger stood at the entrance, yelling at him to return. They might not be willing to stand up to the sweeper, but he was.

He shot his Ruger. The bullets bounced off of its hard exoskeleton. "Shit!"

It turned toward him.

Mitch stood his ground. "Come on you bastard. I'm not going anywhere."

The sweeper shot out a jet of yellow liquid, but Mitch deftly moved out of the way. He put his Ruger away, not wanting to waste any more bullets.

The sweeper charged at him hard, and Mitch back peddled, looking for an avenue of escape and counterattack. With the sweeper nearly on top of him, he backed up against a car. Just before it reached him, he jumped onto the car's hood. It lifted the car off the ground with its pincers. Mitch nearly lost his balance and fell off. He steadied himself and jumped onto the sweeper's back.

The sweeper kicked up. Before Mitch fell off, he reached with his left arm and pulled it around the sweeper's neck. Mitch freed his right arm and punched the back of its neck. He wasn't sure if he did any damage, but if he continued punching, he would break his hand against its shell. Wincing, he pulled back his bloody right fist.

The sweeper threw Mitch off its back. He broke the fall with his arms, rolled over, and landed on his back. Slightly dazed, he tried to get to his feet, but before he could, the sweeper was on top of him. Its bottom pincers came down. He rolled out of the way. It lunged with its top pincers. He did not have time to escape, so he grabbed them with both hands. Despite their incredible force, he held on. Sweat dripped from his brow. His muscles shook from exertion. He gritted his teeth as its bottom pincers thrust towards his abdomen. Mitch let go of the top pincers and grabbed the bottom ones.

He lifted his legs and drove them into the sweeper's underbelly, which was not protected by the heavy exoskeleton. Unable to hold on indefinitely, he let go of the bottom pincers and rolled left. He reached for his knife, located in a holder on his belt. As the sweeper descended, he rammed the knife into its belly.

He breathed a momentary sigh of relief when the sweeper squealed. Orange liquid flowed from the wound as he pulled the knife out. He stabbed the sweeper's belly repeatedly as orange liquid spilled on top of him. He yelped in pain as it burned his skin.

The sweeper stood vertically on its four bottom legs, still squealing. Mitch lowered his shoulder and rammed the sweeper, knocking it over on its back. He climbed on top of it and plunged the knife repeatedly into its belly. He had stabbed it over fifty times when it finally stopped thrashing.

Mitch took a deep breath and slid off the alien. He landed on his thigh, throbbing with pain in so many places that he could not tell exactly what was hurting. He wrapped his arms around his knees and watched the sweeper to make sure that it was dead.

He grabbed its pincers and propped himself up. He tore off his shirt and used it to clean the orange substance that had spilled from the alien's body. After wiping the knife with his torn shirt, he sliced the material holding the sweeper's two human captives. One was a young girl, the other a middle-aged man, who he presumed to be the woman's husband. Both were unconscious but breathing.

Slowly, he walked over to the woman who had fled from Sam and Ron's. Her eyes were open, but she was motionless.

"Please help," she whispered.

"Don't worry. I'll get you out of here," Mitch said.

He sliced through the webbing and pulled her out.

Ginger and Sam ran to him. He glared at Sam, who overzealously patted Mitch on the back, nearly causing him to let go of the knife and inadvertently stab the woman.

"Holy mother of God," Sam shouted. "That was something else. That's the first time I ever saw someone kill an alien."

"You were incredible, Mitch," Ginger said.

A smile crept on Mitch's face despite his fatigue. His skin was still burning, and he would have to treat his cuts to prevent infection, but despite it all he felt damn good. "Let's get these people inside."

## Chapter XI

Mitch stayed inside, not wanting to be part of the spectacle. He took the opportunity to get in a strenuous workout at the hotel gym. It felt good to be hitting the weights and treadmill again. He could hardly believe that killing the sweeper provoked this kind of reaction. It seemed to have awoken the spirits of the people of New Las Vegas.

Ginger remained with him while people paraded outside. They were carrying the dead sweeper on a platform down the Strip while a band played. People were dressed in costumes. Euphoria had spread like a brushfire.

After finishing the workout, Ginger asked, "Sure you want to stay inside? You're the man of the hour."

"I'm positive," Mitch said.

"What you did was a big deal."

"Killing one alien won't make any difference in the grand scheme of things. I'm not going to be satisfied until each and every one of them is gone."

"It is a big deal," Ginger insisted. "You've given us hope. You made us believe that we can stand up to the sweepers."

"Or maybe I just made them angry. Next time there might be twice as many."

"No one knows what's going to happen in the future, Sugar, but you've given everybody a great feeling, and that's a good thing."

He tried to be gracious, but the parade was too much. He thought it wrong to carry a dead alien on a platform and celebrate like they had won a war.

\*\*\*

Later that evening, after the celebration, Sam Arcuri invited Mitch and Ginger to a private guestroom in the casino. Mitch stared at the room's lavish decorations, furnished with a massive chandelier, paintings, Persian rugs, and fine crystal. Plush velvet chairs surrounded the mahogany table. Sam introduced him to representatives of each of the casinos in New Las Vegas. The various casino owners showered Mitch with gifts, giving him cigars, clothes, an iPod, radios, even a sword. Sam and Ron had the head chef prepare him a steak and lobster dinner and had brought a special bottle of champagne for the occasion. Mitch was uncomfortable with the gifts and praise. When he was in the SEALs, his missions had been top secret, and his medals given in private.

Sam asked him to take a seat. "I know you're new in town and still feeling your way around, but you've made a definite impression on us, and we're thankful to have you here. Look, I'm not going to lie to you. I've done pretty well for myself here in New Las Vegas, but I'm not foolish enough to think that things can't be better. Getting more law and order, and becoming more organized would benefit everyone here, myself included. That's the one thing missing that could return Vegas to being a first-class destination. That's why we want you to stay and take charge of this town. You can call yourself the sheriff, the mayor, governor, whatever title you want. Makes no difference to us. The bottom line is that we want you in charge."

Mitch raised his brows. "Sam, that's a generous offer, but you hardly know me. And I just met the other folks. How could you possibly know I'd be an effective leader?"

Sam smiled. "Because you've shown incredible courage and decisiveness."

"I'll be honest, I don't like what this place has become." Murmurs came from the crowd. Mitch proceeded, not caring who he offended. "I have a problem with the general lawlessness around here. You have people killing each other over card games. You have sweepers abducting people. You got strippers, prostitutes, and every form of debauchery. No offense to you, Ginger. I know you're trying to get by, and I fully understand that. After we've lost everything, it just seems frivolous. Millions of people are working as slaves for the aliens, yet here you people are, yucking it up and having a good time, like nothing's changed. It has, from now until forever. I'm sure your intentions are good, but what's happening here just isn't right."

Sam raised his hand. "I understand your concerns. Well, this is your chance to change things and right this ship. We realize our town isn't perfect. We're willing to give you all the support you need. You can choose a staff. We'll give you financial support, vehicles, weapons, land, housing, whatever you need. We think you can turn this into a place where people don't fear alien abduction. We think you can make this into a place that people want to live in and visit."

Mitch got up from his chair and began pacing. "Maybe you're right. Maybe I can fix this society you've created. I'm glad you feel the need for change. I'm flattered that you think

I'm the person for the job, but this isn't what I had in mind when I awoke from my coma. I won't be satisfied with just having a habitable human city. I have greater ambitions. I'm going to reclaim Mother Earth from the aliens."

Murmurs sounded from inside the room.

"I don't know how I'm going to do this. Believe me. I know what the aliens are capable of doing. I was there when they first entered the planet. It won't be easy, but they're going to have to kill me in order to stop me."

Sam put his hand on Mitch's shoulder. "Who knows? Maybe someday you'll do it. I'd be lying to you if I told you I believe it's possible, but you can start in Vegas. Then maybe we can spread to other communities and unite."

Mitch shook his head. "The offer is tempting, but if I take you up on it, I'll be bogged down here. I'm sorry, but I have to move on. You don't need me. I'm a symbol of what could be. You know what needs to be done, so go ahead and do it. You need to assemble a police force and equip them with the resources to get their job done. Elect a mayor or governor and develop laws. Base them on the old laws. Once you have that established, you can build a school, a library, maybe start manufacturing again. We have to become self-sufficient and gain confidence in ourselves. You can do all those things without me."

Mitch could read the disappointment in Sam's face. Sam probably thought he would jump at the offer, and although Mitch liked the man and some of the people he had met in the last few days, he had bigger fish to fry.

***

Mitch was in Ginger's suite packing when the door opened. Her bright smile lit the room. She sat on her bed as Mitch continued to pack.

"Sam asked me to try to talk you into staying."

"It's not going to work, Ginger. I already made up my mind."

"I'm not going to try to talk you out of it."

Mitch paused and regarded Ginger with her thick, pouty lips. "Why not?"

Ginger explained how Sam and the others thought he was crazy about defeating the aliens, but she believed in him. Then Ginger dropped a bomb shell. She wanted to go with him.

Mitch sat next to Ginger. "I don't know. I was planning on traveling alone."

"Is there enough room in that craft of yours?"

"Oh yeah, there's enough room, but I don't know what I'm going to do. I don't know much of anything to be honest. I have grandiose ideas, but no game plan."

"You'll figure it out."

Mitch smirked. "You have more faith in me than I warrant."

"You can't go this alone. I can cook, clean; I'm great at making conversation."

Mitch raised his brows.

"No, I'm serious. You need a woman…for companionship. All those hours traveling by yourself will make you go bat-shit crazy."

"It's going to be dangerous. I probably won't make it out alive."

Ginger would not be deterred regardless of what argument he made.

"All right. You can come along, but you have to follow my rules. You're going to do what I tell you and not question my decisions."

Ginger smiled. "You make yourself out to be a tiger, but you're a real sweet guy."

Mitch closed his suitcase and helped Ginger gather her belongings. She wanted to bring everything, but space was limited, so he made her choose between items to leave behind. Although Sarm's aircraft was big enough for all of her stuff, he didn't know what he might pick up along the way.

"You're going to have to tell Sam and Ron that you're leaving," Mitch said when they were almost finished.

"I know. It won't be easy."

Mitch accompanied her as she told Sam about her decision. He hardly seemed surprised. He gave her his blessing, and said the door was always open if she wanted to return. The same held true for Mitch.

Sam and Ginger left the following morning. He launched the aircraft and watched as the casinos fell from view. Tears streamed down Ginger's face. He squeezed her hand and smiled.

## Chapter XII

Mitch flew northeast of Las Vegas, keeping a close watch on the three-dimensional radar screen. When the visual display was blank, he gave Ginger a tour of the aircraft. They had placed her belongings underneath her cot, located in the opposite side of the vessel from his cot.

"So where are we going?" Ginger asked.

"Toward the Rocky Mountains," Mitch said. "I don't have any real destination in mind. I want to find a populated area and scope out the situation."

Thus far they had seen small groups of people. Mitch was looking for something that resembled a community.

"Why don't we fly east?" Ginger asked. "You got New York and DC."

"I can't imagine it's any better there. I don't want to fly across the country, just to find out that there aren't any people around. Sarm had limited intel on both alien and human settlements since he did not travel much because he was taking care of me."

"I had family in Wyoming," Ginger suggested. "Maybe we could try that."

"The population was sparse in Wyoming to begin with. It's probably more so now, although, it might be a good place to hide out."

Mitch took out the road atlas. He had been to Wyoming for SEAL training. He flipped through the pages. "Canada might work. I've spent some time in Western Canada. Hmm, maybe Alaska."

"That sounds cold. I don't like cold weather."

Mitch raised his eyebrows. "What did I say about not complaining?"

Ginger sat on the co-pilot seat and frowned. "I guess Canada wouldn't be so bad."

"We could try to go outside of North America, but at least around here we'll be able to speak the language. Let's see what's out there, and then we'll make a decision."

"We?" Ginger asked.

"I'll take your opinion into consideration."

After an hour, Mitch put the craft in autopilot, still unsure of where to go beyond surveying the Rocky Mountains. They ate lamb chops and potato salad prepared by the kitchen at Sam and Ron's casino.

As they were finishing, Ginger pointed at the monitor. "Hey, what's that?"

Four large shapes were flying toward them. Mitch gritted his teeth. "Salenkos."

"What are they?"

"Something you want to avoid. We're changing course." Mitch turned left. A few minutes later, they were no longer on the visual display, and he breathed easier.

Later, Mitch caught a glimpse of what he was looking for. They were traveling over the Rocky Mountains in Colorado. Houses mushroomed among the trees and steep hills. They weren't refined like the ones that existed before the invasion. These were crude and likely to have been built by new settlers. Although well hidden in the mountainous landscape, he occasionally spotted people. They were trying to conceal themselves from the aliens, which was a good sign.

"Should we land?" Ginger asked.

"Let's circle the area first."

Mitch scouted the territory closely. He lowered the craft's altitude and flew for a few miles, making a zigzag pattern, eventually returning to his starting point.

"What do you think?" Ginger asked.

Mitch nodded. "Looks good to me. I'm going to find a clear path to land on."

Mitch descended. The area was dense with foliage. It took several minutes before he found an adequate clearing. He gently lowered the craft and touched the ground.

"You're good at this," Ginger commented.

"I'm still learning."

Mitch asked if she was ready, but Ginger fidgeted and expressed doubt about starting a new life. Mitch assured her that she would be fine.

Mitch took his backpack, opened the vehicle's hatch, and walked down the steps leading to the outside. He looked around wide-eyed at an unfriendly-looking group of people. Some had guns, while others had baseball bats, pipes, and clubs.

Mitch tilted his head to Ginger. "Nice and easy. Follow my lead."

He slowly lifted his hands in the air. Ginger did the same.

A man with a rugged brown beard approached them, pointing a hunting rifle at Mitch's head. "Any more in that ship of yours?"

Mitch shook his head. "Just the two of us."

"That looks like an alien ship," brown beard said. "They makin' you infiltrate us?"

"Nothing like that," Mitch replied. "I took this vehicle from an alien. We're alone, seeking friendly faces."

The man's eyes narrowed as he circled Mitch. "Where did you come from?

"Las Vegas. Previously I had been in Southern California."

The crowd continued to grow. A blond-haired kid barely out of his teens was inspecting the vessel closely. Mitch kept half an eye on the kid, just to make sure he didn't try anything stupid.

"I heard there's a lot of people living in Vegas. Is that true?"

"There's a good number of people living there and...passing through." Saying vacationing would sound ridiculous.

Mitch had to diffuse the tension. He lowered his hands, walked toward the man, and suggested that they leave, but brown beard told him he didn't have to leave.

Mitch allowed a slight smile. "My name is Mitch Grace. You can put the weapons down. We're not here for a fight."

"And who's your friend?"

"I'm Elizabeth McNeice."

"We don't want any trouble." Mitch continued moving forward.

The man, who introduced himself as Ethan, lowered his gun, and the others followed suit.

Mitch extended his hand, and Ethan shook it. Elizabeth did the same. Ethan then introduced them to the others who had gathered.

Mitch had a difficult time remembering all the names. There were over thirty people present. They had hard looks on their faces, similar to what he had found in war-torn countries. Certainly not the faces of American citizens. Still, they were friendly and welcoming.

"So, you guys have some sort of settlement here?" Mitch asked.

"That's about the size of it," Ethan replied.

"You keep yourselves pretty well concealed," Mitch commented.

"We had to fly around a few times before we could tell for sure," Elizabeth said. "Mitch has eyes like a hawk. I would never have spotted it."

"I've done my share of surveillance and reconnaissance," Mitch admitted.

"You a military man?" Ethan's face lit up.

Mitch nodded. "Navy SEALs for a decade. I guess we no longer have a military."

"I heard rumors about militias forming, but that's about it. Everyone fends for themselves now and prays the aliens don't bother them."

Mitch had seen enough of that.

"How about I show you two around?"

"That would be great." Mitch looked back at children leering at his aircraft.

"Don't worry about them," Ethan said. "They won't go inside. The kids around here are forced to grow up quickly."

They exited the clearing and walked down a wide trail that sloped into a valley. They passed two houses built low to the ground, as if midgets lived inside.

As if reading his thoughts, Ethan said, "You mentioned before that we're pretty hidden. That's by design. We built these houses into the ground to make them less conspicuous. The houses are spread out to make it look like we have a small population, one that's not worth the effort if you're an alien. If they have infrared sensors, then being under the ground should hopefully mask that."

"I probably would have missed it if I wasn't looking for people."

Ethan led them to a stream. A tin cup stood on a nearby ledge. He took the cup and collected water coming off the rocks. He gave it to Mitch, who drank and then passed it to Elizabeth.

"Wow, that tastes great," she said. "I don't think I've ever tasted water that good."

"We don't have much around here, but we have clean water." Ethan pointed to his left. "Down that way is a road that leads to the valley. We have farms where we raise cows, chickens, goats, and pigs. We also grow crops. We're trying to be self-sufficient."

"How's that working out for you?" Mitch asked.

Ethan tilted his hand back and forth. "We're managing, but we don't have room for error. A bad storm or a crop failure could hurt us."

Thinking of what Sam Arcuri had said, Mitch asked, "Do you trade with others?"

"As seldom as possible. We want to keep a low profile."

"How are the roads in these parts?"

"Mostly intact," Ethan said. "Not so in the surrounding area. Denver and Boulder were burnt to the ground. They're wastelands. We've constructed new maps based on what roads are still drivable. We try to keep the driving to a minimum. Fuel isn't easy to come by."

They turned onto the paved road, which wrapped around a hill leading to a large, drab storage shed. Ethan opened the door, revealing a commercial helicopter. He asked if Mitch knew how to fly helicopters, since their only pilot had suffered a stroke. Mitch told him he had flown helicopters before, and it wouldn't be a problem.

As they began to walk back, Ethan explained how the community formed. "We're a small community. By last count we're around two hundred. A number of us were trying to get out of Utah when it happened. Along the way we met other folks. It was rough at first. We lost a bunch of folks traveling with us. The aliens attacked nonstop. We took shelter in the mountains, and that's how we wound up here. Some of the original group has gone elsewhere. Others have joined us. The only thing we ask is that everybody contributes for the good of the community."

"Does everyone contribute?" Mitch asked.

Ethan nodded. "We had a group of folks who took food but didn't work, so we asked them to leave."

"What did you do before the invasion?" Elizabeth asked.

"I worked for an industrial firm in Utah. I got a civil engineering degree from BYU. I guess that don't mean a whole lot these days. It's funny how things that had been so important before don't matter anymore."

"Your degree might not be worth anything," Mitch said. "But your knowledge is valuable if we want to rebuild our society."

Ethan chuckled. "Rebuild our society? We're just trying to survive, and we're having a helluva time of it."

Mitch did not say anything. Everyone he encountered had a defeatist attitude.

Up the road, two men were climbing a ladder, apparently trying to repair a roof.

"We had a big storm the other day," Ethan said. "Some of the houses got beat up. I can't say quantitatively because no one's keeping records, but it seems that the weather has become more extreme lately. Hotter days in the summer and crazy storms where I just cross my fingers and hope it doesn't do too much damage."

Sarm had mentioned that there had been climate changes since the invasion. There was a team of aliens studying its effects.

They reached Mitch's ship.

"How about you come over for dinner?"

"That would be great," Elizabeth said.

Ethan pointed to the house. "See you around six."

Walking back to the ship, Mitch said, "So you decided to use your real name."

Elizabeth smiled. "Ginger Lynn died when we left Vegas. I want a fresh start."

Mitch put his arm around her shoulder. "There's nothing wrong with that."

He opened the hatch of the craft. They entered, followed by the mystified eyes of the children who had gathered.

***

Along with Ethan, they dined with six others including the community's only physician, Doctor Sherwood. The dinner consisted of vegetable soup, fresh bread and meatloaf cooked in a brick oven. Unlike their counterparts, they did not have gas power, and only a limited supply of electricity from generators.

During dinner, he had the distinct feeling they were being tested. He had nothing to hide and answered their questions honestly. Elizabeth, on the other hand, was less than forthcoming about her past. She did not mention working as a stripper, let alone her brief stint in prostitution. Mitch had no intention of betraying her confidence.

After dinner, they had strawberry shortcake and tea. Ethan said, "On behalf of our humble little community, I would like to invite you and Elizabeth to stay for as long as you like. You're the kind of folk we need around here — good, honest people. And hell, it doesn't hurt that you're a SEAL, Mitch. God forbid we need to defend ourselves, we'd like to have you on our side. We don't have a lot to offer, but we're sheltered from the bad guys. At least they haven't bothered us yet, and there's usually enough food to go around."

Elizabeth beamed. She immediately wanted to agree to stay. Mitch thought they should sleep on it.

For the rest of the evening, the group pitched the merits of their community.

After they left and were walking back in the crisp evening air, Elizabeth extolled the virtues of the community: fresh air, beautiful scenery, great people, and best water she had ever tasted. Mitch had to remind her that she agreed to let him make the decisions without any argument, something she was inclined to ignore.

She hit home when she told him he was wavering on staying here because he was afraid to start his mission. He looked inside himself and found truth in what she said. That was when he agreed that this would be the place in which to settle.

Elizabeth's enthusiasm spread to him. He had the distinct feeling that this was what he was looking for. This group was taking positive strides to rebuild. They were trying to regain their lives. What they needed was someone to take this community even further, and he could be that person. Meanwhile, this could be the base of his operations in his fight against the alien conquerors.

Carl Alves

## Chapter XIII

Gary Daniels shook his head. "Will you look at that? That's the biggest damn tomato I've ever seen. And that cucumber's ungodly."

Mitch wore a wide grin. "And they taste great, too."

Daniels put the tomatoes in a basket. "That's from the fertilizer?"

Mitch nodded.

"Where did you get that stuff?"

"An alien."

Daniels frowned. He looked more like an accountant than a farmer with his wire-rimmed glasses, worn white buttoned-down shirt and black pants with a leather belt. "Hmm."

"Don't worry," Mitch said. "He's one of the good ones."

They brought the vegetables back to the farmhouse. After two months, he had found his niche in this isolated community, locating more fertile ground and improving their farming techniques using the knowledge he had gained from Sarm. Using the nearby stream, he had installed a series of pipes leading to the farm area. From there, he used a surface irrigation technique Sarm had taught him. As a result, their food supply had increased considerably.

He had also helped design and build new roads leading into the valley. Because they didn't have the materials to build asphalt roads, they had constructed dirt roads. His long-term plan was to get bulldozers, earthmovers, and other heavy machinery. Ethan knew where they could find the equipment, but it was not at the top of their priority list.

131

After loading the truck with fruits and vegetables, they drove up the mountain. Mitch had spotted fertile ground ten miles to the south that would make their crops more abundant and prevent future crop shortages.

Daniels pulled the truck up to the storage building where they kept the community's food supply, and Elizabeth waited inside.

Her job was to distribute the food among the households. She picked up a box of supersized squash. "What the hell are you giving these things, growth hormones?"

Mitch replied, "Don't worry. It's perfectly safe."

They put the boxes alongside others filled with lettuce, cabbage, potatoes, onions, and apples. A couple of months ago, the storage area was less than half full. Soon, they would have to look for another place to store food.

When they were done, Daniels offered to drive him in his diesel-fueled truck. Mitch declined, preferring to jog. Although he worked hard, he still maintained an exercise regimen. Sometimes he could hardly believe that less than a year ago, he was dead to the world. He had made too much progress to stop. He was bigger, stronger, and faster than he had been in his twenties when he started with the SEALs.

On the way home, he spotted Ethan Herzberg. He and his crew were building an extension that led from the main road to an area with abandoned houses. Mitch wanted to use the houses for new arrivals so they would not have to use the manpower and resources to build new ones.

Ethan put down his shovel. "Did you have a chance to look at the prints?"

Mitch nodded. He had studied the blueprints for the footbridge last night. "I'm not an engineer, but it looks sound. When will we be able to start?"

"After we finish this," Ethan said. "Maybe a week or two."

"That would be great."

Ethan wiped the sweat off his brow. "Elizabeth said that you wanted to find fishing supplies."

"That's right. The lakes and streams around here are filled with fish. If we get better fishing gear, we could take advantage of an underutilized food source. The old bait and tackle shop in the valley has been completely stripped down. I'm thinking Boulder."

Ethan grunted. "I don't think that's a good idea. What's left of Boulder ain't pretty. Colorado Springs would be better."

Mitch shrugged. "I've been meaning to go there anyway."

"The Air Force base?"

Mitch nodded.

"I was wondering when you were going to make that trip."

"There's been so much to do around here," Mitch said. "I haven't had the time, but it's been on my mind. I can combine the two trips."

He wanted to scout what armament and supplies were still at the base. He imagine much of it had been destroyed but was hoping some of it was salvageable. This would be the start of building his arsenal.

***

"What do you think?" Elizabeth asked, showcasing the strapless, blue sequin dress she had brought with her from Las Vegas that did more than an adequate job of showing off her curves. The dress looked just like the one he had seen Deborah wearing at the officer's ball when they first got together.

Mitch looked up from his desk. He had been reading a book he had borrowed from Ethan. "It's nice, I guess."

"Jeez, can't I get any more out of you than that?"

"I've never seen you wear a dress before. What's the occasion?"

Elizabeth shrugged. "Just felt like wearing it."

Mitch continued reading. Since they landed two months ago, he and Elizabeth had been living in the same house. They didn't so much live together as share space.

Elizabeth began to grow on Mitch. True to her word, she had not made any advances since Vegas. He now thought of her as his kid sister. She had quickly made friends throughout the village. She was a social butterfly.

"So, are you glad we decided to stay?"

Mitch put a bookmark in his book and closed it. "Yeah, as a matter of fact I am. These are good people. And the best part, no aliens."

"That's always a plus. I never thought I would enjoy country living. What about that other thing?" Elizabeth asked. "You know, getting back at the aliens."

"It's easy to get lost in day-to-day activities, but it's about time I started working on that. A couple of months will turn into a year, and then a few years, and so on, and we'll still be living in fear of the aliens, essentially slaves."

"But they don't seem interested in coming our way."

"For now," Mitch said. "It's only a matter of time."

Mitch thought back to the panic in Sarm's voice on the day he left his alien friend. He could very easily have become a slave to the aliens. The thought was still fresh in his memory. He would not rest until that was no longer a possibility.

\*\*\*

Mitch finished welding the last valve on the central pipe leading from the well that fed most of the houses in the village. He wiped the sweat off his brow and handed the propane torch to Ethan. They had taken propane tanks from an abandoned propane distributor an hour south of their community. "That should do it. We should have running water again."

Ethan patted Mitch on the back. "Nice work. I didn't realize you were a plumber."

Mitch shrugged. "I'm no expert, but I've picked up a little here and there over the years."

"Now that the job is done, you want to go back to my place and taste some beer I just brewed?" Ethan asked.

Mitch smirked. "Is it anything like the beer you brewed last time?"

"What was wrong with it?" Ethan raised his eyebrows.

"Nothing, if you like the taste of stale bread."

Ethan frowned. "Come on. It wasn't that bad."

"You're right. It was worse."

"Well, you have to try this batch," Ethan said. "It's much better. I'm using different hops. It's all in the hops."

Mitch put his hands in the air. "All right. Just remember, if this stuff kills me, you'll have to find someone else to work on the pipes."

Mitch put his tools back in his toolbox. They unfastened their horses and rode back to Ethan's house. Mitch preferred using horses to travel to remote places. To prevent the horses from getting injured, only the more experienced riders were allowed to take them in rugged terrain.

When they reached Ethan's modest house, they put their horses in the stable and went inside. Ethan lit an oil lamp, while Mitch sat on a simple wooden chair one of the village carpenters had built. Mitch leaned his head back and closed his eyes. He had been on his feet since four in the morning when Ethan had alerted him of the problem with the pipes. It felt good to sit.

Ethan poured a glass and set it on the table. "It'll be much better this time. The hops, remember?"

Mitch drank the beer. "Well, it is a little better than last time. Not good, but better than your last batch."

Ethan sat down and drank some of his own beer. "Mitch, there is something I want to talk to you about. You've been here for a bit of time now. I take it you don't plan on leaving any time soon."

"I have every intention of sticking around."

"Good. I've been talking to some of the folks who've been here since the beginning. We decided we need to transform this from a place of refuge to a real place to live. We've been doing what we can to survive, but we need to be better organized and structured, and we think you're the perfect person to take the leadership mantel."

Mitch put down his beer and laughed.

"What's so funny?" Ethan asked.

"Oh nothing. I'm just feeling a little déjà vu."

Ethan's brow furrowed.

"Never mind."

"You're a natural born leader. You're exactly what we need. Will you do it?"

Mitch took a deep breath. "Yeah, I'll do it. We can make something good out of this. This will be our base. This is where we start striking back at the aliens."

He pictured the Minister of Science's devious face. In Mitch's mind, this alien was the poster child of all that had gone wrong in his world. He was the face, the mastermind of the invasion. Mitch longed to see him again. They had unfinished business.

## Chapter XIV

Mitch sat at a table inside the village's new community center, which was a converted stable. A clipboard and a stack of papers were in front of him. It was a bright day, and they were using no artificial lighting.

He tapped his pen on the table. "Did you ever take a shop class in school?"

"No, not really," replied the young man with scraggily long hair. He wore a Megadeth tee shirt and a backwards cap.

"Have you ever worked on cars before?"

The young man shook his head.

Mitch sighed. "What did you do before all of this?"

"Um, I don't know. I used to ride my skateboard a lot."

"That won't help. How are you with computers?"

The kid shrugged. "I'm not a hacker, but I know what I'm doing."

"Fine. I'll put you on the automation team."

The kid nodded. "Cool."

"Talk to R.J. Arnberger. He'll get you started."

Next up was Marc Gonzalez. In his late twenties, he looked to be in good shape. Mitch read his information sheet.

"I see you spent time in the military." Mitch always considered this a plus.

"Yes. I served in the army as an Animal Care Specialist."

Mitch surveyed the young man. "Interesting. Tell me more."

"I had always been timid growing up but being in the army gave me confidence. I became more aggressive, not trying to avoid confrontation, protecting those in harm's way. I've also always had a knack for training animals, which I used in the army working with Military Working Dogs. After my time in the army, I trained attack and guard dogs."

Mitch thought about the German Shepherd he and Sarm had been nursing back to health. He hoped Radley was doing well. At least Sarm still had a companion.

He listened intently as Marc told him more about his background working with animals. "We can make use of your skills. Maybe even incorporate some dogs into our military unit."

Marc's eyes lit up. "I would love to be able to help you out with that. I also have experience using all sorts of guns, grenades, claymore mines, land mines."

Mitch smiled. "Consider yourself drafted into my special forces unit. I look forward to working with you."

Mitch's first task in improving the village was to provide a better distribution of labor. He had been interviewing candidates for five hours and was near his limit.

When Gary Daniels brought a steaming cup of coffee, Mitch's eyes lit up. "Thanks. You're a life saver."

"No problem, Chief," Gary said.

Mitch had recruited Gary, who had been a director of a waste management company, to help him. In his previous life, he had a great deal of experience with administrative tasks like hiring and firing.

"Who's next?"

"Sarah Williams," Gary replied. "She's lived past Miller's Bend with her aunt for over two years."

"Background?"

"She graduated high school, spent a year traveling with a rock band. Afterward she worked at a daycare in Utah."

Mitch sipped his coffee. "This should be easy."

Daniels brought her in.

Mitch shook her hand. "I don't think we've met before, but I know your Aunt Denise. I love her apple pie. She's a sweet woman."

"Yeah, she's great," Sarah said. "After my parents died, she's all I got."

"Well, you have us. We're all family."

Sarah nodded. "The people here have been great."

"So, you were a care giver at a daycare facility?"

"Yeah, I love kids. I'd like to have a few of my own."

Mitch smiled. "I might have the perfect fit for you. In the next month, we plan on converting the old Lutheran Church into a school. If we're going to have a future, we need to educate the children. How would you like to work at the school?"

"I don't know. School was never my thing. I barely finished high school."

"You seem bright, and you won't have to teach right away. You can start with taking care of the younger children. At night, you can take teaching classes. Madeline Burke is a retired schoolteacher. She's a little too old these days for manual labor, but she'll be teaching some of our younger folk on the fine points of teaching. In a year or two, you can start teaching music and math to the children."

Sarah smiled. "I never really applied myself in school, but with something that I like to do, I might do better."

140

"I'm sure you will. Everett Griffin's running the school. He'll contact you. Right now we're getting books from schools that weren't totally destroyed. Once we have the books and finish renovating the old church, we'll open the school. In the meantime, we can always use extra help in the fields picking fruits and vegetables."

Mitch shook her hand, and she left.

Mitch conducted three more interviews. When they finished, he said, "Thanks. You did a great job screening the candidates."

Daniels shrugged. "This is a good idea. Since we've been assigning jobs, I've noticed a difference in the folks around here. They have a sense of purpose. If you think about it, pre-invasion most people defined themselves by their job. You ask someone to describe themselves, and they'll say I'm a lawyer, or a nurse, or a student. Take that away, and you take part of their identity away."

"I never really thought about that. I just wanted to find a way to accomplish tasks more efficiently, but I suppose you're right."

Besides assigning people jobs based on experience, talent and interest, Mitch wanted to train people in areas other than their primary job responsibility to create a more diverse work force.

Dr. Sherwood, the community's only doctor, had taken on two assistants. By day, she gave them hands-on training. At night, she taught classroom sessions using textbooks from a nearby university covering various aspects of biology and medicine. It was not quite medical school, but after a few years, she believed the community would have several competent doctors.

Besides this, Ethan Herzberg taught engineering theory and practical application to seven students. There were similar classes in plumbing, nursing, architecture, and agriculture. Mitch encouraged everyone to try a new field.

Mitch was building his own army and required every healthy person to take combat training that he instructed. Most recruits were still in basic training. Before long, his goal was to put them through advanced weapon and battlefield tactics.

Daniels flipped through the pages of his notebook. "This thing never ends. We have seven more interviews scheduled for tomorrow."

Mitch smiled. "That's because more people keep moving in. How many in the last month? About fifty or sixty? Word has spread about our thriving community, and people want to be a part of it. As long as they contribute, I don't have a problem with expanding."

Despite the new residents, Mitch wanted to remain inconspicuous. Instead of clustering houses together, they built new ones further down the valley that were designed to blend in with the surroundings. Periodically, Mitch performed aerial surveillance to make sure that they didn't have the appearance of a thriving community.

*** 

Mitch laid out the outline of the air force base at Colorado Springs in front of Ethan Herzberg. He had made three reconnaissance missions to the base.

"I want to bring a dozen, maybe two dozen people. We won't be able to get everything in one shot, so we'll make a series of runs." Mitch handed him a list of what he planned on obtaining at the base. The list contained fighter planes, helicopters, tanks, bombs, missiles, and artillery. Since it was an air force base, there were more jets than he would typically find in Coronado.

"Wow," Ethan said. "This is serious shit."

Mitch told him that they would need to construct several hangars. He had taken prints of hangars from Colorado Springs as a guide. He wanted to plant tall trees and bushes surrounding the hangars to conceal it. Even if they needed to divert resources, this would be well worth it.

They had acquired equipment from old construction sites and home improvement stores. They now had bulldozers, earthmovers, heavy trucks, and cranes. Gary had expressed some doubt because the construction crew had never built anything like this before, especially in the tight time frame Mitch was requesting.

Ethan raised his brows. "What's the hurry?"

"I've wasted too much time already."

Ethan frowned. "I wouldn't call what we've done here a waste of time."

"I didn't mean it like that. The longer the aliens control the planet, the harder it will be to convince people that we can do something about the occupation."

"Mitch, you really think we can get rid of the aliens? I mean, they destroyed the combined military forces of the world like they were nothing. It was like when the Germans invaded

Poland in World War II, and the Poles tried to fight off the German tanks on bicycles."

"I was in a coma. The aliens never had to deal with me."

"I consider you as close a friend as I have, but I don't know about this."

"Look at it this way; if we get invaded by aliens, we'll be in a better position to fight them off. I told you about Vegas. The people were deathly afraid of those sweepers. They hid and let the sweepers abduct whoever was walking the streets. I said no, it's not going to happen, and killed one of them. It can be done. You just need guts and the will to do it."

After finalizing the plans Ethan said, "There's something I want to talk to you about. It's of a personal nature."

Mitch's brows furrowed. "You know you can talk to me about anything."

"It's about Elizabeth."

Mitch frowned. "What about her?"

"I know the two of you came over from Vegas, and that you've been living together ever since. If I'm overstepping my boundaries, feel free to tell me to mind my own damn business, but I was wondering if there's anything going on between you."

Mitch chuckled. "Me and Elizabeth. Never has been and never will. She's like a kid sister to me."

Ethan pulled out his wallet and took out an old picture. Ethan looked about fifteen years younger in the photo. "Karen and I were high school sweethearts. We got married when we were still in college. We wanted to wait until after graduation, but we were so much in love that we got married right away. She's the only woman I've ever been with. I told you how Karen

144

died in the attack. It left me devastated. I thought if I was ever with another woman again, it would soil her memory."

Mitch put his hand on Ethan's shoulder. Ethan was one of the few people he had confided in about his previous relationship. "I know about loss. The day of the invasion, I proposed to Deborah. I know I'll never see her again, but I can't move on."

"I've really taken a liking to Elizabeth. She's sweet and caring. I feel so damn guilty thinking about her, but I can't stop."

"There's nothing wrong with it. Karen died seven years ago. I know the wound is still fresh, but I don't think Karen would mind. In fact, I'm sure wherever she is at, she'd give you her blessing. I know that Elizabeth's very fond of you. When you come over to our house, there's a little spring in her step and giddiness in her voice."

"Ya think?"

"Oh yeah. You're probably rusty at this sort of thing, so just tell her how you feel."

Ethan smiled. "Maybe I'll do that. Thanks, Mitch. This is what I needed to hear."

After Ethan left, Mitch stared at the ceiling thinking about Deborah. Not that he tried, but even if he wanted to, there was no way he could get her out of his mind. He sat on the floor and buried his head in a pillow. No matter how much he accomplished, he knew he would always be hollow without her in his life.

\*\*\*

When Mitch arrived at his classroom, he was annoyed to see another class in session. Stationed at a naval base in Virginia, Mitch had been tasked with leading underwater demolition training with new recruits. Before they received hands-on training in Puerto Rico next week, the trainees needed classroom time to understand the concepts.

He glared at the instructor, who shot back her own glare. She excused herself and stomped out of the room. "If you don't mind, I'm trying to teach here."

"I can see that," Mitch said. "But I have to teach a demolition class and I have this classroom reserved. I can't afford any delays so I'm going to have to ask you to move to another room."

"Well, you're going to have to go elsewhere. I've had this room reserved for two weeks."

"I have my slides set up for this room. I don't know what frivolous class you have set up here, but I'm set to leave for Puerto Rico in two days with my trainees and we can't afford any hiccups. Underwater demolition is serious business, lady, and I don't want any of the boys to get hurt out there."

She shook her head. "Underwater demolition? Let me guess. You're a SEAL."

Mitch did not respond.

The woman, although undeniably attractive, had a hard edge to her. He couldn't even picture her cracking a smile. She possessed the demeanor of a lion tamer. "You SEALs are all alike. You think you can just smash and bash your way through everything. Well, this is not a combat zone and you can't use your rough house tactics to bully your way into this room. Find another one."

Mitch ground his teeth. The SEAL teams were among the most elite fighting group in the world and deserved special treatment. "I don't know what your function is..."

"It's Lieutenant Norville, Naval Intelligence." She said it with this arrogant tone, like what she did was so much more important than what he did. Who did she think she was?

"I can assure you that your job and the safety of the citizens of this world, I mean our country would be at risk without what I, I mean my group does."

"That's fine, but you're not getting my classroom."

Mitch sighed and walked away. He was taken aback that she had pegged him right away. She was a sharp cookie. It took him a half hour to find another room and he had to wait until she finished before he could do his slide show presentation.

For some reason, Mitch could not shake this confrontation out of his mind. His team operated outside of the rules on combat missions. The SEALs used unconventional methods to take the conflict to the enemy. They did not have the same rules of engagement as the regular army. During a mission, they had the authority to shoot anyone on the enemy side. They used speed and mobility to make the impossible happen. Back home, those same rules did not apply. He hated to admit it, but Lieutenant Norville was right. Despite this, after returning from Puerto Rico, he did not seek her out to apologize.

Three weeks after their initial encounter, Mitch attended an officer's ball at the naval base. He was not seeing anyone special, so he went by himself. He would not normally have gone without a date, but a few men in SEAL team three were leaving for a mission and he wanted to have one more night of revelry with the boys before they left.

On the way to the bar, he stopped in his tracks when he saw Lieutenant Norville eating hors' devours and talking to an officer's wife. Mitch did a double take when he saw her in her blue sequin dress. She looked stunning.

Feeling foolish about their argument, he could not bring himself to talk to her. Instead, he tried to make himself invisible. Steve Galotta, a chief on SEAL team three, was able to coax Mitch into talking after a few martinis.

"Let me take care of this for you, buddy." Galotta patted him on the shoulder. He found Deborah sitting at a table with a glazed look on her face as she spoke to a senior officer.

Galotta waited for a break in the conversation. "Normally I don't do this sort of thing, but my friend's really down. I'm going to be departing in a couple of days. It would really bother me to leave seeing him so down in the dumps, so I told him I would find the prettiest woman in this place and get her to talk to him. I looked around and saw you and said to myself, you know if she can't cheer up Mitch then no one can. Would it be a lot to ask you to come over and talk to my friend for a few minutes?"

Deborah shrugged. "Why not? I've been bored since I arrived. I didn't even want to go tonight but was guilted into it." She followed Galotta. "He isn't hideous, is he?"

"Not at all. He's a good-looking guy. Very popular with the ladies. He's just a little shy."

Deborah gasped as she approached the table.

148

"Hey, Mitch, I want you to meet Lieutenant Deborah Norville. She's a naval intelligence officer. This is my friend, Mitch."

Mitch rose from his seat. "Well, this is unusual." He extended his hand. "Hi, I'm Mitch Grace."

Steve frowned. "Do you two know each other?"

"We had an unpleasant encounter the other day in C Building," Mitch said. "There was some confusion about a room that we both had booked."

"Yes, and you demanded that I leave."

Galotta waved his hand. "Well, that's all in the past. Tonight, we're here to have a good time."

"I agree," Mitch said. "Hey, Deborah, how about you let me make it up to you by getting you a drink. What's your preference?"

She asked for a glass of white wine. When the first slow song of the evening played, he asked her to dance. Several drinks later, Deborah and Mitch were having a great time. They joked and laughed so hard that a rear admiral at the next table asked if they could tone it down. As it turned out, they had a great deal in common. Both received ROTC scholarships from Cal Tech. Deborah majored in Computer Science and Mitch majored in Electrical Engineering. After fulfilling her ROTC requirements, Deborah got a master's degree in computer science. Mitch joined the SEALs. Both had achieved officer status quickly and both were single.

They talked throughout the evening, bouncing from one subject to the next. He was not sure if it was the alcohol that made them so talkative or if they had natural chemistry. They joked about some of the officers and their spouses and were oblivious to everything going on around them. By the end of the evening, both of them had drunk entirely too much.

Mitch said his goodbyes to his friends in SEAL team three and hoped that he would see them again. He never knew when it would be the last time. He gave an extra special thanks to Steve Galotta for doing him this big favor.

His head was nearly spinning when the ball was over. He walked Deborah back to her house. He was tempted to spend the night with her, and Deborah was more than willing. Instead, he gave her a single kiss on the lips and took a cab back to his place, not wanting their first sexual encounter to be based on a night of heavy drinking. He had the distinct feeling that this relationship could be special.

He waited until Monday to give her a call, needing a day to recuperate. He looked her up in the directory and called her office number. When they spoke, she seemed disappointed that he left early the other night. He offered to make it up by taking her to dinner the following night.

Mitch was amazed at how naturally their conversation flowed. After their first encounter, he did not think they could ever be friends. They concluded the evening by spending the night at Mitch's place, much to their mutual delight.

Unfortunately, Mitch's joy was killed the following day when he received an order to go to Ethiopia. A member of the UN Security Council was being held hostage by guerillas, and Mitch's SEAL team was to free him if negotiations did not progress. Normally, he would not have minded this type of mission. He liked to keep his combat skills sharp but did not want to leave Deborah so soon.

When he told her, she accepted it willingly. Before he left, they went out again. It was a magical night. Mitch felt like he was in heaven for one evening. It was that lingering memory that made him strive to get in and out of Ethiopia as quickly as possible.

When hostage negotiations failed, Mitch and his team struck quickly. Under the cover of night, they created a hellacious firefight. The area surrounding the compound where the official was being held hostage was set ablaze. They rescued him without suffering a single casualty or major injury on their side.

Elated by the success of the mission and the prospect of seeing Deborah, his hopes were crushed when his senior officer told him that his team would not be returning home right away. Instead, they had to go to the Persian Gulf where they were responsible for seizing oil exported by Iraq that was prohibited under United Nations sanctions.

Mitch contacted Deborah in Virginia and told her he would not be home for some time. Over the next four months, Mitch's SEAL team seized over five thousand metric tons of oil, halting the flow of illegal oil in the Northern Arabian Gulf. In the process, they captured and arrested three Libyan terrorists.

At long last, Mitch was able to go home. He was crushed upon returning when he found out that Deborah had been sent to Serbia.

Nearly a year after their first date, Mitch and Deborah were finally together again in Coronado, California. Mitch was tentative at first. Perhaps whatever flames they had were now extinguished. Although his feelings for her were still strong, the same may not be the case for Deborah. It was like going out for the first time.

Mitch was relieved to see that Deborah missed him as much as he missed her. They saw each other frequently during the next two months. Sadly, he had to leave for five months.

He never regretted his decision to join the SEALs, but these were trying times. He considered joining another branch of the Navy or retiring from the armed forces, but Deborah encouraged him to stay. He was very good at what he did, and the Navy and his country needed him.

They continued like this for five years. When they were together, they shared joy and ecstasy and happiness. When they were apart, their work kept them busy.

Mitch sighed as he thought about Ethan and Elizabeth, hoping they could find happiness together. As for him, the only woman who ever mattered to him was probably long dead, and he had no interest in trying to find someone to replace her.

## Chapter XV

Mitch stood inside the hangar with his arms folded, alongside Ethan Herzberg and Elizabeth. Not the most impressive hangar he had ever seen, it was sufficient for their purposes. The hangar consisted of a simple steel, portal framed building. It spanned seventy meters in length. The roof and walls were metal sheets welded together and painted red. The construction crew did their best with their limited knowledge and experience.

They had planted tall bushes and trees surrounding the hangar to camouflage it. It wasn't as thoroughly hidden as Mitch would have liked, but he knew before long the growth would become denser.

Elizabeth put her hand on Ethan's shoulder and stared at the stockpile of weapons with her mouth open.

"Hmm." Ethan stepped closer. "I don't even know what we got here."

Mitch stood in front of him. "This is a Pave Low IV helicopter. Its maximum speed is 165 miles per hour with a range of 630 miles. It's got three machine guns inside." He stepped past the helicopter. "We have five MK-82's and three MK-84'S. They're free fall bombs. Here are GBU 27 and GBU 28 missiles. They're laser-guided with a range of six to eleven miles."

Mitch opened a box full of guns. "We have an impressive array of machine guns. We have some M2's, M4 carbines." Mitch picked up an M16 semi-automatic rifle. "This one shoots eight hundred rounds a minute."

Mitch opened a box of Claymore mines and grenades.

"Holy moly," Elizabeth said.

Mitch led them into another room attached to the hangar. "Here's the real heavy-duty stuff. These are cruise and ballistic missiles."

Ethan frowned. "But Mitch, this is what the military used against them."

"I know, but we have the element of surprise. When the Minister of Science invaded, he knew we would counter-attack. He knew about our weapons and tactics, but his technology was so far advanced that we never stood a chance. I know a lot about terrorism. We're going to pound away at them and make conditions such that they won't want to live here anymore."

"I don't know, Mitch. It seems dangerous. We're not an army. We're just survivors."

"All true, but we have one significant advantage over the aliens who occupy this planet, something I guess wasn't exploited the first go around. We will make use of the waterways. They can't or don't. This gives us a significant advantage considering most of the planet is covered by water."

"How do you know they don't use the sea?" Ethan asked.

"Something I learned from an alien friend of mine. The good thing is amphibious attacks are my specialty. That's something we did to perfection in the SEALs."

Ethan nodded. "You might be right."

Mitch indicated he intended on making additional trips to Colorado Springs to tap into their vast arsenal of weapons and then start training their people.

Ethan expressed some interest on inflicting damage on the aliens but was concerned about the repercussions from the aliens. To this point they had been flying under the radar. To Mitch it was worth the risk.

They had some experienced military people. He was planning on recruiting and training new members, creating teams, and arming them. Before long, he would have a little army.

***

Mitch finished logging the inventory from his third trip to Colorado Springs in a database created by a member of the automation team. He couldn't help smiling. It was really happening. In the last trip, they had acquired two Strike Eagle and three Raptor fighter planes. Now, he had his eye on some Nighthawk jets sitting idle at the air force base.

He was pleased with the progress of the military training. His recruits were raw but eager to learn. He targeted the younger and stronger men and women for his new military arm, giving them classroom and hands-on training on guerilla warfare tactics.

In addition, he had set up reconnaissance and watch teams around camp. He didn't think they were at risk of being attacked, but he wanted his troops ready. They went on regular surveillance missions and employed radar systems obtained from Colorado Springs.

Silence filled the room when he shut down his computer. This was typical since Elizabeth had moved out to live with

Ethan. Although he missed her company, he was glad that they were together. The last thing he wanted was to stand in front of their happiness.

A knocking sound startled him.

Steve Minard, one of his young recruits, stood at the door, his face tight with worry. "We were doing surveillance near the New Mexico border by Durango and noticed an unusually large group of people. Then we saw aliens in the vicinity. They appeared to be going down mine shafts. I think the aliens are using them as slaves to work the mines."

Mitch spoke in a deadpan voice. "Right in our backyard."

"It appears so."

"Well, well. Isn't that interesting?" Despite his calm demeanor, his inner fury grew. Human slaves working mines. That would have been him if Sarm hadn't helped him escape.

"I thought you should know." Sweat dripped from Minard's brow.

Mitch sat back in his swivel chair. He knew this moment would come. Now that it was here, he didn't know how to feel. Were his troops ready for real combat?

His mind began working out details of a plan. Before they took action, he needed extensive preparation. He thought of how many people they needed for the mission, whom to choose, and what weapons and vehicles he would need.

"Um, Mitch, what are we going to do about it?"

"We're going to bust them out, Steve."

Mitch's eyes stared out into the distance. He was no stranger to rescue missions, but this would be unlike any he had done before. He reflected on his most infamous rescue as he prepared to get these people out of the mines.

*** 

Commander Parrett called Mitch into his Spartan office and briefed him on his next mission. Private Susan Russell had been captured and was being held as a prisoner of war. They had identified her location, and Mitch had to select twelve men from his SEAL team for the operation. Her capture and imprisonment had already captured worldwide attention, which meant her rescue would also be big news. They had to come back with the soldier without suffering casualties.

Mitch did not want any SEALs still green to combat to make a costly mistake, so he only chose experienced combat veterans.

Russell was being held in a hospital. He knew little about her condition, other than she was still alive. With any luck, she was not badly injured.

A group of marines would provide a diversion by engaging the Iraqis guarding the area. They arrived at the site at dawn via helicopter in coordination with the marine diversion. Mitch's ears buzzed with the sound of explosives and machine gun fire in the background. With their guns raised, they stormed the hospital. Two men carried a stretcher. As soon as they entered a lobby, Mitch spotted an Iraqi guard. Without a moment's hesitation, Mitch put a bullet in the man's head. After taking out the Iraqi soldier, Mitch encountered the doctors and the medical staff, who were surprisingly cooperative as they directed his team to Private Russell.

Private Russell was lying in bed. Clearly in bad shape, her eyes showed recognition as he entered her room.

"I'm Mitch Grace from Seal Team 3. We're here to get you out of here."

His team had escorted the Iraqi doctor who had attended to her into a room. His mannerisms showed that he had been sympathetic to his patients. "Can you please give me her status?"

The doctor nodded and spoke in near perfect English. "She is quite bad shape. Miss Russell has suffered a broken left arm, a broken ankle, and a broken hip bone. If you intend to extract her, you must exhibit great care."

Two SEALs raised her from the bed and lowered her onto the stretcher.

Just then, Mitch heard heavy footsteps along the corridor. He slid to the door leading to the corridor. Just as the footsteps got close, he leaped out and tackled an Iraqi guard. They tumbled to the ground in a heap. As Mitch struggled to his feet, the Iraqi elbowed his head. A white flash sparked in front of him. He blinked hard as the Iraqi lunged at him. Before his opponent could reach him, Mitch connected with an up kick to the man's throat. Mitch rose quickly, put his hands around the Iraqi's head, and drilled him to the nose with his knee. He landed two more knees to the man's head, which rendered him unconscious.

Mitch dragged the Iraqi's prone body to a supply closet and locked him inside. He went back to Private Russell's room, where two members of his team were getting ready to carry her out.

In the background, the firefight had lessened. He suspected that the enemy resistance was not what they thought it would be. As Mitch was continuing to discover, the Fedayeen were either not as strong or as loyal to Sadaam Hussein as he had originally believed.

Mitch held Private Russell's hand. The worst of this nightmare was over. She would receive treatment and then go home, where she would become a war hero.

She smiled and winked. The doctors had administered her heavy doses of drugs, and she appeared mostly out of it.

Mitch and the rest of the team surrounded the two SEALs carrying Private Russell on the stretcher. He was ready for another encounter with Iraqi guardsmen. They ran at a steady pace back to their helicopter. Mitch checked his watch. From the time they had landed to the time they had flown away, eleven minutes had passed.

***

Mitch had set up rotating surveillance units monitoring the mine for the last few weeks. He wanted to remain inconspicuous, so his troops set up camp miles away, and traveled two people at a time. At night, they used infrared cameras and a Global Hawk unmanned aerial reconnaissance vehicle obtained from the air force base at Colorado Springs.

Not surprisingly, the alien security at the mine was lax. The aliens had routed the humans so easily that they no longer considered them worthy adversaries. Apparently, the aliens thought that the human slaves had neither the will, nor the physical strength to escape. If they did, there was always a new crop to replace them.

Mitch hoped that the aliens' arrogance would work against them. Two aliens of a species Mitch had never encountered before guarded the camp. They were humanoid in appearance, standing on two legs. Their faces were sharp and angular with deep-set eyes. Their skin had the color and consistency similar to a salamander. They wore loose-fitting brown robes. The area was not fenced in nor had any physical barrier. Typically, one alien supervised about thirty humans. Neither the guards nor the supervisors appeared to be armed.

A preponderance of evidence suggested physical abuse. The slaves, who wore blue jumpsuits that looked similar to prison uniforms, had faces that looked worn and haggard. Welts and deep bruises were common on the slaves.

This would be the first mission in which they used Marc Gonzalez's trained dogs. He had spoken with Marc at length about how they could use them and felt this would be the ideal test for them.

The night before they attacked, Mitch gathered his team to go over the details of the mission. His skin tingled with a surge of excitement that had always preceded his SEAL missions.

"What if they counterattack?" Darius Washington, one of his pilots, asked.

No doubt Washington expected him to say they would cut and run. "We stand and fight, but it won't come to that if we do our jobs right. Now, I know that many of you are new to this. Some of you have no combat experience, and only a couple of you have ever been in special forces. I'm telling you right now, it's all about execution. Everyone here is a cog in the machine. If each person executes their job with perfection, then we will be in and out of there. Everyone must perform their job flawlessly. Nothing less is acceptable. I chose each of you with the confidence that you'll be able to perform when the time comes."

Mitch walked around the room, looking each member of his new team in the eye. He sensed their apprehension. "How many of you lost a loved one during the invasion?"

"I lost both my parents and my sister," Darius Washington said.

Steve Minard gazed at the floor. "My best friend died, my girlfriend, my mom, my grandparents. I don't know if my other relatives are alive or dead. I've got no one left."

Around the room, the team ran off a long litany of family and friends who had been killed. By the end, grief and anger flooded through Mitch. He ignored the grief.

"This is our time, boys," Mitch said. "You remember what those motherfuckers did. Remember how they took everything we have, and you pay them back. You do that by executing your part of the operation flawlessly."

\*\*\*

On the morning of the operation, Mitch could not stop his hands from shaking. He was more nervous than he could ever remember. His SEAL teams had been physically, mentally, and tactically the best of the best, training in state-of-the-art facilities. As a result, they were equipped to deal with every eventuality. For some of the men on this operation, Mitch had given them their only military training.

They set up their base camp ten miles away. Just before dawn, they advanced. The Jeeps and buses left first. Two Pave Low helicopters followed. Mitch flew in one of the choppers.

The helicopters trailed the land vehicles until they got close to the destination, then flew ahead. They landed to the left of the mine, out of the line of sight of two aliens patrolling the perimeter. When Mitch's chopper touched the ground, he was the first off and led the others on foot.

The commotion attracted the attention of an alien guard. Its green face scrunched together. Mitch knelt down and opened fire with his M-16 sub machine gun, cutting the alien down with a spray of bullets.

Mitch ran forward and bent down as he reached the alien, pointing his M-16 at it. He didn't know if it had a pulse to check, but it looked dead. One of his men was about to shoot it, but Mitch held up his hand.

Leaving the dead alien behind, they ran toward the entrance of the mine. Just then, an alien with a wide body and the face of a hyena came after them on all fours.

"Open fire," Mitch shouted.

As the men started shooting, the hyena alien curled itself into a ball and spun in midair. Mitch's eyes went wide when it repelled the bullets coming at it.

"Holy shit," Mitch muttered. "Stop shooting!"

The hyena alien shot into the air. Mitch pulled out his Colt .44 handgun that he had packed earlier and opened fire. The Colt would be more effective in close range. As was his custom, he always carried multiple weapons to be ready for whatever situation presented itself. He connected twice, causing it to fall awkwardly to the ground. When it reached the ground, it turned and began to run.

"Shoot it," Mitch shouted.

His team fired. It slowed after they hit it repeatedly. Mitch ran after it, and his men followed. After numerous rounds, the hyena alien finally stopped. It turned toward them before collapsing.

Four Jeeps arrived on the scene.

Mitch didn't wait for them. He charged into the mine. It was well lit despite the lack of any recognizable light source. He had been expecting it to be damp and dingy.

He looked around the cavernous interior and paused. He spotted micro-thin filaments floating in the air. Grabbing one and holding it in his hand, he noticed the surrounding air went dark. He had never seen anything like this before. With time, he would have liked to gather these filaments to keep. They would be a useful way of providing illumination without using electricity, but he had bigger concerns right now.

Gaping openings in the earth covered the chamber. He pointed his machine gun from side to side.

"Where the hell is everybody?" Corey Goss, one of his more experienced men, asked.

Mitch shook his head. He thought he would have seen someone by now. He motioned for his team to spread out. Mitch exited the main area and entered a smaller room that looked like a command center. Sophisticated machinery lined the walls.

Mitch pointed outward indicating that there was nobody inside. When they exited, a number of troops clustered around a ten-foot-wide opening in the ground. A grinding mechanical sound emerged from it.

After a minute, Mitch spotted a metallic vehicle below. There were no tracks. The vehicle hovered above the ground, speeding in their direction.

"Back away," Mitch said. "Twenty feet."

With hesitation, they backtracked. By now, the people in the Jeep had arrived. Mitch instructed his men to crouch away from the line of sight of anyone who might be inside.

The vehicle landed on the clay surface surrounding the aperture. Mitch waited two minutes, sweat dripping from his forehead.

A door on the metallic vehicle slid open. Mitch aimed his gun, ready to open fire. A few weary-looking people carrying blue cylinders about the size of a SCUBA tank stepped out. The first man who exited had graying hair on his head and beard. He looked so thin that he appeared ill. Large welts crisscrossed his arms and legs. The man jumped when he saw the troops. Mitch stood and put his index finger to his lips.

The man walked forward. Hopefully his movement had not roused the attention of any aliens. A boy not even in his teens and a young woman who looked beaten down emerged.

Mitch motioned for them to keep coming forward. Fortunately, they did not speak or act like this occurrence was out of the ordinary. Five more people exited. When they got far enough, Mitch stood in front of the entrance, his weapon raised.

After a minute, a humanoid with a reptilian face and tail emerged from the hatch. Mitch shot it twice with his .44. It flew backward and writhed on the floor. Mitch ran over and shot it twice in the head, causing it to stop squirming.

A second alien stepped out of the vehicle. Mitch had not noticed it, but fortunately, Marc Gonzalez had. He commanded a German Shepherd to attack. The Shepherd lunged at the humanoid alien and knocked it to the ground. It had the alien pinned. As the alien struggled to rise, Mitch shot it twice in the head with his .44.

After making sure the second alien was dead, Mitch stepped into the vehicle, which looked like a bus. It had seats along the side and handrails at the top. The cabin was empty.

He exited and walked toward a group of astonished miners. "I'm Mitch Grace. My men and I have come from up north in the Rocky Mountains. When we heard about this slave camp, we decided to do something about it."

"My God. My God." Tears streamed down the face of the first man who walked out of the vehicle. "I thought we would die down here for sure."

"Well, you're not going to," Mitch said. "What's your name?"

"Jimmy McCalister. I can't believe this." McCalister stumbled and hugged Mitch, still sobbing.

Mitch nudged him away. "We've got work to do. How many more people are down there?

"Maybe eighty or ninety."

"Where are they?"

McCalister sighed. "Probably underground in the mines."

"How can we get there?"

McCalister's face turned white. "You can't go down there. There's too many of them."

He told Mitch to wait for the next crew to return. Typically, no more than two aliens stayed inside the transporters, and the next transporter would likely come soon. McCallister also didn't think the aliens would have heard the gunshots since the mines were far below the surface.

Mitch instructed Corey to take the former slaves out to the buses. As soon as a bus was full, have the driver haul them out. He told Jimmy to stay here and help him evacuate the others.

Corey led the former captives to the outside and their freedom.

Just as he was leaving, one of the dogs began barking. A humming sound emerged from an opening.

"All right, people," Mitch said. "Let's get ready."

A few minutes later, a metallic vehicle, similar to the first one, appeared. Mitch wiped the sweat beading down his forehead and gripped his .44 that he had reloaded while waiting.

A heavyset woman carrying a cylinder walked out of the hatch.

McCalister stood in front of her. "It's okay, Becky. Just act like everything's normal."

She nodded. Her eyes drifted to Mitch and the others waiting with their guns. This procession continued less smoothly than the first one. When a reptilian humanoid stepped out of the vehicle, Mitch blasted it repeatedly with his gun.

Once more, Corey Goss led the slaves out of the mine to the buses.

Three more transporters exited the subterranean mines. Each time, Mitch and his troops gunned down the alien on board and freed the slaves.

After the last one, Corey Goss's face tightened. "Before long these aliens are going to notice their transporters aren't coming back."

"Hopefully not before we get everyone out of here," Mitch said.

"It's too late," yelled one of the former slaves, a Hispanic man in his early thirties. "They was grumbling about the delay downstairs. They're coming up."

"Shit," Mitch said. "We have to go down and get them."

McCalister grabbed Mitch's arm. "You can't do that. There's dozens of aliens down there. You won't stand a chance."

"We have to."

"Listen to me," McCalister said. "They'll slaughter you. You don't know what they're like."

Corey agreed, but Mitch hated the idea of leaving anyone behind.

McCalister put his arm on Mitch's shoulder. "You did a lot of good here. You saved a bunch of people. Now you have to save yourself."

Mitch paced the room. "Okay. Before we leave, we're going to do some serious damage." He motioned to Marc Gonzalez. "Have the dogs guard the mine shaft until we're ready to vacate. If they sense any alien vehicles coming, alert us right away."

Mitch and his team planted explosives throughout the top level of the mine including the control room. They timed them to detonate in twenty minutes. With haste, they departed on helicopters and Jeeps back to their Rocky Mountain hideout.

As they flew back, Mitch sat in the back of the helicopter brooding. Corey put a hand on his shoulder. "You can't save everybody. That's part of being a leader. You have to make the tough decisions. We did good today. You have a lot to be proud of."

Mitch sighed. He knew what Corey said was right. He had a mission in the past where he had to leave a captured soldier behind. Even though it had eaten him away inside, none of his commanders had faulted him for his actions. He wanted to save the world, but unfortunately, he wasn't Superman.

## Chapter XVI

Mitch signaled to cut the engines on the landing boats.

The boats sat five hundred yards off the shore on the west coast of Mexico, one hundred miles south of the old US border. There was no longer a United States. For Mitch, the only distinction was the area the aliens occupied and the area the humans occupied. There was too much of the former and not enough of the latter.

Six men manned each of the five landing boats, representing his elite forces. Although they included new recruits with military experience, Mitch had trained most of them himself. At first, he had been wary because they were so green, but he no longer doubted them. They had proven themselves in these terrorist attacks.

When he had time to think about it, he found himself amazed at the irony. When he had been with the SEALs, his aim had been to stop terrorism. He had come to despise the cowards who would kill innocents in their terrorist attacks. Yet here he was, doing things that a few short years ago, he had found to be despicable.

He signaled the men to jump off the boats. He was the last to exit and swim to the shore. Just like the others, he carried a twenty-pound case of explosives.

Over the last six months, he had taken weapons from military bases in the area. They had also been manufacturing their own bullets, explosives, and weaponry. As a result, his men were now well armed.

Mitch watched the other men swimming. He had no difficulty swimming under these conditions since he was used to it, but for some, this was their toughest amphibious operation.

Over the last six months, he had given them rigorous training at a nearby lake. This included rudimentary underwater demolition.

He was glad to see none of the men struggle in their swim to the shore. He gathered them at the shoreline. They ran in single files in teams of six. A month ago, they had taken aerial photos in a nighttime flyby with a helicopter. From intelligence obtained from new members of their community, Mitch knew this was a trade center for the distribution of deuterium and krypton, two noble gases in high demand among the aliens that they used human slaves to mine for.

Tonight, Mitch wanted to put a dent in their operations. Their targets were six high-rise buildings off the coast. These remarkable structures reached the heavens and had been constructed in a fraction of the time it would have taken people to build inferior buildings.

At the base of a building, Mitch's team broke up and circled the perimeter. Mitch ran to his spot at the rear of the building and set a timer to detonate the explosives.

The night was eerily quiet. He expected resistance. In earlier raids, they had encountered unsuspecting aliens who had to be dealt with. Using the element of surprise, they had suffered minimal casualties.

After checking the timer to make sure it operated properly, Mitch ran back to the reconnaissance point at the shoreline. Corey Goss was the only person to return before him.

He took a moment to catch his breath while waiting for the others to return. Over the next two minutes, they trickled back. The team leaders performed a headcount. One man was missing. Mitch gritted his teeth. They could not afford any delays, but he couldn't leave anyone behind.

Mitch looked at his watch. "I'm going back for him."

Before he left, Steve Minard, the missing team member, ran toward the shore. "I had a problem with the timer. I had to tinker with it, but I was able to set it."

"Good," Mitch said. "Let's roll."

Mitch ran into the warm night water and swam out. Without the pack of explosives, swimming was easier. When he first started with the SEALs, he found night swimming intimidating. As a child, after dark he often sat on the beach watching the waves crash on the shore, thinking that if he went into the water, the sea would swallow him, and no one would save him. His entire body shook before his first night swim. Just like most of his fears, he conquered it by doing it.

When he reached the landing boat, he pulled himself onto it. He then helped pull the others inside. When everyone was in the boat, he started the motor, and rode north to Coronado. He looked at his watch. A deep rumble came from the sky as four Nighthawk jets and two hijacked alien vessels soared through the air.

They had jet fuel, a form of kerosene, obtained from the Coronado Springs air force base, and then later at an abandoned Sunoco refinery, where Mitch had discovered an underground storage area with hundreds of barrels of the fuel waiting for them to take.

Mitch waited in anticipation for the fireworks to start.

The explosives were to ignite as the fighter planes attacked, creating an assault designed to look and sound devastating.

He grimaced when the first explosive detonated. It took place too early since the fighter planes were not ready to strike. Soon enough, a cacophony of bombs bursting sounded as more explosives detonated and the air strike commenced.

He pumped his fist as the first building tumbled to the ground. This magnificent piece of architecture was no longer.

He could not help but remember the images on the television screen he had seen when the World Trade Center collapsed. He had just started with the SEALs and was training at a base in Virginia. He had never felt so much rage and fury in his life, yet here he was doing the same to the alien bastards who controlled his planet.

The night sparkled with intense light as another building lit on fire. Before long, it crumbled to the ground.

Mitch steered the landing boat away from the action as the third building collapsed.

He had told the pilots to get in and out, wreaking as much havoc as possible. They had accomplished their task, and now it was time to leave. He wanted to avoid a confrontation with the aliens. Thus far, hit and run tactics had been effective, causing the aliens to pull out of a trade center he had targeted.

After another building had turned into a flaming heap of rubble, the fighter planes changed direction and began to return. Mitch held his breath. A few minutes later, alarms sounded. By this point, his pilots were far away. Mitch was confident his landing boats would remain inconspicuous. Since the aliens made minimal use of the planet's waterways for travel, it wouldn't be likely that they would capture him.

Before long, the trade center began to fade from view. The only thing left was a trail of smoke.

*** 

The drive back to their base in Colorado had been fruitful. On the way, they found an abandoned gas truck full of diesel fuel, which they could use. One of Mitch's men, who had been an experienced engine mechanic in his old life, got the truck running after tinkering under the hood. They drove it back. Oil was a precious commodity. They always sought out fuel sources, while harnessing alternative energy sources. They had become adept at using vegetable oil as a fuel source after modifying the engines of some of the vehicles to accommodate it. Most recently, they had turned to solar power. They were also in the process of restarting a nearby nuclear power plant and an oil refinery.

Mitch had also been in the process of securing as many electric vehicles as possible. They had mostly been using them in their day-to-day operations. Any way they could conserve fuel was an option they considered.

They arrived late the following morning in Colorado after having set up camp in Utah the previous night.

When Mitch arrived, Elizabeth had been guiding a tour for a new group of dirty and disheveled settlers. Among them was a boy not yet in his teens who looked like he was made of patches of skin clinging to a skeleton. The gaping holes in his shoes matched the ones in his pants. He had outgrown his shirt, its sleeves extending just past his elbows.

Elizabeth ran over and hugged Mitch. "Thank God you guys are back. How did it go?"

Mitch didn't answer right away. "Good."

"Is that all you're going to give me?" Elizabeth asked.

Mitch hesitated. When he was with the SEALs, he gave information on a need-to-know basis and never to a civilian. That veil of secrecy died when the United States armed forces died. His people had a right to know. They were all in this together.

"It was a success. We got in undetected, destroyed some buildings that are valuable to the aliens, and got out. Hopefully, they'll leave like the others after we attacked them in the San Fernando Valley."

"You have no idea how worried I get whenever you guys leave. I don't know how you do it, knowing you might not come back. Ask Ethan. I'm a nervous wreck."

Mitch chuckled. "You would never make it on one of our teams being jumpy like that."

"Well, I'm glad you're back." Elizabeth gave him a peck on the cheek. "See you later."

She ran off to join the new settlers. He surveyed the expanding community. It had grown so much since he had first landed with Elizabeth. They had started a second town five miles away, maintaining the same principle of remaining inconspicuous, and camouflaging their construction. As they grew, that had become increasingly difficult.

It was a risk worth taking. For the first time, they were starting to live and not just survive. At first, they had concentrated on basic necessities such as food and shelter. After Mitch took charge, he had prioritized educating the children, and building his military forces.

Since then, he had taken it a step further. They had created their own woodworking shop. With all of the new people coming in, they needed lumber for new construction and furniture. He had recently started new projects such as re-opening an abandoned steel mill and creating a facility to manufacture electronic parts and equipment.

Mitch yawned. He had not been getting more than three or four hours of sleep a night for the past week. He had so much to do, despite delegating responsibilities. Strolling toward his house, he stretched his aching muscles.

He pondered about what he could do to hurt the aliens, something that was never far from his thoughts. They had to be agitated due to the disruption of their activities, but not to the point where they were making an all-out search to find the culprit of these hits.

"Earth to Mitch," Ethan said. "I've been calling to you for the past couple of minutes. Are you okay?"

Mitch nodded. He had not even realized Ethan was there. "Yeah, sure. Just thinking, that's all."

"So how did it go?"

Mitch gave him a recap of their last mission but could tell something else was on Ethan's mind. "What's been happening since I've been gone?"

"I've received intelligence reports about a new alien settlement close to the Nebraska border," Ethan replied.

Mitch gritted his teeth. "That's too close for my liking."

"My thoughts exactly. The question is what do we do about it? That close, they're bound to find out about us, but if we attack, they'll retaliate."

"We're going to have to get rid of them."

Ethan gulped. "You mean, like take them out?"

"That's exactly what I mean."

Mitch had no qualms about raising the stakes. Still, he had a hard time reconciling killing innocent aliens. His friendship with Sarm was proof that there were good aliens out there. It was something that frequently kept him up at night, even when he had time to sleep. All the same, he was willing to accept the collateral damage. He knew that his obsession with destroying the aliens was probably unhealthy, and some of his actions were regrettable, but there was no limit to what he was willing to do to achieve his goals. The aliens had made an enemy they could not afford to have.

## Chapter XVII

Mitch had gathered over one hundred fifty of his troops in the community center. The center was a multi-purpose room that acted as a meeting place, dining room, concert hall, and in this case a war room. Standing on a stage in front of a podium, Mitch addressed his troops, who sat on folding chairs. Normally, he outlined his plans on a blackboard, but with this many people, he used an overhead projector.

The audience gave him rapt attention. There were no side conversations, or people staring at the ceiling.

"It's going to be a little different this time, boys." Mitch paused, realizing there were a number of women here. He still had a hard time getting used to that. He had always fought alongside men. Although he wasn't crazy about females on the front lines, he didn't have the luxury of being choosy.

"Up until now, we've hit and run," Mitch continued. "It's time to raise the bar. There's an alien settlement northeast of here, a little too close for comfort. When you have pests in your house, you exterminate them, and that's what we're going to do."

Murmurs sounded. The troops had concerned looks.

"Everyone here has seen the devastation the aliens have caused. I'm the only one who didn't see the totality of their invasion, but the aliens have gotten fat and lazy. They think we're insignificant and pose them no harm. Their defenses are a joke. Despite our numerous attacks, they still haven't adequately defended themselves." Mitch paused. "We're going to use that in our favor.

"Our reports indicate that there are between eight and twelve aliens here." Mitch clicked onto his first slide. "These are pictures taken from the Global Hawk." He used a pointer and traced over a sharp, angular structure. "This is the center of their activities. I'm not sure what their business is and I don't care." He went to the next shot. "These are modular houses. Our goal is to attack while they're inside. They seem to be nocturnal and congregate inside of these modular units in the early hours of the morning. We're going to strike them from the air and finish them on the ground. Then we clear the area."

Jay Menza, a former marine, raised his hand. Menza was five years younger than Mitch. He had a long scar that ran from his eyelid to his jaw. Long and lean, he was one of the most athletic men on Mitch's team. "I get the part about killing them, but why do you want to clear the area afterward?"

Mitch stepped in front of the projector and faced the audience. "This settlement has been around for less than a week. My hope is that the other aliens they deal with don't know about this location and won't know to look around here if they try finding it. Any other questions?"

There were no more.

"This won't be easy. It's our most dangerous mission yet, but we have to protect what is ours. We might not have much, just this little patch of ground, but it's ours."

Mitch gave specific instructions for each of the teams. "We leave at 0400. I have confidence in each of you. Tomorrow we fight for more than just our little community. Tomorrow we fight for humanity!"

All of the other missions they had conducted were table setters for this one. This would take his fight against the aliens to a new level. So much of his future, of the community's future would ride on this. Failure was not an option.

***

Mitch contacted Corey Goss on the radio. Despite a sleepless night fret with worry, today he felt calm. If he could kill the sweeper and those aliens at the mine, he could handle this. Cruise missiles had served him well in Iraq, and he had faith they would work here. Granted the US military had used these same weapons, but he had the element of surprise in his favor. In a way it was fortunate for him that the aliens routed the humans in the first go around, since there was still quite a bit of armament left that went unused.

"Are you ready?" Mitch asked.

"We are," Goss said. "I wished we could test them first."

"They'll work. These missiles cost a million a pop back in the day."

On the other end of the radio, Goss commented, "I never fired one off of a ground launcher before."

"I have."

"Is the accuracy any different than from a destroyer?"

"No," Mitch replied. "It works the same way. We didn't normally fire cruise missiles from ground launchers in the old days because we attacked the enemy from the sea. Don't worry, Corey. It'll work. If not, we still have air and ground support."

"All right, boss."

Steve Minard looked at him with wide, anxious eyes.

Mitch took a deep breath. "All we can do is wait. Get ready to move."

"Yes, sir," Minard said.

"You're not in the army, Steve. No sirs around here."

"Right...Mitch."

The ground troops stood around an array of vehicles including two tanks, six Jeeps, two vans, two converted buses, and a truck. All were outfitted with machine gun turrets.

Mitch gave last-second instructions.

A roar came from the west followed by a cruise missile flying overhead. A second cruise missile followed closely behind.

Mitch pumped his fist in the air. "Let's get them!"

He jumped into his Jeep and led a procession of vehicles to the alien camp. He looked out the window as the cruise missiles soared out of view. Up close, they were an awesome sight.

Mitch signaled Corey Goss on the radio. "The birds just passed. We'll find out soon if they hit their mark."

Goss said, "I hope these aliens didn't go for a stroll."

If the aliens were inside the buildings, and the missiles hit the targets, then his ground troops would have little work to do.

Five minutes later, the convoy was near their destination when the fighter planes soared above them. The jets moved out of Mitch's line of sight. Explosions rippled through the air. He closed the windows of the Jeep when a blast of hot air roared from the explosions.

At the bottom of a hill, a raging fire came from the two modular housing units as well as the work area. Dark towers of smoke rose high in the air. Shiny black material that looked like glass littered the nearby ground.

Machinery similar to what Mitch had seen inside Sarm's laboratory lined the alien's lab. He still had not seen any aliens, dead or alive.

Jay Menza, the Jeep's driver, asked "So, are we going to see some action?"

Mitch shrugged. "It's hard to say. The missiles hit the targets, but they might not all be dead."

Jay slowed as they neared their destination. Even with the windows closed, the intense heat radiated into the Jeep.

"Stop the car." Mitch stepped out of the Jeep and surveyed the area, moving his M16 from side to side.

The other ground troops filed out of their vehicles and gathered near Mitch.

He faced them. "Let's move in. Search and destroy."

Mitch wore military issue Teflon undershirt and socks, the same he had worn during the Gulf War. They were designed to prevent perspiring even in intense heat. He also wore gloves and a mask, but no body armor.

He stepped over the shiny black material that the building had been constructed from as he entered the burning buildings. A sizzling sound came from behind him. He turned and spotted an alien with four legs and a set of wings writhing on the floor. Its body and face consisted of a shredded gray exoskeleton. Its face was a gelatinous mass with no form. Its wings were on fire and still beating.

Using his boot, Mitch pinned the beating wings, trying not to touch the fire. It stopped moving. He contemplated putting a bullet in its face, but that didn't seem necessary.

"Mitch," Steve Minard shouted.

He stepped over the rubble. Minard was pointing his machine gun at a prone insectile-alien.

"What do you think?" Minard asked.

Mitch kicked it so it was flat on its back. "It's dead."

They continued walking to the other side of the modular residence. Minard yelped. Underneath the rubble, two alien tentacles wrapped around Minard's feet and yanked him down.

Mitch slung his M16 to the side and tried to drag away Minard. It wasn't going to work. The alien's grip was too strong.

Mitch opened fire on the alien at close range. After thirty bullets, it stopped moving, and Minard pulled himself free. He kicked the alien for good measure. It had eight gangly appendages with an abdomen and a thorax like a spider. There was little left of its face to see.

Minard gasped. "Holy shit. These bastards don't die easy."

After searching the rest of the house, they found three more dead aliens. The group gathered around Mitch.

"There should be more. Let's see what they found in the other building." Mitch began coughing from the intense smoke.

Most of the ground troops stood with guns ready. Jay Menza walked in his direction.

"What's the status?" Mitch asked.

"Three dead aliens inside," Menza replied.

Mitch frowned. "That's it?"

"That's all we found."

"Keep looking."

Menza's body tensed, and his eyes went wide. "Watch out!"

Mitch turned in time to see an insect-like alien descending on one of his men, who was looking the other way. The alien landed on the man's back and wrapped its four legs around his neck and shoulders. The exoskeleton that covered its face slid away. Like a jellyfish, it covered the man's face with its own. He began thrashing.

Mitch pulled out his gun but didn't have a clean shot. The others had their guns drawn but did not fire.

Mitch ran, found an opening, and fired at the alien's torso, but it would not let go. He fired again. The bullet pierced its exoskeleton, and a large chunk of blue flesh flew off.

"You got to be kidding." Mitch grabbed the alien and pulled with all his strength.

It finally released. As it hovered in the air just above Mitch, a thunderous greeting of gunfire tore the alien apart as everyone shot at once. Within seconds, it crashed to the ground.

Mitch bent to inspect his horribly disfigured soldier. Skin had been torn off his face. He coughed up blood once, twice, and then his head rolled back.

"Shit." He grabbed the man's wrist. No pulse.

He turned and looked around at the group of soldiers behind him. Their eyes all asked the same question.

"He's dead," Mitch said. "Make sure there are no more aliens around. Then we'll give him a proper burial and clean up."

Mitch busied himself by searching with the others. Twenty minutes later, he was convinced they had killed all the aliens.

Mitch instructed two of his troops to dig a hole and bury the dead soldier. He gathered the others and said a few words and a couple of prayers, trying his best not to get choked up despite the torrent of emotion inside him.

He wasn't sure if it was because he was older, or the world had changed, but the death of his comrades affected him worse than it used to. They were like his children. It was worse late at night, when he was alone, and serious doubt crept in. What were they really accomplishing? Was it worth losing these brave men and women?

## Chapter XVIII

Here are where the sewing machines will go." Sandy McGowan pointed to a room with six workstations. They had what looked like simple wooden tables with yarn, thread, and other sewing materials. Nearby the workstations were bins that had various fabrics.

Mitch yawned. Although he was interested in the community's new clothing manufacturing facility, he had barely slept lately, and it was catching up to him.

Sandy led him to another room. "This is where we'll produce wool." The room had large tubs to scour the wool, a dyeing station, a station to comb the wool, and finally a spinning frame.

Mitch smiled. "You've done a good job."

"Well, the people here need new clothes," Sandy said.

He excused himself after Sandy finished the tour. Tomorrow, he planned on inspecting a nearby tool and dye shop. He wanted to manufacture mechanical items needed for construction. They had already started making circuit boards and computers. They were becoming self-sufficient, raising their own food and making various goods.

He jogged home, trying to get in some extra exercise. On the way, he ran into Bruce Dennison, who Mitch had put in charge of getting the nuclear power plant back into operation.

Mitch took a moment to catch his breath. "Moose, I've been meaning to talk to you about the plant. How are the upgrades coming along?"

Bruce had spent his previous life as an operations instructor at a nuclear power station, spending most of his time teaching people how to run the reactor plant. He had the most nuclear power operational experience at the community. Mitch also felt a kinship with Bruce, who he affectionately referred to as Moose, because of his background in the navy, having served as a ballistic mate in a nuclear submarine.

Bruce sighed. "Slowly. The biggest problem has been getting or making replacement parts. We've made some progress. Slowly but surely, we'll get the reactors up and running."

"Great. Let me know what resources you need. That would be a huge benefit if we can start using nuclear power."

"Mitch, I'm all for getting another fuel source, and I think we can get the power plant up and running, but we need to step carefully here and avoid making the same mistakes we made in the past. Back in the day, disposing of the nuclear waste and byproducts was always an issue. Typically, the government found Native American reservations to dump the waste. We need to be smart about how we handle our nuclear waste. It's bad enough what the aliens have done to the planet. We shouldn't contribute to the decimation of Earth."

Mitch nodded. With all of the things on his agenda, it was easy to overlook important details. Fortunately, he had good people to whom he could delegate the work. "You're absolutely right. I want you to hold town forum discussions to discuss the matter. Set up time at the community center, and we can brainstorm."

"Good deal." Moose was about to leave when he stopped suddenly. "I do have some good news. We've made strides converting the cars from gasoline to biofuels. Two this week. There's been a bit of a learning curve, but we're getting there."

After Mitch had learned about Bruce's pre-invasion passion for restoring old cars, he set him to work in helping convert their existing gasoline-powered vehicles to ones using biodiesel, but primarily vegetable oil. Given the existing lack of refinery capacity, Mitch was trying to move away from the use of petroleum where possible.

Mitch patted him on the back. "Good work. Keep me updated."

Mitch finished his run. When he got to his house, a note posted on the front door stated, "Interviews with new citizens. Meet me at Community Center 2 at noon."

Mitch looked at his watch. "Damn." He was late, so he extended his jog to the second Community Center.

Last night, he had eaten dinner with Ethan and Elizabeth. She had suggested they name their new communities. Mitch thought it a good idea but didn't have any good names. Elizabeth suggested they run a contest to name the new towns, so he gave her the task of spearheading this effort.

On the way to the community center, he smiled at the sight of a group of children at play. These kids had changed dramatically since he first landed. Before, they looked wary and suspicious. They had been missing out on their childhood. Now, all children were required to attend school, and they acted like normal kids.

He slowed as he spotted Ethan driving toward him in a pick-up truck. He stopped in front of Mitch and rolled down the window.

Mitch extended his hand. "Hey, Ethan. Haven't seen you around the last few days."

"I went to investigate that oil refinery in Utah."

"Oh yeah. I forgot all about that." With so much going on, Mitch had a hard time keeping track of everything.

"I went along with a few engineers. I think we can get it operational. It'll take work. We'll have to allocate manpower from other tasks, but it'll be worth it."

Mitch nodded. "It will definitely be a worthwhile project."

"There's a good amount of capacity in there right now. It should last us a while." Right now, the community could produce enough biofuels to support itself, but as it grew, it would need more of that land for farming food crops. If they expanded their farms too far and wide, they risked the aliens detecting signs of their community.

"What's the time frame on the refinery?" Mitch asked.

"Two months."

Mitch nodded. "Good. One of our Gulf of Mexico contacts said he knows a group of people who are drilling for oil. Maybe we can work out a deal."

"Could be. You look tired, Mitch. You should get some sleep."

Mitch shook his head. "I can sleep when I'm dead. I'll see you later."

Ethan waved and drove off.

He jogged to the community center, where Gary Daniels stood at the front door drinking coffee.

"Hey, Mitch, I'm glad you got my note. I meant to tell you last night, but after the second glass of wine, it slipped my mind."

Mitch waved his hand. "No worries."

Mitch followed Daniels to the back office where they conducted interviews. He handed Mitch a stack of papers containing background information on each of the new residents.

Mitch felt surprised at the weight of the stack, and Daniels informed him they had forty-seven new applicants. Mitch didn't like turning anyone back, especially if they could contribute, but he wondered if they were getting too big, which could lead to discovery by the aliens. The community now had eight thousand residents, a staggering number considering they had just over a thousand when Mitch first arrived. He knew that people sought out this place seeking a better life. People felt safe here and had a sense of worth. Attacking the aliens gave them pride and hope.

Mitch didn't have to do these interviews. Daniels was more than capable of placing the newcomers into jobs. He would be lost without the man's administrative help, but this allowed him to meet the new people. Otherwise, he wouldn't recognize half of them.

Mitch buried himself in Gary's notes. One caught his eye, a software engineer who worked for the military. There was an emergency room nurse from Illinois. He also wanted another physician. Dr. Sherwood needed help. Her staff consisted of three experienced physicians and a few others in training. The injuries sustained by Mitch's military occupied most of their time.

He had barely scanned the papers when the first applicant walked into his office. The man had a mohawk and tattoos across his arms and shoulders. This was going to be a long day.

\*\*\*

Mitch's eyes felt heavy halfway through the interviews. He wanted to tell Daniels to reschedule them for another day, but he had time this afternoon, and might not later.

The lady with the wire-rimmed glasses who sat in front of him had been talking for the last several minutes about how she had used conflict resolution to diffuse a tense situation between two lawyers at a firm she had worked for. He searched his mind for an appropriate job for a lawyer. Normally, Gary wrote suggestions at the bottom of the sheet to make things easier for Mitch, but in this case, he had not written anything. After hearing the woman speak, he could see why. Their growing community did not need lawyers.

Mitch twirled a pencil and interrupted her speech. "Have you ever taken knitting classes?"

The woman frowned. "No, I haven't."

"Hmm. Gardening?"

The woman shook her head.

An idea struck Mitch. He waved his index finger. "Have you ever done contract law?"

The woman smiled. "Why, yes I have."

"The other day I was thinking we could use somebody with savvy negotiation skills for trading. I think you could help here. What do you think?"

A bright smile lit the woman's face. "That would be positively delightful."

"Good. Contact Ethan Herzberg. He lives on the third house on the left on Maple Street."

Coming from outside, Gary Daniels had a concerned look as he told Mitch they had a situation. A group of people just arrived, who had a military look, whatever that meant. They had heard about the community's operations. Their leader, a woman, demanded to see the one who has stood up to the aliens, although Mitch didn't consider what they did standing up to the aliens. Furthermore, the woman wouldn't take no for an answer.

They still had nine interviews left. Mitch didn't like the idea of people barging in here and making demands. He was trying to put together an orderly society with rules and respect.

Mitch sat as Gary walked out of the room.

From outside someone said, "I don't have time to waste. I need to speak to the one who has defied the aliens."

Mitch's heart nearly stopped beating. For a moment, everything around him disappeared and the only thing that mattered was the voice. *That voice. It couldn't be.*

"We've come a long way. Now please help us out."

Mitch leaned against his desk. "Oh my God." His voice was a high pitch squeal. "Deborah."

He leaped over the desk, leaving a flurry of flying papers behind him. He nearly tore the door off its hinges. It was her. "Deborah!"

"Mitch." Her jaw dropped. Tears streamed down her cheeks.

Deborah looked much like he remembered her, except her face was a little harder, and her eyes more intense. She wore faded blue jeans and a dark blouse. Her brown hair was lighter than he remembered, but she still had the same infectious smile. Mitch hugged her, lifting her off her feet. He never thought he would see her again, and now that he held her in his arms, he never wanted to let go.

## Chapter XIX

Late into the night, after Mitch had met with Deborah's people and had introduced her to the community at large, they found themselves alone in his home. He was surprised to find that he was nervous. He had to remind himself that he had been alone and intimate with Deborah many times. Granted, it had been years ago, and the world had changed drastically since them, but this was still his Deborah, the woman he loved and cherished, so why were his hands shaking?

His skin tingled when he touched her hand. Staring at her, he found himself unable to form the words he wanted to say.

Deborah initiated the conversation. "So, Mitch, it's been a long time."

"Ain't that the truth. Longer for you than for me, but all the same, it has been a while."

For a moment, Mitch wasn't sure what to do. What if she no longer felt the same way about him?

She erased all doubt when she drew him in and pressed her lips against his. Mitch closed his eyes, savoring her taste. Their kisses grew ravenous, their hunger more than evident. When he kissed the nape of her neck, Deborah tilted her head and moaned softly.

Mitch's hands moved down her shoulders and wound their way to the buttons on her blouse, where he deftly began to unbutton them. Deborah in turn removed his shirt and rubbed his shoulders and chest. Before long, Deborah's bra found its way to the floor. His fingertips gently caressed her breasts, and she quivered. He kept his touch light as he worked his way

193

toward her nipples. He swirled his hands toward her nipples before kissing one and then the other.

Deborah arched her body backward, inviting him in. At first, he had been concerned that his movements would be clumsy and awkward, but he surmised there are things one doesn't forget. It becomes like muscle memory.

Mitch took her into his strong arms and brought her to his bedroom. She stared up at him, neither saying a word. It was just like old times.

He laid her onto the bed and pressed his bare chest onto hers. They resumed kissing aggressively and passionately. His desire was so strong that he thought he was going to explode. He had to slow down, savor the moment.

"You have no idea how much I missed you," Mitch whispered in her ear. "Not knowing whether you were alive or dead drove me half out of my mind."

Deborah kissed his neck. "I know exactly what you were feeling."

Of course she did. That was stupid of him. He was about to apologize when she put a finger to his lips, sensibly shushing him. He licked her finger delicately.

"Make love to me," Deborah said.

He slowly entered her. She gave a low moan at first, which began to rise as he pressed harder into her. Before long, they were both swept up into a rolling crescendo of emotion. Mitch wanted the feeling to last forever. Deborah cried out in ecstasy, and he did the same. After it was over, he lay down next to her, nearly out of breath. Perhaps it was the longing he had felt over the years since they had last seen each other, but he never remembered it feeling so good.

*** 

Mitch put a grape in Deborah's mouth and grinned as she ate it. The last three days had been like living in paradise. Every day was Christmas Eve.

For the first time since he had awoken from the coma, he had forgotten about the alien occupation. Soon, he would have to return to reality, but for now, he savored every moment with the woman he thought he had lost.

Deborah pulled herself up to a sitting position. They were lying on blankets in Mitch's living room. Mitch nuzzled his head on her lap. He felt so alive. The world once again had meaning.

"Mitch, I know these last few days have been great, but we need to talk about what happened."

Mitch frowned. "I wish we didn't have to talk about that day, or anything that has to do with aliens."

Deborah stroked his hair. "We need to, and I need to get back to my people. Garth wants to discuss our plans."

Garth Williams was part of the group that Deborah had arrived with. He was a former colonel in the US army with fiery red hair and a massive scar on his forehead.

Before they left, Deborah wanted closure on what happened to Mitch during the invasion.

Mitch sighed. He hated thinking back about that day. "It was hell. The aliens were crushing us. I shot this one that was

195

eating a soldier alive. I wanted to pull out and regroup because there was nothing I could do. Then, I got caught in the path of an alien that looked like a wooly mammoth with metallic armor. I tried to get out of its way, but it was lights out. What about you?"

"I was inside trying to get ahold of all branches of the military. We even managed to reach the president."

"Did he make it out alive?" Mitch asked.

"I have no idea. Nobody has seen him in years. For at least a few weeks he had been commanding the military from a secret location. Then he dropped out of sight and stopped giving radio broadcasts. He may have died or abandoned ship. Who knows? After that, the country fell apart."

Mitch had heard stories about the one-sided battles that took place afterward. Deborah explained how it was over in a few weeks. Every major city had been decimated. Entire countries had been wasted, and any formal military had disbanded. Survivors went into hiding.

Mitch went to the kitchen and poured a glass of water. He drank some and handed the glass to Deborah. "I've thought about that day a lot. I've pondered the chances of you surviving. Sarm and I discussed it often, and my conclusion was that you died. How did you make it out?"

"We didn't know how bad things had gotten until they hit the building. It was going to collapse, so I got out of there. I ran down the steps praying that the building would hold. When I got outside, it was smoke and fire and explosions everywhere. You couldn't go more than ten feet without running into a dead body."

Mitch paced the living room.

"When I left, most of the aliens had vacated. I looked everywhere for you. It was tough, just trying to avoid becoming alien roadkill. I had a couple close calls. I was cornered by this one alien and shot it. It wasn't enough to kill the thing, but at least it fled."

Mitch propped his arms on the windowsill and looked outside. The sunny, cheerful day had grown dark.

"I couldn't find you, and I had to leave if I wanted to stay alive, so I got in a Jeep and drove north, sticking to the back roads. LA was a war zone. I kept driving until I reached Vandenburg Air Force Base. From there, I joined a counterattack against the aliens."

Mitch scratched the back of his head. "They must have carted me away by then."

"In all of the confusion, it was hard to see anything. Most of the place was on fire. Buildings were coming down. Bodies littered the ground, but yours wasn't among them."

Mitch gazed at her. "Maybe it was best you didn't find me."

Deborah frowned. "What do you mean?"

Mitch explained how Sarm revived him, and that in the end it was for the best that Deborah didn't find him, because he would likely have died without Sarm's advanced medical techniques.

"Someday I'd like to meet Sarm. I owe him so much for saving you."

Mitch smiled. "He's an interesting cat, for an alien."

For a while, neither said anything. They sat on the blankets and held each other. Mitch sighed. The unbridled bliss of getting to know Deborah again had come to an end. Like it or not, they had to get back to the real world.

Mitch asked Deborah about her military group, which was less organized than Mitch's group, and acted more like a militia. According to Deborah, Mitch's

exploits of defying the aliens were legendary, a comment that made Mitch laugh since they lived hidden away from the captors of the planet.

Her group was spread out in Nebraska, Iowa, and Kansas. He wanted their respective communities to join together, but more importantly he wanted Deborah with him, now and forever.

***

With Deborah at his side, Mitch sat across the table from her four-person entourage. Wanting to keep this meeting informal, he volunteered Ethan's house for dinner. Ethan had a modest one-bedroom house. As with the rest of the houses, it was small and efficient. The dining room doubled as an office, and the kitchen had a laundry basin. Knowing Elizabeth's culinary skills left a little to be desired, he recruited Sandy McGowen, who made a world class meatloaf, to help.

Elizabeth and Ethan served food as Mitch engaged in small talk with their guests. He felt comforted that Deborah chose to sit by his side, instead of with her party.

Ethan, who earlier had entertained the guests, had told him that Garth Williams was antsy. He had intended on talking to

Mitch the day they had arrived, but that changed when Mitch met Deborah.

Before dinner, Corey Goss said grace. Goss attended the non-denominational services on Sunday unless he was on a mission. Growing up in Alabama, his father had been an ordained Baptist minister. Before they attacked, Goss always led the troops in prayer.

When he finished reciting his prayer, Elizabeth served vegetable soup.

Mitch cleared his throat. "Deborah brought me up to speed on your operations. I had her put together a list of your heavy artillery, vehicles, and aircraft. You've done a good job. However, we're incredibly shorthanded against the aliens. Their weaponry and physical attributes far eclipse anything we have."

"Despite that, you've made inroads against them," Garth said.

"We have," Corey Goss admitted. "But not by battling them head-to-head. We've hit them when they've been unprepared."

Mitch nodded. "We've been successful because we know our limitations. We use our strengths to our fullest advantage. Corey took you on a tour of our facilities."

"Yes," Garth said. "It's impressive. Deborah and I were hoping to come to an agreement with you about sharing intelligence and coordinating operations."

Mitch folded his arms. "To be completely honest, you don't have a shot against the aliens."

Garth looked like he had been slapped in the face. His eyes narrowed as he stared at Mitch.

"It's true, Garth," Deborah agreed. "That's why we came here. We lack organization and manpower. We act like a militia, and we've mostly fought other people."

"We've had to defend ourselves," Garth said in a defensive tone.

"I'm not saying you're wrong for what you've done," Mitch said. "You have to do what you can to survive. I'm giving you a reality check. Currently, you aren't even a pesky fly to the aliens. Join forces with us. We can use your experienced people and equipment."

Garth stared at Deborah. "You know I trust you. Forget about personal feelings and past relationships. Do you think this is a good move? We've always prided ourselves on our independence."

"I suggested it to Mitch. We've been able to go it alone thus far, but the only chance we as people have against the aliens is to unite. I've worked with Mitch. He is more than capable as a leader. This is our best option."

Garth glanced at the others in his group. They each nodded or gave him a signal of affirmation. "Okay. We'll do it."

Mitch smiled and shook Garth's hand. "I would like you to set up a base twenty-five miles south of here. Corey and I have scouted an ideal spot to extend our operations. He can help you organize this move."

Elizabeth brought out a tray of meatloaf, along with rolls of bread and a tub of butter. Corey Goss grabbed a roll and buttered it. "It's the right choice. We'll be stronger if we stand together."

Ethan brought out a couple of pitchers of his home-made beer for the guests, which seemed to be much appreciated. Mitch was feeling on top of the world, almost as if the aliens truly did not control the planet.

*** 

With a full stomach, Mitch strolled hand in hand with Deborah back to his house. He felt oxytocin flowing through his brain just being near her.

They walked on a well-worn footpath. There still were not many paved roads in the community, but there were a number of walking paths.

As they made their way home, they marveled at their good fortune in surviving the alien invasion when so many had died. From their perspective, it was nothing short of a miracle.

Mitch said, "It's been more than six years for you. You've probably moved on, but for me, it's been just over a year. I've thought about you every single day since I woke from my coma."

Deborah's smile faded. "How can you say that? I haven't moved on and I've never gotten over you. Trying to survive and create a resistance movement has been the only thing keeping me going. If not for that, I don't know what I would have done."

Mitch wished he hadn't said that last part. At least things were getting back to normal. When they had dated, she always got mad at him for saying the wrong thing.

They entered his house on this quiet evening. Most nights people went to sleep early and woke up early. The lights might attract the aliens, plus Mitch wanted to conserve as much energy as possible since they were mostly using batteries and solar power.

Mitch lit a few candles. He dreaded asking his next question. "So, are you going to go back with Garth and the others?"

Deborah pressed her lips together. "They can manage."

Mitch breathed easier. He didn't think he could stand being apart from her. "Good. There's a lot of things I want to go over with you. I haven't had the benefit of consulting another naval officer."

"Is that the only reason you want me to stay?"

Mitch kissed her upper lip and held her tightly. "That's not the only reason. I would like you to live here at Casa Del Mitch."

"Now that sounds like an offer I just can't refuse."

Exploring her body with his hands, Mitch said, "Then don't."

## Chapter XX

"From the information we've gathered, they have settlements here, here and here." Deborah pointed to two spots in New Mexico and one in Texas on the large, worn-out paper map of the United States. Mitch had borrowed it from one of the schoolteachers and had taped it to the wall in the conference room. "If we remove them from those locations, then we can clear a path toward the Pacific coast of Mexico, which we know is an alien hotbed."

Corey Goss folded his arms. "First of all, we don't know how credible that information is, and second, it won't be easy to drive them out."

Mitch removed a pair of glasses that had been fashioned by their new optometrist. Sadly, he was becoming far-sighted as he got older. "Corey's right. Maybe there's another way. We could get there by sea. We would have free reign since the aliens barely use waterways. If we put together a strong fleet, we can attack from the ocean."

Garth Williams tugged on the strands of his fiery red beard. "How are we going to put together a fleet? All of the naval bases have been destroyed."

Mitch had heard the same thing. Their network now extended from Alaska to Mexico. In addition, they had encountered others coming through, gathering intelligence, and using it to populate their information database.

"Unless the base in Ingleside is still operational," Mitch said.

Garth shook his head. "I think you're chasing a phantom there, Mitch."

A man who had staggered into camp first told Mitch about the Ingleside naval base, located twenty miles northeast of Corpus Christi. When the man arrived, he had a high fever and was hallucinogenic. Dr. Sherwood diagnosed him as having a poisonous snakebite that had deteriorated his nervous system. He lasted a month. Before he died, he had told Mitch about this naval base with an impressive fleet kept hidden from the aliens. He might have discarded this as the ravings of a dying man if a couple from Mexico hadn't corroborated the story.

Mitch stared at the map. "I'd like to send a small team to investigate the Ingleside base. If it doesn't pan out, then at least we've gathered intelligence. If Ingleside is operational, then I'd like to talk to their leaders. Anyone maintaining an operational naval base must be inclined to combat the aliens. Corey, assemble a team."

"I'll get right to it, boss," Corey said.

"But what's the long-term strategy?" Garth asked. "What will clearing a path through Texas accomplish? I'm guessing the aliens won't take too kindly to that."

Mitch folded his arms. "You're probably right. They'll likely retaliate, maybe wipe us out, but the way I see it, in the long run, they'll either turn us into slaves or kill us. They keep us around because they need slaves but can't use everybody just now. They're harvesting us so to speak. We're well shielded here and have eluded them thus far, but that won't last forever."

"Maybe," Garth conceded. "But what can we realistically do against them? We saw how things turned out the first time our governments tried to fight them."

Mitch shook his head. "We're not going to beat them in a straight-out war. They're too powerful, too advanced."

"What if we use nukes?" Garth asked.

A month ago, they had secured nuclear missiles from an abandoned silo in Utah. They had put them in underground storage.

"Absolutely not," Mitch insisted. "What would be the point of getting rid of the aliens if our planet is uninhabitable? The fallout would be devastating."

"So where does that leave us?" Garth asked.

"Our best chance is to terrorize them to the point where it isn't worth living here anymore. There must be other planets they can take over. It's a long shot, but it's our best bet."

Deborah's brown eyes radiated intensity. She appeared to have little difficulty separating their personal life with their military strategy. "It's like you said. We're doomed either way. I'd rather go down fighting."

Mitch nodded. He wasn't sure if he was taking his people in a path to suicide or redemption. All he knew was that he studied all of his options and concluded that this was their best path.

\*\*\*

Inside his office, Mitch finished typing a memo to his captains detailing current equipment inventory and instructions on how to distribute the equipment. The room was the size of a closet. He used a retrofitted laptop computer and a printer that broke down once a week. For illumination, he used a small, battery-powered lamp. Other than that, the office was filled with stacks of military manuals and maps. He had just hit the print button when knocking sounded at the door.

Deborah peered out from the kitchen, where she was getting dinner ready. "Can you get that?"

"Sure thing," Mitch opened the door and found Ethan Hertzberg standing hand in hand with Elizabeth. They were engaged and getting married next month. Ethan had already asked Mitch to be his best man. They didn't have much in the way of laws, so this wouldn't be a legally binding marriage. It was mostly for the community to have something to celebrate.

Mitch shook Ethan's hand and gave Elizabeth a hug. "Ah, my favorite couple. Thanks for coming over for dinner."

"I'll give her a hand," Elizabeth offered.

Mitch raised his brow.

"I can cook," Elizabeth insisted.

Mitch frowned.

"Well, I'm sure I can help out." Elizabeth went to the kitchen.

Ethan smiled. "Ah. She's not much of a cook, but she tries."

"So how are the wedding plans going?" Mitch asked.

"Beats me," Ethan said. "I've been so busy I haven't had much involvement. Elizabeth tells me it's going to be a real communal affair."

"That's good. A wedding will give people a reminder of the way things used to be."

Ethan nodded. "I suppose you're right. Before we eat, I wanted to let you know that Jay Menza's team came back from Kansas. The settlements there got hit hard by the tornadoes."

A week ago, Deborah had received radio contact from her old group. A series of tornadoes had hit the Kansas area, so Mitch sent a team to investigate.

Mitch sighed. "That's what I figured. What are the conditions?"

Ethan informed him that many shelters were in rubble, they suffered serious crop damage, and most of their belongings were destroyed. Mitch insisted they send a truck with food and supplies from their reserve, even though they were supposed to trade their excess food with a group from New Mexico for electronic parts. It was important that people stick together.

"Sure thing. You know, you've changed over the past few weeks."

Mitch frowned. "What are you talking about?"

"You're different."

Mitch folded his arms. "Would you care to elaborate?"

"Since Deborah's been here, you're less on edge. Not easy going, but less intense. It works for you."

Mitch chuckled. "I'm glad you think so, but I doubt it. Socially, I may have mellowed, but I still hate the aliens."

Whether or not he had mellowed, he couldn't judge, but one thing was certain, he was loving life ever since Deborah stepped back into his world.

*\*\**

In his office, Mitch received a radio call from Gary Daniels. "Steve Minard just arrived. He needs to talk to you."

"Tell him I'll be right there," Mitch said.

Minard had just come back from a reconnaissance mission to find out if the Ingleside naval base was operational. It was a long shot, but he kept his fingers crossed.

Mitch closed a manual on a radio transmitter he had been reading. They wanted to build their own, but they had to have a full understanding of how the old ones worked. Since he had experience with radio transmission, he volunteered to lend his expertise.

Walking at a brisk pace, it took fifteen minutes to reach the military vehicle hangar.

When he arrived, Corey Goss had just finished debriefing Minard's team.

Minard had a wide smile. "You were right. Ingleside has a functional naval base. Before you get your hopes up too high, their fleet is about twenty five percent pre-invasion capacity, and much of what they are using is in need of repair."

"It's a starting point, and it's a hell of a lot better than what we have now."

"I spoke to the commander of the base," Minard said. "Apparently our reputation precedes us. They heard about our exploits and they're interested in talking to you."

"Perfect. When?"

"The sooner the better."

Mitch was busy next week. Perhaps the week after that he could leave. This Ingleside deal was important. The others would have to take care of things in his absence.

Mitch asked Minard for a full rundown of everything he had learned. Fortunately, Minard had been observant.

Mitch sniffed the air. "I think I smell…"

Minard cut him off. "Smoke."

They both rushed out of the house. In the distance, Mitch could see the unmistakable flames. It still wasn't close to the community, but it seemed to be everywhere. Wherever he turned, he saw fire.

"Son of a bitch," Mitch muttered. "How did this thing start?" It hadn't been dry lately. Just three days ago, they had a good, soaking rain.

"I don't know," Minard said.

Corey Goss ran toward them. His dark-skinned face was pale and haggard. Mitch had never seen him like this.

"We got big problems, boss," Goss said.

He had a terrible feeling that things were about to take a dramatic turn for the worse. "Yeah, I see the fire. We need to get it under control."

"No, that's not it," Corey said.

"What is it?"

Goss stared hard, unwilling to speak, until Mitch gestured for him to continue.

"Two alien ships just landed."

"Son of a bitch," Mitch muttered through gritted teeth. "Have they attacked?" Of course, they hadn't attacked. He would have heard if they did.

"No. This two-headed alien came out. Said he wants to talk to Mitch Grace. He said you better come, or they'll level us."

Mitch took a deep breath. "Okay. He wants to see me. Then take me to him."

As Mitch followed Corey outside, he felt surprisingly at ease. What could they do to him that he had not already experienced? His main objective was to keep the community safe. He had worked too hard to see it go down in flames.

## Chapter XXI

Mitch wanted to do something about the fire surrounding the community, but he had the distinct feeling that the danger posed by the fire and the aliens were one in the same.

He knew it was a matter of time. There was no way they could operate so boldly without attracting the aliens' attention. He hoped before that happened, his forces would have mounted a major offensive.

*Why the hell does he want to talk to me?*

Mitch followed Goss, who said, "Looks like trouble, boss."

At the edge of the town center, two enormous ships, about twice the size of luxury cruise liners, loomed in front of him. They were long and thin with shiny surfaces that glistened in the sun. They had smooth edges, unlike Sarm's sharp and angular vessel.

In front of him stood a two-headed alien with spikes running down its back, the same damn alien that had tried to capture him when he had fled Sarm's compound. Based on the look the alien had given him back then, Mitch knew that he wouldn't give up his pursuit so easily.

At the top of its neck, the spikes divided, and a set ran up each head. It had smooth, green skin and the face of a tortoise. Its blue lips smacked even when it did not speak. This thing was ugly even for an alien.

"Mitch Grace, I presume." The alien's words came out of its left mouth.

Mitch nodded slowly. The heat from the fire was building. Sweat was pouring down his neck. He considered his possibilities. If he was quick enough, he could shoot the alien, but he didn't know what repercussions would come from the ships.

"That's me." Mitch felt no fear. Perhaps because he had spent so much time with Sarm, he was no longer intimidated by them. "How can I help you?"

The alien's right head nodded, while its left head turned. Watching this creature was disorienting. The alien informed him that he had pissed off the ruling federation, and they had placed a substantial bounty for his capture.

*So, this is it.* He had a good run. He helped assemble a new society after coming back from the grave and gave people hope.

"And you intend to collect this bounty?" Mitch asked. "I won't go down easy."

"If I intended to dispose of you, you would already be dead. As you may have guessed, we are responsible for creating the fire. We have completely encased your community. There is no way out other than to go through a wall of flame. However, just as we have created the fire, we have capabilities of extinguishing it as well without a single member of your community being harmed. You eluded me once, Mitch Grace. Nobody eludes me."

"So, what do you want with me? Is this a personal matter since I bruised your ego, or is this about a reward?"

Ruje moved forward, but his casual stance did not indicate that he was looking for a fight. "I seek no reward, nor is this personal. You have showed amazing resiliency and courage in the way you escaped me and have defied the ruling government. You are a fighter. That is why I have sought you. I have made agreement with Mogenheim, the chief marshal of Santanovia, that if I capture you, I can use you for the Games. You would be under my custody. I will mold you into a fabulous attraction that many will eagerly pay to see. This will generate more revenue than by collecting the bounty."

Mitch sized up the alien. "The Games? What the hell are you talking about?"

"Let me use a historical parallel. In your civilization's ancient history, your Romans enjoyed gladiator challenges. Am I right?"

Mitch nodded.

"The Games have similarities to your gladiator fights. In Santanovia, we have humans fight against each other in an arena to the death. It is great sport."

"You sick son of a bitch," Mitch said.

The alien's right face had a half smile, and half a grimace. "What you must find understanding for is that the beings living in Santanovia have much work. This planet has become a commerce center. Having such hard work without entertainment leads to trouble. The Games create an outlet for aggression to prevent violent crime."

"Better we kill each other," Mitch muttered.

"Now you have the correct mindset. The Games have been quite profitable. My arenas attract many guests, and because workers in Santanovia have large incomes, they are inclined to spend it at the Games. You have a wonderful planet."

"It was until you got here."

The alien threw its head back and squealed. "I enjoy your wit."

More members of the community gathered, including Deborah. She grabbed Mitch's hand. "What's going on? They can't take you."

Mitch wanted to turn to her, to reassure her that everything was going to be all right, but he ignored Deborah. He needed to concentrate on the alien and didn't have much time. The intensity of the flames was increasing.

The alien gave Mitch the ultimatum to surrender, or he would destroy the settlement.

Mitch's brain raced to find a way out.

"You can't do that," Deborah said. "We'll fight you."

"That would be foolish," the two-headed alien said in its low grumble. "Apparently the fire is not enough to convince you. You humans are a stubborn people. Perhaps a demonstration is necessary."

The alien pulled out a yellow device. He uttered something Mitch couldn't understand.

A white pulsing beam fired from the vessel at a tree. Where the tree had stood, there was nothing, not even ashes.

Mitch's mouth opened wide. He tried to hide his astonishment, but he doubted he was that good of an actor. He had never seen a weapon so powerful.

There were screams in the background.

His instinct was to fight, but how could they fight against a weapon like that? If he didn't cooperate, they would destroy his community.

"You made your point. I'll go with you if you promise to not harm the others and put out the fire immediately without any destruction of property or injuries to my people."

The alien's body jiggled. "Agreed."

Deborah grabbed his hands. "You can't let them take you."

He sighed, his hands trembling. Just a few weeks ago, he was on top of the world after reuniting with the love of his life, and bam, just like that, it was over. He had learned six years ago that life wasn't always fair.

"Look, Deb, we don't have a choice. You saw what that thing could do, and it would be nearly impossible for us to extinguish the fire even if we didn't have the aliens to contend with. They'll destroy us, you and me included. One person's life isn't worth it. We've put too much work into this. I'm not going to risk it all."

Deborah cried. "No. I lost you once. I'm not losing you again." She turned to the alien. "Take me with you."

Mitch stared into her eyes. "Absolutely not. I need you here. I need you to run this place and continue our resistance. There's no one else more capable than you to take my place."

"Please, Mitch," Deborah pleaded.

He saw the desperation in her eyes, but there was no viable alternative. He pulled her close. "I have to go with them. We can't risk it. Don't worry. I'll be back. I'm a survivor. If they couldn't kill me that first day of the invasion, they're not going to kill me now. I'll figure a way out of this mess."

Mitch kissed her tenderly on the lips.

"I love you, Mitch."

He brought her head to his chest and stroked her hair. "I've always loved you. I will come back. It's a promise." One he had no idea how he was going to keep.

"This is very touching." The two-headed alien's words dripped with sarcasm. "But it is time to leave before your camp in is flames. Bid your farewell."

Mitch hugged Deborah. He didn't know what to say to the others, so he said nothing.

He walked alongside the alien to one of the massive ships. He looked back at the place he had helped develop into a haven for humans. He could only hope it would stay that way. The alien had promised to spare his people if he cooperated.

It felt like his heart had been ripped out of him once more. Deborah was the one woman he truly cared for, yet he could never spend more than just a brief period of time with her before having to leave. Sometimes life just wasn't fair.

A few feet away, a hatch opened. Mitch took a deep breath as a ramp lowered. He stepped on the ramp, followed by his captor. The hatch closed so quickly he didn't have time to look back.

## Chapter XXII

Once inside, Mitch watched through a porthole as the vessel circled around the community, releasing a silver jet of liquid. The effects were remarkable. The fire was out almost on contact.

"Are you satisfied?" the two-headed alien said.

Mitch nodded. He at least had some solace that the community wouldn't burn to the ground.

An alien that slithered on the ground like a snake escorted him to a cell. Mitch hung his head low and didn't resist. He would not go down without a fight, but now was not the time or place. A door that stood more than twice his height slid open. "Inside." The alien made a buzzing sound after speaking. Mitch stepped inside and the door closed behind him. When he turned, the snake-like alien was gone.

The cell was austere yet brightly lit despite the lack of a visible light source. He looked for those micro-filaments he had seen in the mines but could find none. He knocked on the metallic surface of the dull grey wall.

Mitch crossed his arms and stared at a slab, the same color as the wall, hovering in the center of the room. He could not find any legs, nor anything protruding from the ceiling to support it. "Hmm." He bent and tapped on it, expecting it to move, but it remained motionless. He tried to push it, but it did not give. It defied all laws of physics. He sat on the slab. Although the exterior seemed metallic, he sunk into it. Much to his surprise, it felt comfortable. The very top of the seat had a thick cushion.

Mitch sighed, feeling a mixture of depression and dread. Things had been going so well, especially with Deborah back. He knew they couldn't defeat the aliens, but maybe they could make the aliens leave. Now, what was he going to do? How would he fulfill his promise and return to Deborah?

Still not sure of the stability of the slab, he leaned back and locked his fingers behind his head.

The minutes ticked by. Since entering the cell, he had not seen another being.

A half hour later, the alien that had originally abducted him appeared. "Are you enjoying your accommodations, Mitch Grace?"

Mitch sat up. "It's not exactly the Ritz Carlton."

The alien's first head stared at him, while the second head shook back and forth.

"Never mind," Mitch said.

"Perhaps for future times, I can let you roam if you provide reasons to trust you. Based on your exploits, you are likely to take over my ship."

Mitch shrugged.

"I see, you are a man with few words. My name is Ruje."

"What the hell do you want with me?"

"I want you to generate income for me. Several ventures I have require considerable sums of monetary units. You will generate large incomes for me or face death. Have we an understanding?"

"What do you want me to do, rob a bank?"

"You will be my gladiator."

"Oh yeah, your Games. You know, my civilization did that back in its early days. We've progressed since then. I thought you aliens are supposed to be so much better than us."

Ruje's left head twirled. "The Games provide a method of releasing aggression and currency from the spectators."

"Great for everyone except the competitors."

Ruje shrieked. "Not so, Mitch Grace. Success in the Games brings greater glory to the competitors. Some have risen to be intergalactic stars, gaining wealth and fame. I wouldn't suspect a human can do so well because of your physical limitations, but among humans, you can become the top competitor."

There was no way in hell he would fight another person. They had taken so much away from him; they weren't going to take away his dignity. Ruje would probably kill him when he refused, but he would deal with that later. For now, he played along with this two-headed freak show.

"I need you strong and fit. I will give you nutrition to optimize your physical strength, and an exercise regimen that will enhance your conditioning. The more I gain your trust, the more freedom you will have. Your group would have been annihilated before long. It is your fortune that I found you first. You are still alive and can enjoy a satisfying life. This is a new beginning for you. It will have its rewards. I can provide female human companions if that is your interest." Ruje laid a leathery hand on his shoulder. "I am your friend. Do as I ask, and you will live well, providing you win at the Games. Do not even think of an escape."

Ruje pulled out a yellow transmitter and spoke into it in an alien language. A minute later, an alien with a green oval head and four tentacles approached his cell. It was three feet in height and had cold black eyes.

"This is Takano, our physician. She will implant a device that will allow me to track your movement over vast distances."

Mitch jumped off his floating cot. "I don't think so."

Ruje grabbed Mitch's wrist. He tried to pull away but could not budge. He gritted his teeth. The alien had incredible strength.

"You have no choice. You need not worry. The procedure is harmless. Takano, implant the subject."

Takano slithered a tentacle at Mitch. Cupped in it was a dull, flat object. She pressed it against Mitch's skin.

Ruje let go of Mitch, who felt revulsion when the cool object, roughly the size of a half-dollar, sunk into his skin. He expected to feel intense pain, but he only felt a twinge. He stared at his arm, his mouth wide open. A vibration radiated through his body. It surged through his shoulder and teeth. Mitch groaned, not so much in pain, but at the strange sensation. Just when he thought the sensation was going to drive him crazy, it stopped.

He took a deep breath and shook his head.

Ruje's left face smiled. "I said it would be painless. You had momentary discomfort, but that is nothing for a gladiator."

Mitch balled his fist. "You fucking bastard."

Ruje's eyes narrowed. "No need to use your tongue's abusive language. I am your friend, the best one you have, but make no mistake, you belong to me. I could have you executed. You live because you bring value to me, so cheer up as you humans might say, and let us maximize this partnership."

Ruje extended his leathery hand.

Mitch backed up a step. "I don't think so. I may be forced to work for you, but we're not friends." Shaking this alien's hand would tarnish his friendship with Sarm.

Ruje's face was expressionless. "Let us leave the human, Takano."

Mitch folded his arms as the two aliens left. He expected to feel repugnance from having this tracking device implanted into him, but he felt nothing, only a sinking feeling that he was more than just a prisoner; he was a slave.

After pacing about the room for several minutes, Mitch yawned. His hands sunk to his knees. Suddenly, he felt bone tired. It had to be the tracking device.

Mitch took a couple of wobbly steps and collapsed on the cot. "Ohh." His head turned to one side and sleep came quickly.

***

Mitch opened one eye to find a white ceiling above him. He closed his eye, still groggy. He wanted to get up, but had no strength, so he propped himself on his elbows. Scanning the cell, from the corner of his eye he spotted Ruje. He slid off his cot and tried to stand, but his balance was poor, and he stumbled to the floor.

Ruje lifted him. "Your slumber was long for a human. You were asleep for fifteen of your Earth hours, double the normal length of sleep for your kind."

Mitch yawned. "Fifteen hours and we're still in the air. Where are we going?"

"To your old city of Los Angeles."

"How can we be in the air for fifteen hours and not have reached Los Angeles?"

Ruje laughed. "As your people would say, this hasn't been a direct flight. We stopped in your old country of Mexico."

Mitch shook his head. "Damn. I slept through that."

"Apparently your revolt against those who control Santanovia has made you weary. I have enjoyed following your exploits."

Mitch rolled his eyes. He had enough of Ruje's compliments.

Ruje lifted a tray encased in metal and removed the cover. Inside was an oversized plate of green mush. "I have brought you food."

"You call that food," Mitch said. "It looks like vomit."

"I had it tempered to the palate of your kind. You will no doubt find it enjoyable."

Mitch furrowed his brow. "I have plenty of doubt."

"Please eat."

Mitch's stomach rumbled. He cast a wary glance at the alien, then took a spoon from the side of the tray and dug in, chewing reluctantly at first, and then with more vigor. "Not bad. It tastes like a good steak."

"You are so filled with doubt, Mitch Grace. You need to find trust in me."

Mitch continued eating, savoring the food.

"Eat until you are full. This food is rich in vitamins, proteins, and nutrients that will give you strength, mass, and agility. If you are still hungry when you have completed the plate, I can get you more."

Mitch ignored Ruje and concentrated on his food, still ravenous.

When he finished, he leaned back and put his fork down. "My compliments to the chef. That was excellent."

"I am glad you enjoyed. We will be landing shortly. Follow me. You no longer need to remain in your cell."

Mitch had to play Ruje's game to buy himself time. That meant dropping his hostility and gaining Ruje's trust.

They walked down a hallway. Unlike his austere cell, the rest of the vessel was colorful and decorated with three dimensional murals and sculptures.

They passed aliens of all shapes and sizes. A number of tall, slender aliens sat around a bar. Instead of drinking from glasses, they had tubes attached below their necks.

The vessel was much larger inside than it looked from the outside. The ceilings were at least forty feet high, capable of housing some of these gigantic aliens.

An alien with light blue skin and features closely resembling a woman walked toward them. Her hair was green, and she had large lips. She was slight in stature, only reaching Mitch's shoulders. He found her strangely attractive.

"So, this is the human who caused so many problems." The alien's voice sounded like it was coming from behind a metallic screen. Her soft hand caressed his chest and shoulders. "Hmm. Very firm. Nice well-developed muscles."

Ruje's four eyes narrowed. "Mitch Grace is not your plaything, Merelda. I have big plans for him."

"As do I." Merelda leaned in, her large breasts rubbing up against him. "A girl has to have fun. I've read your contemporary women magazines. I know how to seduce a human male, and what a male to seduce."

"Have you duties to attend?" Ruje asked.

"I've finished my duties, so I wanted to meet our new human friend." Merelda leaned her head back and winked. "I like your style, Mitch Grace. You have the ruling council of Santanovia in an uproar. I hoped you would succeed. It is your planet."

"You got that right. It is my planet." He sounded foolish. This alien had him all twisted.

"Obviously it's no longer his planet," Ruje said. "Otherwise, his people wouldn't be hiding. I would like to show Mitch Grace the rest of the vessel."

Merelda purred like a cat. "I am here for you, Mitch. I'm sure you will have many needs, and I can satisfy those needs."

"Um, right," Mitch said. "I'll keep that in mind."

Ruje kept a set of wary eyes on Merelda as she left. "I require your focus on the tasks set forth."

Mitch nodded. "You'll have it." He liked the idea of dissension among his captors. If he pitted one against another, it might help him find a way out.

Several winged aliens flew past, causing Mitch to duck his head. Overhead, several aliens flew at low speeds on hovercrafts. Ruje continued to talk. In awe of his surroundings, Mitch didn't listen to half of what he said. As he looked around the ship, he realized it had multiple levels. Up above were crosswalks. It was hard to gauge just how large this craft was, but to this point he had seen at least a hundred aliens. He had not seen anything like an engineer or navigation room.

"And your impressions of my ship?"

"It's really something."

"As we travel, you will be able to explore the vessel. Stay away from Merelda. She makes conquests of males both of your species and others in an insatiable manner. She will only bring you trouble. In fact, if memory serves, one of my human male slaves killed another over her. Bad business. Ah, we shall be landing in your old Los Angeles momentarily. Take a seat. I had them specifically prepared for humans."

The chair's length was about his height. It was shiny and black. Tilted at a strange angle, it almost appeared to be a recliner. He sat on the chair, and as soon as his body settled into it, the chair began to shift.

"At ease," Ruje said. "It is merely scanning your body and making adjustments based on your height and weight. It is designed to adjust for optimal comfort."

Mitch settled back. It would take no time to reach his old headquarters in Colorado in this vessel, but to him it seemed like a lifetime away.

## Chapter XXIII

Mitch enjoyed the cool water running down his body after finishing another of Ruje's intense workouts. He didn't know if it was the workouts or the nutrition, but he was bigger, faster, and stronger than he had ever been in his life. He had always had a solid build and good conditioning, but now he had rippling muscles throughout his body.

At first, he resisted the idea of training to be Ruje's gladiator, but increasing his physical capabilities would help him escape, so instead, he embraced it. After seeing the results from the first week of training, Mitch had become obsessed with getting better. Even Ruje had expressed his appreciation for Mitch's efforts.

Mitch turned off the water and left his private bathroom. He reached for a towel on the rack but found none. Stepping out of the shower, his eyes lit up. Merelda stood in front of him holding his towel.

She taunted him by shaking the towel. Merelda showed up at least once a day to flirt with him. He wasn't about to tell her that he had no interest in having sex with her, something she had propositioned him with twice. Even if Deborah wasn't in his life, he couldn't see himself sleeping with an alien, but perhaps he could figure out a way for her to help him escape.

She held the towel in front of her.

Mitch stepped back into the shower. "Do you mind if I dry myself off?"

"I prefer you wet."

"If it's all the same with you, I'd rather be dry."

Merelda shrugged. "If you wish."

Mitch took a step back when Merelda came forward. "Mitch, why are you afraid of a little girl like me? I am just trying to help. Why do you resist me?"

"Well, there is the little fact that your kind took over my planet?"

"I had nothing to do with that. I am only here because I am under Ruje's employ, and he decided to come to this barbarian planet."

Mitch gritted his teeth. *Barbarian planet. If it was so bad, then why did they stay?*

"Let me help you." It was hard to tell what type of clothes Merelda was wearing because it blended with the color of her skin, making it difficult to see where the clothes ended and her flesh began. Whatever it was she was wearing left very little to the imagination and accentuated every possible curve.

She toweled him off, groping him in the process. Part of him was repulsed, and part of him felt aroused. He had to stick to his plan.

He took the towel from her and dried himself off properly. "Do you mind giving me a little privacy while I dress?"

Merelda pouted. "Why do you insist on taking away all of my fun?"

"Ruje wouldn't like it if he found you here. He told you to stay away from me."

Merelda laughed. "Since when do you follow authority? Isn't that how you got here in the first place, by resisting the aliens who control your planet?"

"I guess we're kindred spirits. Now would you mind turning while I get dressed?"

Merelda threw down her arms. "If you insist."

Mitch quickly got dressed in black pants and a sweatshirt. He had to remain elusive in order to maintain her interest. "You can turn now."

"I preferred you without your clothes."

"This leaves more for the imagination," Mitch said.

Merelda ran her long, thin, green fingers along his chest. "When are you going to let me bed you? I know you want to. No one will have to know."

Mitch straightened up. With his head, he motioned behind Merelda. Standing there was the two-headed green alien with the face of a tortoise, standing alongside a heavily muscled human male.

Ruje cleared his throat. "There is need for you back on the ship."

Merelda turned and smiled. "I was checking your gladiator. He seems to be progressing well."

"Well indeed." Ruje kept his four eyes on her.

She grabbed the hand of the man standing next to Ruje and pulled him toward her. She kissed him deeply and gripped firmly onto his buttocks. The whole time, she locked eyes with Mitch. She pulled back, closed her eyes, and blew him a kiss.

Ruje growled, and Merelda and her boy toy made themselves scarce. Using a mirror in the bathroom, Mitch checked the cut underneath his left eye that he had suffered while sparring with another human captive. Ruje had over a dozen human prisoners who stayed in an apartment building nearby, including Merelda's boy toy. Five were actively fighting gladiators. The others were in training. Ruje had provided Mitch with his own lavish apartment, while the others lived together.

"You had a strong session of training," Ruje said. "I think you are nearly ready."

Mitch gritted his teeth. He didn't mind the training, but he did not want to fight. "Is that right?"

"Oh, yes. You will have much success. I had weapons furnished for you. I am sure you will see them as satisfactory. Follow me."

"You sure know how to treat a prisoner."

"You are not a prisoner, Mitch Grace. You are an employee. I provide well for you in exchange for future services."

Ruje could call it what he wanted, but Mitch felt like a prisoner. He followed Ruje out of the training facility, which used to belong to the Los Angeles Dodgers baseball team.

Inside the cavernous, domed building, the weight and exercise equipment had been replaced by high tech machinery that Ruje's people had designed for his human gladiators. Mitch had never seen anything like it before, but after using the equipment for a month, he did not doubt its efficacy.

Ruje pressed a button that opened a door. Inside, an alien who had a body of a caterpillar molded an alloy with a laser beam torch.

Ruje grabbed his wrist. "Over here, Mitch. Pay attention. This is important. As I mentioned, I had weapons created for you. I lack doubt that you will find them useful."

Ruje held a black cylindrical device attached to a wrist band. He pressed a button at the bottom of the band, and a blue blade shot out. "When you come close to your opponent, this will allow you to slice him. Be careful, it is very sharp."

He took a cloth sack with a blue, crystalline powder. "I have tempered this substance found in a distant galaxy with your epidermal cells. It will not react with your skin, however if it encounters your opponent's skin, it will create a sensation of how do you call it when fire touches you."

"Burning?" Mitch said.

"Yes, burning. The effect will be intensified if it encounters the mouth or eyes."

Mitch's brow furrowed. "Is this legal?"

Ruje's right head nodded. "I have verified with the commissioner of the Games, and the commissioner has deemed these weapons acceptable."

"Not very sportsmanlike."

"Sportsmanship does not win fights." Ruje took out a vial with black powder. "This powder upon reacting with the atmosphere will create a jet of flame which you can use to burn your opponent."

Mitch crossed his arms, and Ruje showed him additional devious weapons he had secured. Mitch had no interest in using these at the Games, since he had no intention of fighting any man or woman.

Ruje's face took a serious demeanor when he asked Mitch if he was ready to fight.

Mitch didn't know how to answer that. Every time he been in combat, there was a reason for it. He couldn't imagine fighting for sport. Reality hit home when Ruje reminded him he would be fighting for his life. His first bout would be tomorrow.

Mitch waited for Ruje to leave, before picking up some sparring gloves and working on a simulated human android that was trying to defend against Mitch's strikes. Mitch had pounded the holy hell out of this android, which seemed not to sustain damage despite the beatings it took.

He needed a plan. Back in his former life, he had killed more people than he cared to remember. Now the idea of harming another human repulsed him. The Games were fights to the death. How was he going to get out of this? He prided himself in his ingenuity, but this problem had him stymied.

## Chapter XXIV

Mitch took a deep breath as he stared at the thousands of aliens in the arena. He couldn't understand their chants, but knew they wanted blood.

Since Ruje had informed him about his first bout, he had been filled with anxiety, desperately wanting to get out of it.

During the procession in front of the stadium, Mitch had felt physically ill when the aliens had cheered the gladiators. Nothing he had done with the Navy SEALs could prepare him for this, since he did not kill for sport.

He stepped onto the grass field. A clear, hard material separated the spectators from the competitors. The stadium reached to the heavens. It had to be at least the height of a fifty-story building and three football fields long.

The aliens roared their approval. Mitch focused on his opponent. Across from him was a large black man who had at least six inches and fifty pounds on him. The man's nickname was the Predator, but his real name was Bob Brennan. Although he was not one of Ruje's slaves, Mitch had seen him around at Ruje's training facility fairly regularly over the past few weeks. Unlike Mitch, he was no rookie. According to Merelda, he had six bouts under his belt. Obviously, he had won them all. He raised his arms, and the aliens cheered.

The referee, an alien of Ruje's species, stood at the center of the arena. Mitch and his opponent walked toward the referee. Sparks shot across the sky, signifying the start of the fight.

Mitch's opponent raised his fists. Spiked straps ran across Bob's massive pects. He wore red and yellow face paint for the theatrical element of this competition.

The Predator closed the gap between them.

"I won't fight you, Bob."

Bob's brows furrowed. "What do you mean? We have to fight."

"I won't fight you."

The Predator's face tightened. "What's wrong with you? They'll kill us both. They came to see us fight, and if that don't happen, we're gonna have some pissed off aliens."

Mitch shook his head. "I won't fight you."

The referee approached Mitch. "What is wrong with you, human?"

"I won't fight this man," Mitch replied.

The referee shook both its heads, and all four of its eyes swirled. "What is the meaning of this?"

"I will not fight another human."

The Predator stood back, crossing his arms across his chest.

The referee spoke into a radio while the audience grumbled.

A minute later, Ruje entered the stadium. He spoke in an angry tone. "Mitch Grace, you will fight tonight or die."

Mitch stepped in front of Ruje. "You want me to fight tonight? Fine. But I won't fight this man. Tell the crowd that I'll take on any alien who thinks they can crush a lowly human."

Both of Ruje's faces were impassive. "Interesting. I think that can be done, assuming I find a challenger." He returned to the underground portion of the arena.

Mitch took a deep breath. Thankfully, Ruje decided to go with his plan. For a second, he had thought he was dead.

"I hope you know what you're doing," the Predator said.

Mitch shrugged. "Not really."

"You're either crazy or you're...no forget it, you're crazy."

Mitch waited, his stomach tied in knots.

Ruje's voice chimed in the loudspeakers. Mitch felt disoriented when a cacophonous blend of sounds stemming from individual speakers on the spectators' tables sounded throughout the arena.

A loud roar emerged from the stands.

Bob stood in front of him shaking his head. "You're just plain crazy, that's all. You got a better chance against me than one of them. What are you thinking, man?"

Mitch didn't respond. He would rather take his chances against an alien.

The referee approached Mitch. Just like Ruje, he had two heads. Oddly enough, one head was larger than the other. Entirely clad in white, he had four large, bulbous eyes and thick lips. "Ruje has informed me that he has posted your challenge to all in attendance. We must wait to discover if there have been any acceptances."

Mitch stretched his arms. If he was right about the aliens' disdain for humans, he would find a taker.

Murmurs came from the crowd. Mitch looked up. Apparently Ruje had found a challenger, an alien with the lower torso of a snake with thick scales and an upper torso that resembled a gorilla. It had a muscular physique with dark patches of hair. Four heavy arms emerged from its powerful upper body. Its long, thin face lacked a nose. Just like the rest of the aliens, it was damn ugly.

The Predator patted Mitch on the shoulder. "Good luck, man. You're going to need it. At least you gave me a chance to live another day."

Ruje walked toward him. "Mitch Grace, the response from those in attendance had an overwhelming effect. Apparently, they would like to see you battle a non-human. Unfortunately, I will have to accept this short-term gain, because it is unlikely that you will live."

The announcer introduced the alien. Sparks shot into the air. It was time to fight.

Mitch raised his fists and circled right as the snake alien pursued him. He had to buy time to figure out how to kill this thing. Its upper body looked powerful, so it would be a mistake to get too close. Its snake-like lower torso moved with great quickness.

It slithered at him. Before he could react, it smacked him in the side of the face with an open hand. He had never been hit that hard. Mitch took a couple steps back trying to regain his senses.

The alien came forward and swung with a closed fist. He avoided the first shot, but it hit him with its lower hand. It swung around and connected with another blow.

Damn. He couldn't take too many more of those shots. He backpedaled to get out of range but wasn't prepared when it lashed him with its tail across his chest, knocking his wind out and sending him crashing onto his back. *Holy hell.*

Blood dripped down Mitch's nose and mouth. His head felt like it was going to explode, and his ribs ached.

It was time to dip into Ruje's bag of tricks. When the alien first presented him with these weapons, he had been disgusted that Ruje wanted him to use them against another person. He had no problem using them against this creature.

Mitch took out a black pouch from inside his vest. The crystal powder inside had been tempered to his skin but would burn another person. This alien's upper torso appeared similar to his own, so he might be able to use the substance against it. First, he had to get closer.

The alien whipped its snake-like tail, but Mitch dodged it. He then darted toward it. When he was five feet away, he stopped and poured the crystal powder into his hand. He threw the powder into its face, neck, and upper torso.

The alien howled, flailing its four arms. A hush overcame the crowd. Its tail whipped back and forth but could not reach Mitch. Drool dripped down its mouth, and its eyes bulged.

He jumped on the alien's back. It tried to shake him off, but he held on, not about to let go of his momentary advantage.

He punched the back of the alien's head, hurting his hand in the process. He wrapped his arm around its neck. The alien thrashed, so he wrapped his legs around its waist. He punched the back of its head several times, trying to slow the alien down.

It still wasn't showing any sign of weakness, so Mitch squeezed harder. It tried to reach him with its four arms but could not pull him off. With his free arm, he elbowed the back of its head and neck. He then wrenched down, causing the alien to fall backward.

They both crashed onto the arena floor. The alien was suffocating him, so he flipped over so that he was on top of the alien. He then slipped his arm underneath its neck and began to choke it once more.

The alien got to a vertical position, hauling Mitch along with it. It slithered across the arena toward the stands, while Mitch held onto his choke-hold. Mitch braced himself as it lunged against the rail.

Pain surged through his back and shoulder, but he would not let go. What the hell was it going to take to kill this thing? A human would have been long dead.

The snake alien slithered from the wall and charged at it again. At the last second, Mitch flipped over to the other side of the alien's body, avoiding impact with the wall. They crashed, this time the alien taking the worst of the blow.

Once more, he punched and elbowed the back of the alien's head.

"Just die already, you bastard," Mitch said through gritted teeth.

Without warning, the alien collapsed.

The referee ran over to the struggling combatants, but Mitch would not let go, not until he knew it was dead. The referee pulled him off his opponent. Mitch tilted his head back, taking in a deep breath. A hushed silence overcame the arena.

"You are the winner." The alien raised both of Mitch's arms.

Mitch sank to his knees and gave an elated cry. He had not thought he would make it out of this fight. It felt like the alien had hit him with bricks.

Mitch stood, startled when the audience gave a resounding roar of approval. He wasn't sure how to react. The last thing he wanted was to give these blood-thirsty aliens satisfaction.

The more cunning side of his mind thought he could use this to his advantage. He pumped his fist in the air and saluted the aliens. They cheered wildly. He walked closer to the stands, raising both fists in the air.

Ruje strode in his direction with a wide smile on his ugly face. At the center of the arena, Ruje spoke. His words translated in the speakers at the various tables, giving off a cacophony of sound. The aliens let out a frenzied roar.

Ruje congratulated him. "You defy notions that are held of you. With reluctance, I must let it be known that I wagered against you, but I can be glad to be proven wrong. The money I lost in the wager is small compared to the revenue you will bring. I lack doubt that your popularity will expand with this victory."

Mitch didn't let Ruje's plans bring him down. He had just killed one of the hated alien bastards with his two hands and a little trickery from Ruje. Now, he had to figure out a way to keep his promise to Deborah and return home.

## Chapter XXV

Bob Brennan threw a left, right combination. Mitch side-stepped the first punch and ducked the second punch. Brennan wouldn't let up, sending a front kick, which grazed Mitch's abdomen. He was being unusually aggressive in their sparring session.

Following their almost fight in the arena, Ruje had purchased The Predator, as he was known in the Games, from his owner to train with Mitch. Normally, they got along fine, but today Brennan was coming at him hard.

Brennan charged in at him, but Mitch sprawled to avoid being taken down. While in the clinch, they both tripped to the mat. Mitch got to his feet and reached his hand to help his opponent up, when Brennan inexplicably slugged him in the jaw.

The blow stunned Mitch, sending him to the mat. "Hey, what the hell was that?"

Instead of a response, Brennan landed a knee to Mitch's head, which nearly rendered him unconscious. He regained his senses enough to scramble to his feet, grab both of Brennan's legs, lift him, and slam him hard to the mat. He punched Brennan twice to the face. When Brennan turned away from the punches, Mitch put his arm underneath his neck in a choke-hold.

Mitch controlled him but did not put any pressure on his opponent's windpipe. "Now what the hell was that all about?"

Brennan continued to struggle underneath him but could not escape the choke-hold.

"It would be real easy for me to choke you unconscious right now. Do you want to fight or do you want to talk?"

In a choked breath, Brennan managed to say, "I'm done."

Mitch let go of the choke hold and helped Brennan stand. "Now what's your problem?"

Brennan took a step back, his face in a tight snarl. "You're the problem. Me and Merelda, we used to have a good thing going. She'd come and visit me once or twice a week and we'd have a good ole time. I figured once Ruje bought me from my owner, I'd be set. But no, she's all enamored with you. She ain't showin' me any love anymore."

Mitch raised his hands. "Look, man. You have it all wrong. There's nothing going on between me and Merelda. Now, as far as who she chooses to show her affections to, that's up to her. She's a grown alien female. She can do what she wants."

"Bullshit. You poisoned her mind with all your Gladiator crap."

Mitch gritted his teeth, trying to keep his anger in check. "You think I asked for this? You think I want to be fighting to the death in an arena against aliens who are physically superior to me? Face facts, Bob. You're a slave. You have no freedom. Why would you begrudge Merelda for choosing who she wants to be with? The aliens have taken everything away from us. You should value freedom above all else."

Just then, Merelda came walking toward them. Her skin color had turned pink. Based on the icy glare she gave Brennan, she must have heard their conversation.

"You need to leave," Merelda said.

Meekly, Brennan collected his gear and left.

Merelda also vacated the training area. Mitch stared at her intently as she was leaving, glad that she was on his side.

\*\*\*

Mitch shut his eyes, getting in the proper mental state for his fight. As usual, Merelda was with him. She had insisted on taking the role of his manager. At first, he had been reluctant, but now he found her invaluable.

With her slick hands, she massaged his neck and back. "Your largest obstacle is the lashwhim's agility. It is extremely quick. Although it can't fly, it can take long leaps. However, it is not exceptionally strong. You can overpower it."

Mitch nodded, listening carefully. Her advice in the last few fights had saved his ass. He might not care for her motives, but she had an extensive knowledge of alien species and was well-versed in hand-to-hand combat.

"I'm assuming it won't be easy to get close to this thing," Mitch said.

"Turn over."

Mitch flipped onto his back.

"No. That will be your challenge, Mitch, but I am confident you can overcome it. It shouldn't be as difficult as the farmone you defeated."

Mitch nodded. "I certainly hope not. I still can't believe I made it out alive."

"Your resourcefulness led you to victory. I checked the betting lines this morning, and you are the favorite. You have gained respect."

This would be the fifth time Mitch stepped into the arena to battle an alien. After his first fight, Merelda had told him he was the talk of the intergalactic sporting world.

For each of his fights, Mitch had been scheduled to fight another human. Ruje knew he had no intention of doing so, but his slave master used it as a ploy to increase the drama. He would refuse to fight his human opponent, then challenge any alien in attendance. Unlike the first time, Ruje had planted opponents in the stands to accept his challenge.

Mitch had relished killing the aliens. When he was with the SEALs, he never took pleasure in killing. Aliens were a different story. He wanted to kill every last one of them.

Ruje had told him earlier this week that they would skip the pre-fight drama. Mitch had become an intergalactic fighting superstar, and there was no longer a need for this charade. Aliens now traveled from all corners of the universe to watch him fight. He had even caught the attention of the great Salandar, the most vicious and brutal killer the Games had ever known. Merelda had told him tickets to these events fetched astronomical sums. In addition, they broadcasted his fights to many solar systems. Ruje treated him like a prince, giving Mitch anything he wanted, save for the one thing he truly craved—his freedom.

The most surreal aspect of his new fame was doing interviews broadcasted to distant galaxies. After the first few, he had convinced Ruje to stop the interviews so he could maintain a mysterious persona.

Meanwhile, he was doing all he could to turn himself into a fighting machine. He followed Merelda's training regimen religiously, even suggesting more strenuous and taxing exercises that would push him farther than he thought possible. He was also working closely with Takano, who was developing a formula that would both strengthen his bones and make them more flexible.

Merelda stopped massaging him and brought him to his feet. Her skin had turned bright red, as was customary right before he entered the arena. It was her battle mode. Based on her intensity, it seemed like Merelda was the one going out there to fight. "I wish you well. I know you will win."

"Thanks for the confidence."

Merelda drew him in close, her face a few centimeters from his. "After you win, I think a ...private celebration would be in order."

He had already told Merelda that he was tied to Deborah, but the alien didn't think that should make any difference to their relationship.

"Having sex during training will make you soft. I can't afford that. I have to be in absolute peak physical conditioning or I'll die out there."

Merelda pouted. "There is no evidence to support your claim. That is merely a myth. It's not fair. I should get rewarded for my effort. Ruje only scolds me."

"That's because he knows if I succumb to you, it'll hurt my ability to fight."

Merelda crossed her arms. "Normally you scoff at what Ruje says. Now that you want him to support your philosophy, you act as if he is an expert."

"Ruje knows about fighting at the Games."

The announcer called Mitch's name.

Before he had a chance to protest, Merelda gave him a full kiss on the lips.

Mitch stepped out to thunderous chants of "Gladiator", a moniker that Ruje had given him, and the aliens had taken to immediately.

His opponent entered to boos and jeers. The audience had embraced him strongly because he was an underdog. It was the classic American sport story.

This was the first time Mitch faced a smaller opponent. The lashwhim was short and wiry. It had smooth brown skin and a sunken face. Its lower extremities looked rubbery, and it had no feet. Covered in light brown fur, it had large flaps of skin on its side.

Mitch and the lashwhim moved to the center of the arena.

Mitch tried to get in its head. "You ready to meet your maker, double ugly?"

The lashwhim snorted, spitting brown saliva.

"I'm going to take pleasure putting you out of your misery."

The lashwhim shrieked.

Blue sparks shot across the arena. The fight was on.

Mitch shot in at the lashwhim, trying to heed Merelda's advice. It backed away like a blur, and he caught nothing but air. Before he could react, the lashwhim leaped at him and used its razor-sharp claws to slash his face.

Mitch wiped blood from his face.

It was one thing to know in advance that the lashwhim was quick, but he couldn't truly grasp its amazing agility until he saw it for himself. How the hell was he going to catch it?

He got ready to meet another attack. This time, the lashwhim spat a jet of saliva at Mitch's face, causing him to scream. When he was an undergraduate, a classmate had accidentally spilled diluted hydrochloric acid from a beaker onto his hand. This felt just like that. Without thinking, he hit the ground and rubbed dirt onto his face.

A rumble came from the audience. Mitch looked up in time to catch the lashwhim flying at him. He moved, and it missed his face with its clawed hands, striking him in the chest instead and knocking him to the ground.

Mitch grunted. Merelda had told him he had a strength advantage over the lashwhim, but after that blow, he wasn't so sure.

Mitch got to his feet as the lashwhim backed away. He had to fight it in close. At a distance, it would destroy him.

He put his fists to his face, which still ached from the saliva. "Come on, bastard. Bring it on."

Mitch had no idea if it understood him, but it advanced. The lashwhim leaped at him as the crowd chanted "Gladiator". Mitch took a glancing blow to his shoulders and chest. Feigning injury, he clutched his right shoulder and howled.

When the lashwhim jumped on him again, Mitch grabbed it and held it in a bear hug. It tried to wriggle free, but he squeezed tightly. Once he had a solid grip, Mitch tilted his hips and swept the lashwhim, driving it hard into the ground. Mitch hammered it with heavy punches, causing its head to bounce off the dirt.

Mitch pressed the button on his right sleeve, releasing a dagger near his wrist. With a slashing motion, Mitch tore its face and neck, causing green fluid to surge. He continued slashing with his dagger until fluid covered the lashwhim.

Mitch only stopped when the referee pulled him off. The alien was dead.

As soon as the referee pronounced Mitch the winner, he raised his fists in the air and turned to the crowd. The arena shook from the booming cheers of spectators.

Mitch played to the audience, not because he needed their adulation, but because it was part of his plan. He fully intended to fulfill Ruje's wishes of becoming a great gladiator. With some luck, it would be his ticket to freedom.

***

Mitch caught the legs of the winged creature as it flew by him. "Holy shit!" He flew through the air along with his opponent. Merelda had told him his best chance was to ground this alien. If it fought him in the air, then he was at a significant disadvantage. Judging by his bloody arms and ribs, she was right.

Just before they hit the guardrail, he pulled the alien down. He was far stronger than he had been when Ruje had first captured him.

The alien crashed into the railing. A loud crunch sounded as its head and neck hit metal.

It staggered on the ground. Mitch sprung to his feet, ran to the winged alien, snarled, and grabbed its head. Viciously twisting its head as if it were a cork, he tried to wrench it from its shoulders.

Bones crunched as he turned its head at an impossible angle. The crowd cheered as he fed their blood lust. Hoping to satiate their need for a violent death, he wrapped his thick arm around its neck and squeezed, causing its eyes to bulge out. The referee stepped in and stopped the fight, pronouncing Mitch the winner.

After the closing ceremonies, Mitch walked through the arena exit past another dead alien. He was amazed at how far he had come since his first fight. He had become overwhelmingly popular because the aliens had never thought a human could win. They considered humans mentally and physically inferior — not surprisingly since they had taken over Earth in a few days.

Merelda and Ruje waited in his private dressing room.

"Well done, Mitch Grace," Ruje said. "I have signed an agreement with three new solar systems to broadcast your fights. Your popularity continues to rise."

Mitch nodded. "Did you look at the drawings for those new weapons?"

"Yes. I remember when you objected to using weapons. I did not realize then that it was because you wouldn't use them against your own kind."

Merelda smiled. She leaned in and rubbed her body against his hot and sweaty upper torso. "Mitch is popular because he is of great character, only fighting against species thought to be superior to his own."

"I just picture my opponent as one of the bastards who took over Mother Earth."

"I have selected several opponents for your upcoming fights. Merelda will go over their strengths and weaknesses."

Mitch shook his head. "I'm not taking any of those fights."

Ruje's left face tightened. His right face remained blank. "What is your meaning?"

"I've made more money for you than you ever could have expected. I've killed dozens of fighters. My time serving you is over."

Ruje's eyes narrowed. "Mitch Grace, I value you, but you must remember your place. You belong to me."

Mitch went face to faces with Ruje. "Look, I can continue fighting for you, but one of these days, an alien will defeat me. Hell, I've nearly bought my ticket a few times out there. Here's my proposal. I want one more fight— against Salandar."

Merelda gasped. "No, Mitch. You know not what you speak of."

"You would not last a minute," Ruje said. "Do you wish to die?"

Mitch shook his head. "I want out, and I know that in order to get you to agree, I have to give you something. You'll make more from this one fight than my next ten, if I even lasted that long. If I win, you give me my freedom."

Merelda put her hand on his shoulder. She was near tears. Her skin turned a light shade of pink. "What good is your freedom if you're dead?"

Mitch was taken aback by her concern for him. He had always just assumed she wanted sex from him, but he could see that there were more to her feelings than just the physical. For the first time, he felt a twinge of guilt for leading her on the way he had. "This is no life for me, and I won't go on doing this. This way, I have a fighting chance."

Merelda frowned. She had often spoken of Salandar, the great champion, one of the greatest in the history of the Games. He had defeated all challengers for years, brutalizing his opponents before finishing them.

Prior to becoming a superstar in the Games, Salandar had been in prison for murder. He had committed many crimes for which he had never been convicted. His manager got him released to participate in the Games. Since then, he had bought his freedom with his earnings, but never stopped fighting because he enjoyed hurting his opponents.

Mitch counted on Ruje being too greedy to pass on this. If Salandar was as big a deal as Merelda made him out to be, combined with his own breakaway popularity, the fight would be a massive draw.

A glint formed in Ruje's turquoise eyes. The alien put a hand up to each face. "I could promote the fight as the Gladiator against the unconquerable Salandar. If the Gladiator can do the impossible, he would gain his freedom. The marketing possibilities are endless."

Merelda grabbed Mitch's hands. "Please don't do this. Salandar will kill you."

Mitch ignored her. "What do you say, Ruje?"

"Very well, Mitch Grace. I accept your proposal. I wish you luck. You will need it."

Reconquest Mother Earth

## Chapter XXVI

Merelda sat in front of Mitch with a grim expression. She looked less human than normal. "It is not too late to withdraw. We can claim you had a debilitating injury while training. You will not miss your face."

"The expression is lose face."

Merelda grabbed his hands. "That doesn't matter. The only thing that matters is that if you fight today, you will die. I do not wish to see that happen."

"Look, all of the fame and accolades I've achieved, none of this means anything to me. All I want is my freedom."

Merelda gave an exasperated sigh. "And why is this so important to you?"

"These alien invaders took my planet. Earth wasn't perfect before all of this, but at least we humans were in charge of our destiny. They robbed us of that."

Merelda shook her head. "You act as if you are the only who has had your planet conquered. I assure you that you are not. My home world has been occupied for three generations. My kind no longer even seeks independence." A forlorn look took over Merelda's face.

Mitch touched the soft skin of her face. "I'm sorry. Is that why you are helping me?"

Merelda playfully pushed his chest. "I am helping you because I want to have sex with you, you silly human."

"Look, I get your concern, but what I need from you is strategy to defeat Salandar."

Merelda was adamant about his safety, but Mitch was equally adamant about the choice he made.

Merelda threw her hands in the air, her blue-green face turning purple. "Don't you think I would have given you instructions if I knew how you could defeat Salandar? He's unlike any being I have seen. Salandar is a genetically engineered mix of three races, all vicious fighters, the perfect killing machine. None of his opponents have even inflicted any damage upon him. He is a thug, convicted for killing three members of my species, the Zohn, at the Festival of Light for no reason." Merelda turned away from him. "And he killed my ex-lover at the Games."

"I'm sorry."

"I don't want to lose you the way I lost him. I am not Ruje. I care about you, Mitch. Rumor is that he has killed many more beings whom he has not been convicted for. He has no weaknesses."

Mitch crossed his arms. "He has to. No one's invincible."

"I have viewed all of Salandar's previous combats. If he has a weakness, I can't find it."

Neither said anything for some time. A few minutes later, Ruje entered the room, his hands raised in triumph, his two faces grinning feverishly. "Today is indeed a grand and glorious day. Dignitaries from the universe will grace us in their presence. The current rumor is that the Minister of Science has a special guest of honor, Zolmethier, the Grand Emperor of the Twelve Circles."

Merelda gasped. "Zolmethier?"

"It appears that even the Grand Emperor would like to watch Mitch Grace battle the great Salandar. It is a bit of a surprise when you consider that Zolmethier loathes the Minister of Science yet will be in his presence today."

"Why's that?" Mitch asked.

Ruje waved his hand. "I try not to concern myself with the political arena. The battle arena is far more of interest. It is a long-standing grudge between the two, perhaps the reason why the Minister of Science has not been able to rise higher in his political career."

"Interesting. Then I guess I have something in common with this Grand Emperor."

"Your popularity is so vast that even Zolmethier has become a fan of your work. There can no longer be doubt that I am the foremost promoter of the Games." Ruje laughed. "With all of this attention I may be forced to stop pursuing my less legal activities. No matter, my fortune will be vast."

Merelda had clued him in on some of these illegal activities. Ruje had his hands involved in all sorts of criminal endeavors such as black-market smuggling, brokering deals for assassination, forging documents, and space piracy.

"Just don't forget our agreement," Mitch reminded him.

Ruje laughed so hard his heads spun and his large torso jiggled. "Mitch Grace, if you defy the thirty to one odds against you, I will release you. I wish you well, human. You have provided with me much revenue, and I will speak upon you with reverence. Beat Salandar. You have good humor for a human."

Mitch walked up to Ruje, grabbed his left face and glared at him. "I will beat Salandar. If you want to increase your take today, then bet on me to win."

"Very well, Mitch Grace. I will wager upon you." Ruje left the room.

Merelda slammed the door. "Let's review everything I know of Salandar."

Mitch nodded. The entire world doubted him. It was the way he wanted it.

*** 

Thunderous chants of Gladiator greeted Mitch as he entered the arena.

The ground shook under Salandar's large feet as he emerged from the tunnel.

Mitch stared at his opponent and swallowed hard. "Holy mother of God. What did I get myself into?"

Salandar was enormous, thirty feet in height. His torso looked like it had been chiseled from granite. Dark, green eyes sunk into his impassive face. His skin was the color of dirt. His clawed hands were almost the size of Mitch's body. Three spiked horns came from his head. A long, jagged tail protruded from his posterior. Short wings stuck out of his back. The alien didn't have a recognizable mouth, just a circular maw that looked like it could swallow Mitch whole.

What the hell was he going to do against this thing?

As the announcer addressed the audience, Mitch's legs felt weak. He had signed his own death warrant.

He closed his eyes, clearing his mind of everything besides his hatred for the aliens.

After the announcements, he and Salandar walked to the center of the arena. Salandar looked down on him as if he were an ant to be stepped on and crushed.

In the weeks leading to this, Mitch had endured numerous interviews with the intergalactic press. Ruje, hell bent on promoting this event, had forced Mitch to take these interviews. All Mitch wanted to do was train. Physically, he was at his peak. His speed, strength and agility had become superhuman thanks to the training regimen and dietary supplements Ruje and Merelda provided. If this was his old life, he could have dominated whatever professional sport he chose on sheer athleticism and physical conditioning, but this was no game. This was life and death.

Sparks shot into the air, signifying the start of the bout. Salandar brought his massive fist down at Mitch. He ran out of the way. His fist left a huge indentation in the dirt. If he hadn't gotten out of the way, Mitch would have become hamburger.

Mitch kicked Salandar's left leg. He might as well have kicked a stone wall. Salandar did not flinch. He picked Mitch up by his armor-plated suit and flung him across the arena. Mitch landed with a thud and grunted.

"Shit!" Mitch rolled away as black bolts flew in his direction. He thought he would be able to get away in time, but a bolt struck his left shoulder.

He screamed as a stabbing pain radiated from his shoulder. He clutched his arm, looking for the object that had pierced him, but there was nothing there, only the busted armor plate from his outfit and the missing flesh from his shoulder.

Mitch back-pedaled, trying to come up with a plan. Before he caught his breath, more black bolts shot from Salandar's tail. He dropped to the floor, lying flat on the dirt as the projectiles skimmed past him.

He removed a spear that one of Ruje's engineers had fashioned for him. It was lightweight but deadly sharp. He flung the spear at Salandar, wincing from the pain in his shoulder.

Mitch's heart sunk when his opponent knocked the spear aside like it was a twig.

Fighting from a distance wasn't going to work, especially with those bolts from Salandar's tail, so he ran at the alien, only to be swatted away.

Mitch collapsed. It felt like Salandar had smashed him with a sledgehammer.

Mitch couldn't move. He groaned, his chest feeling like it had been crushed. He took two shallow breaths. The earth shook. He turned his head as Salandar stomped on the ground.

"Please, no," Mitch muttered as the alien bounced toward him. Salandar took a giant leap. Mitch rolled left, the alien just missing him. He got to his knees, and Salandar picked him up with his massive hand.

He gasped for breath, the armor only doing so much to protect him. He had the feeling that Salandar was holding back, that if he really wanted to, he could crush him. Mitch hated the idea that he would spend his final moments having this sadistic alien toy with him.

He wriggled loose before prying apart Salandar's fingers. He broke free only to face a long drop to the dirt.

Sweat, blood and grime covered his face. He limped in-between Salandar's legs, positioning himself underneath the giant. Salandar looked around, giving Mitch a temporary reprieve. Too bad this fight didn't have rounds like a boxing match.

He took out his knife and stabbed Salandar's leg. If the alien felt the blow, he didn't indicate it. He pulled the knife out, and Salandar walked across the arena.

Mitch licked his cracked and bleeding lips as the audience chanted, "Gladiator." They had not given up on him.

"Come on, Salandar, give me an opening."

With surprising agility, the alien whipped his tail at him. With no way to avoid the blow, Mitch braced himself for impact. The blow jarred his body, knocking him off his feet. He sailed through the air, only stopping when he landed head and shoulders first into the railing that separated them from the spectators. He flopped face first into the dirt, feeling beyond numb. He wished Salandar would end it quickly, but the alien apparently intended on pulverizing him until his body gave out.

"Deborah," Mitch mumbled. *Have to keep my promise. Can't let her down.*

Using a railing, he pulled himself up to a standing position. Salandar shifted from one foot to the other, shaking the arena floor. The alien then brushed his feet on the dirt like a bull ready to charge. He bent down, exposing three horns. If Salandar gored him with those horns, he was done.

Instead of charging like a bull, Salandar levitated and flew even though his wings did not flap. Just before impact, Mitch drew a deep breath and jumped. He wrapped his arms around Salandar's neck, only to be thrown off when the alien crashed into the guardrail.

Mitch landed softly on the ground. For a moment, the alien didn't move. Mitch's mouth curled into a smile. *Finally, something positive.*

The smile dissipated when Salandar stood with an angry snarl. Mitch back-peddled. Chants of "Gladiator" grew louder as a rudimentary plan formed in his clouded mind. Ruje had given him a vial of black liquid. Against smaller opponents, it would stick to their skin and restrict their movement. The more the opponent moved, the further it would seep into their flesh. Salandar was too large for the substance to have an effect on him, but the liquid was super slick.

Mitch took out the vial. As Salandar ran toward him, he threw it on the ground and got out of the way. Salandar skidded before falling face forward.

If he was going to beat Salandar, he had to take advantage of this opportunity. He climbed on Salandar's back. What the hell was he going to do? The alien's neck was too thick to choke. He had already stabbed it. Punching or kicking would break his hands or feet before hurting the alien. He noticed that the end of the alien's tail was exposed, unlike the rest of his body, which was covered with that granite-like exterior.

Mitch ran down the alien's back as Salandar rose to his feet. He pulled out his knife and stabbed the exposed end of his tail. Salandar's howl echoed throughout the arena.

"So you can feel pain?" Mitch continued to stab.

Salandar howled so loud that Mitch's eardrums felt like they were going to rupture.

A seam along the alien's tail caught his eye. He wasn't sure if it stemmed from an injury, or if it was part of the alien's body, but it looked vulnerable.

Mitch ran his knife up the seam. Amazingly, the alien's external shell came apart. Salandar moved from side to side. Mitch continued to slice upward, before putting the knife back in its sheath. With two hands, he pulled the shell up and buried his fists into the alien's exposed pink flesh. Salandar shook, but Mitch hung onto the shell. He removed the knife and sliced upward, peeling apart Salandar's protective shell, working his way up the alien's back.

Salandar tried to swat him, but couldn't reach far enough with his short and squat arms.

Mitch stabbed at his flesh. Fluid oozed as Salandar jumped up and down. Mitch had to grab mounds of flesh to prevent himself from sliding off.

Mitch pulled apart a wide opening, slid underneath the shell, and went inside Salandar's body. Using both hands, he lifted the shell so that it hung off the alien's body like a flap of skin. He grabbed pink flesh for leverage and worked his way to the front of the alien's torso. Despite the darkness, he spotted what he thought were organs. Mitch plunged the knife into the soft organs.

Salandar convulsed. Sticky fluid gushed around him. Mitch stabbed with short strokes. There wasn't enough room to get leverage behind his blows, but he didn't think it mattered.

By the way the alien's body shook, he had done massive damage.

Mitch's body shifted as Salandar jumped up and down. He wasn't going anywhere until this son of a bitch was dead.

Like a madman sick with bloodlust, he plunged his knife into the alien. Salandar let out a giant shudder. Mitch's body turned sideways as the alien dropped to the ground.

Mitch felt nauseous. He had to get out. Grabbing chunks of thick flesh, he lifted himself, fighting back the urge to vomit.

He propelled himself forward until bright sunlight greeted him. A muted roar came from the crowd. The fluid covering his head muffled his hearing.

Mitch heaved himself out of Salandar's body onto the arena floor. The referee approached Mitch and raised his hands. He pulled back, dazed and disoriented. He looked down. Salandar was dead.

Merelda ran onto the arena with a towel in hand. He felt broken down. Somehow he managed to stand on shaky legs. Merelda wiped him with the towel. She said something that he couldn't understand. After she had removed most of the fluid from his ears, he made out what she was saying. "You did it, Mitch. You beat Salandar."

Mitch nodded. He pumped his fist in the air to acknowledge the audience. The arena shook. This was the loudest he had ever heard it.

When Merelda hugged him, he felt as if his body might crumble. He had taken punishment in his time as The Gladiator, but nothing compared to this. Luckily, Takano was a wizard at patching him up.

Ruje walked out on unsteady legs, acknowledging the crowd. Ruje slapped his shoulder, causing Mitch to fall to his knees. The two-headed alien picked him up. "Well done, Mitch Grace. I am glad you convinced me to wager upon you. There has never been a more masterful performance in the history of Games. Your name will live forever."

Mitch didn't care about that. He only wanted Ruje to keep his end of the deal.

As if reading his mind, Ruje said, "It is with the most pleasure that I grant you your freedom." The speakers inside the arena translated his words to the aliens in their own language.

The audience roared their approval.

In his ear, Merelda shouted, "He announced that you have gained your freedom with this victory."

Mitch wiped his face with the towel Merelda had given him. "I feel like shit. I need to see Takano."

"When this final ceremony has completed, she will treat you."

"I wish Ruje would get on with it."

Mitch's body throbbed. He did not know or care about what Ruje was saying to the audience. The ceremony dragged for all of eternity until something happened that woke up Mitch. Coming from his platform inside the arena was a four-foot alien with white hair on his head, a ferocious face, and sharp claws. Mitch had met him over eight years ago. It was the Minister of Science.

An incredible rage built inside Mitch. He no longer cared about his pain. This son of a bitch had taken over his planet for no particular reason other than because he could. He was the reason Mitch had to fight to the death against Salandar in this arena. He was the reason he had been separated from Deborah. He was the reason that billions of people had died.

Ruje met the Minister of Science in the middle of the arena. After the Minister addressed the crowd, he and Ruje walked in Mitch's direction.

"What's wrong, Mitch?" Merelda asked.

*How dare that alien piece of shit come to congratulate me!* Mitch lost control. His time in the military had instilled discipline within him, and it pervaded every facet of his life. If he looked at the situation, detached and from afar, he would have frowned at what he was about to do.

He dropped the towel and charged at the Minister of Science. "You bastard. You fucking alien bastard! I'll kill you."

Ruje stepped in front of him. "What is the meaning of this, Mitch Grace?"

Mitch kept running, his fists clenched. He wanted a pound of flesh from the Minister.

Someone tackled Mitch from behind. Tasting dirt, he looked up and found the referee on top of him. He struggled to push the larger alien off.

"Get the hell off me! I'll kill him."

Ruje lifted Mitch off the ground, and restrained him. "What are you doing, Mitch Grace? This is an outrage."

Merelda pulled Mitch away. Meanwhile, the Minister of Science, wearing a devilish smile, didn't move.

Even with all these people separating him, Mitch still tried to get at the Minister. When the alien moved toward him, the arena hushed.

Nobody prevented the Minister from advancing toward Mitch. "That was well done, Gladiator. I congratulate you on your victory."

There was no way to get at the Minister. Too many aliens blocked his path. In his current condition, it wouldn't be a good idea anyway. He stopped struggling. "It's not over yet. You haven't seen the last of me."

Mitch moved away and felt a massive wave of dizziness. His legs gave out and he collapsed in a heap, losing consciousness.

## Chapter XXVII

As Takano sealed a gaping wound on Mitch's shoulder with a laser, Merelda paced around the room, located inside of Ruje's training center. It served as a combination surgical suite, physician's office, and convalescing center that was loaded with sophisticated machinery. Ruje spared little expense in keeping his athletes healthy. They were like work horses to him. "You are fortunate that you were in front of a large audience in the arena and many more viewing live around the universe. Your outburst at the Minister of Science could have resulted in your being imprisoned or worse."

Mitch bit back the pain. Normally Takano's anesthetics were effective, but these wounds were the most severe he had ever suffered. "I couldn't help myself. You can't understand what it was like when I saw that bastard."

"You think you're the first being whose homeland has been occupied? It has happened repeatedly throughout history."

Mitch cringed as Takano inserted a syringe into his abdomen. "Maybe I'm just sensitive."

Takano slithered across the floor and put away the syringe, then screeched something Mitch couldn't understand.

"Stay completely still for the next procedure," Merelda instructed.

Mitch nodded and the alien fed a tiny scope into Mitch's abdomen. He watched in lurid fascination as this device entered his body. Amazingly, he could not feel it as it penetrated him.

Takano was nothing short of a wizard with her advanced instruments and techniques.

Mitch's stomach tightened as the pain intensified. He clenched his fist and did his best to stay still.

After two minutes, the pain receded and Takano removed the probe. She had been working on him for the past two hours, and he hoped they were nearly through.

Merelda stood in front of him, her voice low. "It was not wise to confront the Minister like that. He is not known to forgive. You must make yourself scarce."

Mitch's face narrowed. "I'm not going to hide and I won't stop until I reclaim the planet."

Merelda folded her arms. "Or wind up dead."

"If it comes down to that."

"It will. Mitch, this is a losing proposition. Why do you want to stay here? There are opportunities around the galaxy for someone of your skills and fame. You can do great things."

"That doesn't interest me."

Merelda's blue-green skin turned a shade of purple, showing her annoyance.

Ruje entered the room. "I enjoyed the stunt you perpetrated in front of the Minister. I never liked that scoundrel. Of course, I would not show my displeasure in that manner." Ruje exchanged words with Takano. "After Takano is finished, she will remove your tracking device and you will be free."

A few minutes later, Merelda handed Mitch a vial. "Drink this. It will extract the tracking mechanism."

"With pleasure." Mitch downed the bitter green liquid. His eyes opened wide. It seemed like the inside of his body shifted.

Mitch got to his knees and retched. He looked up, but the aliens remained impassive. It felt like he was going to vomit out his insides. Mucous came out of his nostrils, and blood rushed to his face.

Mitch opened his mouth, and a small black critter came out. Takano gathered the critter inside of a blue box.

Ruje extended a hand and raised Mitch to his feet. "You are free, Mitch Grace. However, our relationship is not required to be at a conclusion."

Mitch's brow furrowed.

Ruje raised his hands. "I am not asking you to participate in the Games, although an occasional special attraction event would do well. With your current level of fame, I could utilize you. I intend to expand my promotion of the Games to new galaxies. With you as my ambassador, my level of success would be grand. I would compensate you greatly and you could become quite wealthy."

Mitch wanted to laugh, but it would hurt too much. "You want me to work for you? You have to be kidding."

"This is not a joke," Ruje said. "This is a legitimate business proposition. I will even draft a contract. Merelda can review it for you since you seem to have trust in her."

"There's no need. I don't doubt your sincerity. You wouldn't make this proposition if you didn't stand to profit from it, and I'm sure I could have an easy, comfortable lifestyle with this wealth, but my place is with my people. As soon as I collect my belongings, I'm going back to them."

Ruje's left mouth formed a frown. On his right face, his eyes narrowed. Mitch often found it disorienting that although the faces had identical features, they often performed different actions. "You have no future on this planet. I do not doubt your courage, but your people lack military might, not to mention that the other species are entrenched on your planet and will not leave. It is a lost cause."

Mitch was too tired to refute him. "You might be right, but I don't care. I'm going to return to my people, and I won't stop until your kind are gone."

"It is a noble ambition, Mitch Grace," Ruje said. "If you have a change of mind, my offer for employment will still have standing."

"I'll take that under consideration." There was no consideration. He was going back to Deborah and his people.

***

Mitch packed several bags. He hadn't accumulated much, so it didn't take him long, mostly packing many of the fancy gadgets that he had used during the Games. Ruje had not expressly forbidden him to take them, and Mitch had not asked his permission.

"I guess I'll be going," Mitch said.

"And what is your intention, to walk back to your settlement?" Merelda asked.

Mitch shrugged. "Sure."

"Don't be silly. I will take you. I have time off due to me. Not that I care. I was serious when I told you I will no longer work for Ruje. I detest the way he has treated you, and although there are certain love interests whom I will miss, it is time for me to move on."

267

"Merelda, do what's best for yourself. He's just a businessman trying to make money. Things turned out fine. Hey, if he hadn't captured me, and one of the Minister's bounty hunters found me instead, they would have killed me."

"Regardless, it will take time before I secure employment, so I will remain on this planet until then. If you need anything, contact me." She handed him a shiny, metallic cylindrical device, and wrote something on a translucent sheet that the aliens used as paper. "These are my coordinates. Punch them in to contact me. We may no longer be together, but I can still help."

"Thanks, Merelda. You're the best."

"We will be at your old settlement in twenty minutes."

"That's quick." Mitch sat next to Merelda and harnessed himself in an oversized chair.

She punched digits into the controller and spoke into a receiver. An alien replied to her, and she turned to Mitch. "We're ready."

After a rough takeoff, he began to doubt Merelda's flying ability. The craft screamed through the sky.

Merelda put the craft on autopilot and leaned back. "There's still time for me to take you to my bed before we arrive."

Mitch shook his head. "It's nothing against you, Merelda."

Merelda waved her hand. "I know. You're attached to Deborah. Is it common for your kind to have monogamous relationships?"

"Not for everybody, but that is my societal norm."

"Most species in the galaxy aren't like that."

Mitch shrugged. "I can't speak for other species. I can only speak for what's in my heart. For me, there's no one else besides Deborah. I really appreciate everything you've done for me. If I was ever to have sex with an alien, you would be the one."

Merelda laughed. "Well, I admire your perseverance. You have principles and stick to them, even though it would be easier to have them abandoned. Your Deborah is lucky. Would it be a correct assumption that you will resume your attacks on the invaders of your planet?"

Mitch said nothing.

"I will not betray you."

Mitch nodded. "I'm going to keep hitting them until they leave."

"It could be helpful if someone provided you with inside information. A being with many contacts. How would you say? During some of our pillow talk I am able to find out a great deal of information. That is my little secret about how I can know so much about many things I should not be privy to."

Mitch's brows rose, trying to stifle a laugh. Who knew her voracious sexual appetite would work in his favor? During the time he had been Ruje's slave, he had seen her with about a dozen lovers, both human and alien. "You would be willing to help me?"

"I care for you, Mitch. Of course I would help."

Mitch fidgeted as the Rocky Mountains came into view. He still wasn't sure if Deborah and the others would be in Colorado. Any number of things could have happened in his absence. The group could have disbanded, although that was unlikely since they had formed prior to his arrival in Sarm's ship, and they would likely stick together without him.

More likely, aliens could have attacked. If Ruje had found them, others could as well. Perhaps some aliens would have been out for revenge after his terrorist campaign.

Realizing they had been discovered, the group could have left the area, although it would be difficult to abandon a place with such good infrastructure.

His heart raced when he saw people. They were too high up for him to tell if they were his people.

Merelda leaned back. "No doubt you are excited to be back."

"Anxious is more like it. I just hope my people are still around."

"They are."

Mitch's brows arched. "What are you talking about?"

Merelda stretched her arms behind her back in an unnatural fashion. "Your people are still there."

"How do you know that?"

"My observers report to me about them." Mitch's voice rose. "Why have you never told me?"

"It would not have done any good to speak of this while you were working for Ruje. It would only have added to your frustration. When you challenged Salandar, I wanted you to be completely focused on the battle."

Mitch shook his head. "You should have said something."

"It was for the best. Trust in me. I realize you have hatred for those who took over your planet, but I am not one of them."

More people came into view. He scanned the concealed houses and buildings. If he hadn't known what to look for, he would not have found them.

As Merelda's ship descended, people from the community gathered. They would be wary to find an alien ship overhead. He just hoped they didn't open fire.

When they got close to the surface, he recognized familiar faces and smiled broadly. It was good to be back.

Mitch wasn't expecting such a rough landing when the ship hit the surface. His bruised body did not appreciate the jolt. The aches and pains that had been somewhat under control now flared. Merelda needed to improve her navigational skills. He was pretty sure the craft had inertial dampeners, but apparently, she was not interested in using them.

"I will leave you to your people, Mitch. It is not my place to intrude upon your reunion."

Mitch unstrapped himself. "I appreciate everything you've done for me. You're the reason I'm still alive." He kissed her forehead. "It's a debt I can't repay."

"There's no debt. You will contact me soon."

Mitch nodded. "I'll be in contact with you. Don't do anything that will get you in trouble."

Merelda smiled. "I can be discrete, and normally I get what I want. You are the only one who can seem to refuse me." She opened the hatch leading to the outside.

Mitch waved to her as he walked down the ramp. He took a deep breath as the sun glistened on his face. He was home again.

## Chapter XXVIII

Ethan was the first to greet Mitch, lifting him up in a big bear hug. "Mitch Grace, as I live and breathe. I thought you left us forever. God, it's good to see you."

Mitch recognized most of the faces in the crowd.

Elizabeth hugged him, tears streaming down her face. "I can't believe it's really you." She buried her head in his chest.

As Elizabeth clung to him, the others surrounded him, patting him on the back and giving him their well-wishes. It sounded as if a million people were trying to talk to him at once.

When Elizabeth let go, he spotted Corey Goss at the back of the crowd. Corey was hard to miss since he stood a head taller than anyone else. He fought through the crowd, and they clasped hands.

"I'm glad you're back, boss. I knew you'd return. I kept tellin' the others, we can't let up for a minute, because Mitch will be back, and we got to be ready. We've got a lot of work to do."

Mitch wanted to say something but was too choked up. He rarely let his emotions overtake him but being here after all this time was overwhelming.

Fortunately, Ethan came to his rescue. "Work? We haven't seen Mitch in two years. We have plenty of time to work. Tonight, we celebrate."

A loud cheer came from the crowd.

"How did you get out, boss?" Corey asked.

Mitch took a deep breath. "It's a long story. I'm just so glad to be back; I don't have the words to express it."

"We're glad to have you," Ethan said. "Those first few months were trying, but we stayed together. Now that you're here, things are going to get better. I can feel it."

Mitch nodded. "Where's Deborah?"

"She left a few days ago to scout an alien encampment," Elizabeth explained. "She's supposed to return today. In fact, she should be coming back soon."

For a moment the attention shifted away from Mitch as Merelda's ship energized. With no fanfare, she launched. In the blink of an eye, her vessel was no longer visible. Mitch waved good-bye. For all his hatred of the aliens, he wouldn't be alive if not for the kindness two had shown him. He fully intended on taking her up on her offer to help in his guerilla war.

"What was that all about?" Ethan asked. "Did you get a ride on an alien taxi?"

"Not exactly. That was Merelda. She's a good friend and will make a good ally."

"I'm sure you have a story to tell us," Ethan said. "I can't wait to hear it."

"And you will, but first I want to settle into my old place and wait for Deborah."

Elizabeth frowned. "Your leaving crushed her. Normally, she has everything under control, but she was on the verge of losing it those first few weeks. Then one day, she just resigned herself to what had happened and carried on."

Ethan nodded. "She's done a great job, too, taking the leadership mantel of Libertà in your absence."

"Libertà?" Mitch asked.

"The new name of our community. It's Italian for freedom."

Corey Goss took Mitch's duffel bags. "Let me help you out, boss. I'll walk you down to your pad."

As they walked, he couldn't stop thinking about Deborah.

\*\*\*

Corey stayed an hour, going over what they had been doing from a military and intelligence standpoint. Mitch's mind drifted. Before long he would resume his old role, but for now it was hard to get out of his Gladiator mindset.

After Corey left, Ethan and Elizabeth visited, bringing fruit and freshly baked bread. He ate and drank heartily, not so much from hunger, but because it was nice to eat food prepared by people.

Ethan got a call on his radio. "Deborah's here."

Elizabeth kissed Mitch on the cheek. "We'll see you tonight."

Ethan patted him on the back. "We're going to have one hell of a celebration because our prodigal son is back."

Mitch chuckled. Ethan was usually more reserved. He was touched that his return had affected Ethan in this manner.

He sat on a simple, wooden chair and waited. Ten minutes later, the heavy sound of running came from outside, followed by the fumbling of a doorknob. The door opened and Deborah stood at the entrance with her hand covering her mouth. She dropped to her knees. "Oh my God. It really is you." She sobbed on the floor.

Dropping to his knees, Mitch wrapped his arms around her. "I promised you I would come back. There was no way in hell I was going to break that promise."

For a few minutes, neither spoke. They were on their knees hugging and kissing until Mitch lifted her to her feet.

"What happened to you?" Deborah asked.

Mitch grinned. "Would you like the long or the short version?"

"Give me the short version." Deborah kissed him passionately. "We have catching up to do."

***

Judging by the attendance of the festival in Mitch's honor, the community's population had decreased. Before they arrived, Mitch and Deborah walked hand in hand, casually wearing shorts and tee shirts. "Tell me what happened right after Ruje took me away,"

Deborah paused, her hand on her face. "Some people got scared. They thought it was a matter of time before the aliens returned for the rest of us. I was worried too. We talked about relocating, but where would we go? It would take too long to build what we had here. Not to mention that if they found us here, they could find us elsewhere. Secretly, my motivation was that if you escaped, you would look for us here."

"I'm glad you stayed the course."

"Some left. Nobody stopped them. It's never been our policy to make folks stay if they don't want to, but newcomers have arrived since then."

"I didn't want you to go with me because I needed you here to keep this together."

Deborah sighed. "I didn't realize it at the time. I was so broken up about them abducting you. Over time, I realized that

276

if we're going to survive as a race and take back what's been stolen from us, then what we have here is our best shot."

There was plenty food and beverage at the celebration. The community had raised animals in abundance. They had also grown a new vineyard nearby. The wine wasn't good since they were still experimenting with the grapes. At first, they had issues with downy mildew and black rot. Later, the vines were infested with mites and mealybugs.

So many people wanted to talk to him that it was hard to spend quality time with anyone. Toward the end of the evening, Deborah suggested he address the crowd.

He stood on a podium that they typically used for entertainment purposes. The community had several talented musicians and singers. Before he spoke, he scanned the radiating faces in the audience, swelling with pride.

"I just wanted to thank everyone for giving me such a warm reception," Mitch said.

"Speak up," someone in the back of the crowd yelled. This was greeted by laughter.

"I'll try. Before long, everyone here will have heard about what happened to me, so I'll spare the details, but I wanted to share a few things. I faced death repeatedly in the past couple years and was in some tough spots. It would have been easy to give up. I knew I had to come back to you. I couldn't let them beat me because we still have many things to accomplish here.

"The aliens have taken so much from us. They took away our land, our freedom, our possessions, and the society we built, but one thing they haven't — and can't — take from us is our spirit. Although I despise them, in a way I'm thankful because they have reawakened something in us, and that's the unflinching will to never give up, never let up an inch, and do whatever it takes to survive. Everybody here shares that. If not, you would never have made it this far. For that, I thank each of you.

"But surviving isn't enough. We have to take back what is ours. The easy thing to do after having battled aliens in gladiator fights would be to go into hiding and live out the rest of my life. There's no way in hell I'm doing that. Now, more than ever, we have to fight back. I've lived among the enemy. They're motivated by profit, power, and greed. They don't share our strong will, and that will be their downfall."

Nods of ascent and murmurs of agreement emerged from the crowd.

"We can beat the aliens, but we're going to need the same dedication and commitment you have shown in the past. By going after the aliens, we risk exposing ourselves, but it's worth the risk. I don't know about you, but I don't want our children to have to live like this. I want them to have a planet of their own, and not to be slaves, living in fear of being captured or killed."

The murmurs turned into shouts. People raised their fists and shouted their agreement.

"Tonight, we celebrate. Tomorrow, we take it to the aliens in a way they haven't experienced before."

Mitch stepped off of the podium and joined his table with Mitch, Ethan, and Elizabeth. He lost himself amidst their chatter. The Minister of Science had made a severe miscalculation by letting him live. Mitch would make him rue the day he had made this egregious error.

## Chapter XXIX

After sleeping in his old bed next to Deborah, Mitch was ready to work, but first, he had to know everything going on in the community.

He met with Gary Daniels, who had assumed most of the community's administrative tasks. Gary produced spreadsheets and reports detailing work assignments for each adult and teen. He had charts outlining food production and storage. Fortunately, they had a strong crop season. They had attempted to grow different types of fruits and vegetables, but some had failed because of the climate.

As Mitch poured through the sheets, he looked up at Gary. "We've been lucky that we haven't been hurt by crop failures or bad storms. What happens if we have a bad season?"

Gary tilted his head. "It would be tough, but if we dig in, we could survive. With a couple more good years, we should have enough surplus of grain and wheat to get us through. If we got hit hard, we'd have to depend on trade. Fortunately, we've identified farmers growing crops on their own."

"How are our fuel levels?"

"Strong. We've been maintaining a refinery down south. At any given time, there are at least a dozen men and women working there. We rotate people, so we have different folks who know how to maintain and operate the facility."

"Good. What about the nuclear power plant?"

Gary smiled. "I'll let Bruce Dennison update you on the status since he's been the brains behind the operation. We're about ninety percent there to getting it operational once again.

There have been small hiccups along the way that keep prolonging the process."

"That's great news. I'll have Bruce give me a tour of the facility."

As they walked through the community, Gary showed him the new farming area. Mitch felt like a celebrity. Everywhere he went, people wanted to talk to him, hug him and shake his hand.

Gary said, "Since you've been gone, you've become a legend, especially with the newer members. They've heard of your exploits. With these gladiator fights against the aliens, I can only imagine your legend will grow."

Mitch shrugged. "That might not be a bad thing. I don't need adulation. It was weird enough getting it from the aliens, but if I can get people to do things they might not ordinarily be willing to by using the power of persuasion, then it will make life easier."

Gary stroked his graying beard. "Don't let it get to your head. The last thing we need is one of those megalomaniac cult leaders like Jim Jones."

Mitch grinned. "Don't worry. Deborah would put me in my place."

When he was done touring with Gary, he stopped by the medical center and met Dr. Sherwood. They had two experienced physicians and three more in training. They couldn't put them through medical school, but they got hands-on-training along with schooling using old textbooks.

"We need better supplies," Dr. Sherwood said. "We have vaccines and medications from nearby abandoned pharmacies, but the problem is that these drugs are expiring or already have expired. It would be great if we could formulate drugs on our own."

Mitch crossed his arms. The facility looked like a pre-invasion doctor's office. "We have scientists and engineers with backgrounds in the pharmaceutical industry, but we don't have the facilities. There's no way we could build that around here, either. Our best bet would be to take over an old pharmaceutical facility and revamp it. It's too bad I'm not in contact with Sarm anymore. His medical knowledge and techniques are far more advanced than ours."

"Maybe someday you can look him up. I'd love to learn from him."

"That's a good idea." He missed the big, green alien and thought about him often.

After lunch with Deborah, he spent the rest of the afternoon visiting people. He was pleased with the progress they had made in his absence. They had gotten too comfortable in their existence, and his capture served as a harsh reminder of the conditions they faced. He had to instill a belief of vulnerability so that they would always be on their guard.

Later that evening, he and Deborah stayed inside. It was like their second honeymoon. Although they were not married, he counted their first reunion as a honeymoon of sorts.

"You know, our little home has felt empty without you," Deborah said.

Mitch looked around. Their small house still looked the same. It had very little furniture. They had a few chairs, a kitchen table, a desk, and a bed. Everything in the house was made by members of the community.

Deborah massaged his powerfully built back and shoulders, mentioning how massive he looked.

Mitch explained that it was from the long hours of intense training along with Ruje's diet. They spoke about fighting inside of the arena, and the thrill of killing aliens, satiating his thirst for revenge.

Deborah stopped massaging him. "You're filled with rage and hate. It scares me sometimes."

It scared Mitch as well, but he needed that if he was going to accomplish his goals.

Before going to bed, Deborah made him promise never to leave him again. He brought her in close and buried the side of his head into her bosom before falling asleep.

***

Early the following morning, Corey Goss and Garth Williams briefed him on what had happened from a military viewpoint. Deborah had already told him that they hadn't made any attacks on alien targets in the past two years since he had been gone.

Mitch drank tea and ate corn muffins Corey had baked.

"So, who wants to give me a rundown?"

Deborah stood. "I will." Whenever they talked strategy, she was all business. It was like they didn't even have a personal relationship. "After your abduction, we wanted to keep a low profile. There was no telling how much the aliens knew about us."

Mitch interrupted her. "I can clarify that. The aliens who run this planet saw us as a nuisance, but never wanted to dedicate resources to find us. For the most part, the aliens here are involved in commerce. The purpose of our planet is to further their ventures. They don't have a real law enforcement or military force. That initial invasion was coordinated by the Minister of Science using hired mercenaries. After they decimated us, those mercenaries left. The Minister still employs some in case he needs muscle, but they're not nearly as strong as they used to be, and the Minister of Science isn't inclined to spend the money required to bring those mercenaries back."

Garth's eyes narrowed. "So, you're saying we actually have a chance against them."

Mitch shook his head. "Absolutely not. It wouldn't take much for them to mobilize the forces necessary to crush us."

"But if we hit them hard, then they might do that. Right, boss?" Corey asked.

"It's possible." Mitch motioned for Deborah to continue.

Deborah cleared her throat. "We haven't been sitting on our hands. We have done extensive combat and weapons training. When we strike again, we'll be more prepared. Most of the men and many of the women are capable of fighting. Sadly, most of the children know how to use guns and grenades."

There was no avoiding it. It was part of living in this strange, new world.

"The most important thing is that we entered into an alliance with the Ingleside naval base," Deborah said.

Mitch's brows rose.

"Right now, we have twenty of our people working with them to get the base to a combat-ready level. They have two aircraft carriers, a squad of fighter planes and numerous ships. It's likely the only base of its kind left."

Mitch smiled. "That's great news. I'm surprised the aliens haven't destroyed it."

"It's like you said, they don't think we're a threat to them," Garth said.

Mitch narrowed his eyes. "We're going to make them pay for their arrogance."

"We've never been more ready to fight," Deborah said.

Mitch leaned his arms against the windowsill, feeling invigorated. The last two years had not been a waste. His community had made strides, and so had he. "We have to hit them hard. We have the weaponry and personnel to do it. I've gained valuable intel about the enemy. I know where and how to hit them to make it count. They're not going to suspect an immediate attack. Even if they did, the only ones who know our location are Merelda and Ruje. I trust Merelda implicitly, and Ruje is actively trying to recruit me to work for him.

"We start tomorrow. Corey, I want you and Garth to take two hundred of our people to Ingleside. Deborah and I will mobilize our forces from here. We'll contact you on the radio. Meanwhile, Merelda will help coordinate the attack."

Garth folded his arms, and the others in the room glanced from Mitch to Garth with worry in their eyes. Garth expressed his distrust of Merelda, but Mitch assured everyone that he would not be alive without her. This seemed to satisfy them. Garth wasn't the only one suspicious of Merelda. Gary had confided in him that about a dozen of the citizens did not want to have any dealings with her.

Mitch glanced at Deborah. The intensity in her eyes mirrored what he felt. This was the time to cripple the aliens and drive them off the planet.

After the meeting adjourned and the others left, Mitch held onto Deborah tightly. He wished for a simpler time where their biggest problem would be scraping together enough money to pay a mortgage or raising children and making sure they were on the straight and narrow, but he and Deborah had never known simpler times. Even prior to the invasion, they had always been involved in some war or global conflict. Perhaps it was what made their relationship so strong. He kissed her forehead, glad that they somehow had managed to stay together through it all.

## Chapter XXX

Mitch spoke into the audio transmitter. "Talk to me, Merelda."

She spoke in hushed tones. "I will transmit the coordinates. You must make your attack after nineteen hundred tomorrow. The complex will be abandoned for seven hours."

"Don't worry. We'll attack precisely at that time."

"Will I see you again, Mitch?"

"No. We have to be in and out as quickly as possible."

Merelda grumbled. "Then perhaps next time."

"We'll see. Thanks for your assistance."

"I am glad to help."

They ended their communication. Moments later, coordinates appeared on the transmitter Merelda had given him. He jotted them on a pad of paper.

They were going to strike the heart of the aliens' data center, which held two buildings filled with sophisticated telecommunications equipment. Merelda had told him it was state of the art and extremely expensive. This would be a huge blow. Hopefully, it would make the aliens want to discontinue their commercial enterprises here. According to Merelda, many had voiced their displeasure to the Minister of Science after the last attack.

Merelda was insistent that they only attack infrastructure and minimize collateral damage. Mitch would have liked to take out some of the aliens, but he needed Merelda's help, and he had to abide by her conditions.

The last time they had attacked, Mitch, Deborah and Corey had met Merelda to scope out their target, a large alien community south of old Mexico. Since Los Angeles was their current target, it would have been too dangerous for Mitch since he would be too easily recognized, so Merelda had done all of the preparation.

Mitch walked out of the Comm Center and gazed at the crashing waves of the Pacific Ocean. During the previous week, they had transported an aircraft carrier and fighter planes from Ingleside across the Panama Canal to Coronado, Mitch's old training station with the SEALs.

There was no way of telling if the Panama Canal would still be in working condition until they actually went through it. Fortunately, the aliens infrequently used the planet's waterways, so Mitch's fleet faced open seas.

He turned when he felt a hand on his shoulder and relaxed when it was only Deborah.

"What did Merelda say?" Deborah asked.

"She gave us the green light. We can strike tomorrow at nineteen hundred."

"Good. You should give the flyboys a pep talk. They're nervous."

Mitch frowned. "This isn't their first aerial attack."

Deborah nodded. "I know, but they sense that this one's bigger and riskier than the others. Plus, they look up to you. Hell, some idolize you. None of *them* have ever killed an alien in hand-to-hand combat."

"All right, I'll talk to them. That sort of thing was unnecessary in the SEALs. Everyone had a job to do and they did it with little discussion."

"Well, we live in a different world now. Dinner will be ready in fifteen minutes. That would be a good time to talk to the pilots."

If Merelda was right, tomorrow would accomplish one of two things. It would frustrate the aliens enough so that many would pack their bags and leave or force the Minister of Science to hunt down Mitch. Undoubtedly, when he had tried to attack the Minister after he fought Salandar, this had become a personal matter for the alien.

***

Mitch grabbed Corey Goss's arm before he boarded his fighter plane. Corey would lead the aerial strike. Besides being their best flier, he had iron nerves. He had been in tight situations and never showed trepidation. Mitch would direct the attack from the carrier.

"Listen, anything goes awry, you get the boys out right away. We can always hit them some other time. Bring them home safe."

Corey nodded and clasped hands with Mitch. "You know I'm going to do my best, boss." Corey got into the cockpit of his jet and the others followed suit.

Shortly thereafter, they took off. Mitch said a silent prayer as the jets soared through the sky. Before long they were beyond the horizon.

On the radio, Corey said, "Smooth flying so far, boss. We picked a good night."

"Good to hear."

The skies had darkened, and the sea was tranquil. They were using sophisticated missiles with a guidance system supplied by Merelda.

Others had expressed doubt about Merelda's sincerity, but not Deborah. Immediately, she seemed to dislike the alien. Mitch got a sense that she realized Merelda held a torch for him and resented her for that, but Deborah's professionalism overtook personal feelings and she never voiced any mistrust about Merelda.

"We've reached the coast," Corey said. "Still none of them salenkos in the sky."

Mitch spoke into his radio. "Pray you don't run into any of them. Our fighter planes wouldn't stand a chance. What's your ETA?"

"Three minutes and forty-five seconds."

Deborah stood nearby, her hands folded, her face a mask of intense concentration. "Let's turn the carrier around."

Mitch nodded. When the jets returned, they would sail back through the Panama Canal. They didn't want to be near the coast after the attack. He looked at the seconds tick by on his watch.

"We're now flying over the alien community," Corey said. "No visible signs of defense."

"What's your ETA?"

"One minute and twelve seconds."

Mitch's heart fluttered. He closed his eyes as if his added concentration would help the fighter planes, wishing he could be in the air with them.

"The target is in sight," Corey said over the radio.

"Hit them with everything you got."

"You got it, boss."

The men and women on the carrier stood on the deck looking at the horizon. Bright lights flashed in the sky. Seconds later massive booms sounded. Mitch put his fists to his face waiting for the next radio contact. Deborah touched his arm.

Corey's voice rang through the radio. "Target one has been hit." Heavy rumbling sounded on the radio. "Target one is down."

Mitch pumped his fist in the air. There was a brief outburst before everyone quieted.

More explosions came from the former Los Angeles.

"Target two has also been destroyed," Corey said. "I repeat, target two is down."

The crew gave a raucous cheer.

"Great job," Mitch said. "Now get your butts back here. We're heading home."

"Copy that, boss," Corey said.

"Any aliens trailing you?" Mitch asked.

"None that I can see, and I don't plan on giving them an invitation."

Mitch hugged Deborah. "This is going to hurt those bastards. There's going to be some real pissed off aliens."

"When will you contact Merelda?"

"Not until we get back to Colorado. She'll assess the damage, and then we'll figure out our next move."

"Prepare the ship for landing," Deborah said. "Then we sail south."

\*\*\*

Mitch woke with a jolt. For a moment he thought he was still on the aircraft carrier on the night they had bombed the alien establishment in Los Angeles. It was only when he glanced at Deborah sleeping soundly beside him that he realized he was in his bed in Colorado.

He woke from a dream that blended past and present so fluidly that it seemed real even though the situation was impossible. *It was the first day of the invasion. The Minister of Science and his original contingent of aliens had been inside of a cage on the naval base in Coronado. Mitch ran out of the building and found the cage open. He sprinted in an attempt to lock the cage, but he was too late. The aliens had escaped. Outside was Mitch's present community in Colorado. The aliens attacked the unsuspecting children, shredding them apart. It was a gory scene as the aliens indiscriminately ripped off their heads and limbs and tossed their dying bodies aside like garbage.*

If only Mitch had been able to close the cage door and shut out the aliens, then he could have prevented this gruesome violence. Just like a decade earlier, he couldn't stop the invasion.

Mitch couldn't get his last confrontation with the Minister of Science out of his head. The alien had aggravated Mitch to no end with his smugness and arrogance. He could only hope these most recent actions had caused the Minister serious consternation.

What if it didn't work? What if blowing up these two buildings only served as a minor nuisance, despite Merelda's claim that they hampered the alien operations? What else could he do? There were few options left, and the likelihood of retaliation increased with every attack.

He would have to try something bolder and riskier next time. He was on a collision course with the Minister of Science. One of them would bend or break. The path had been set in motion, and nothing could stop it.

## Chapter XXXI

Mitch smiled as Merelda's ship landed in the same location she had dropped him off a month ago. A group from the community had gathered to watch the vessel.

"Her spaceship isn't very big," Ethan commented.

Elizabeth nodded. "Nowhere near the size of the one they carted you off in."

Mitch shrugged. "This one's built for speed."

"So, we finally get to meet your alien friend," Ethan said.

The hatch opened and Merelda emerged, moving with the grace and elegance of a feline. "I am glad to see you brought a welcoming committee."

Mitch gave her a hug. "It's good to see you. These are my people." He motioned toward those who had gathered.

Merelda looked around. "I like this place. I can see why you wanted to return. If the ruling council of this planet saw this, they would dismantle it immediately."

Mitch said, "Hopefully they'll never find out. We like to keep a low profile."

"Hello, Deborah." Merelda extended her hand.

Deborah shook it. An icy chill entered the air. "It's nice to meet you again."

Mitch clutched her arm. "Let me show you around."

While the others disbursed, Mitch, Deborah and a few others gave Merelda a tour of the community. He kept it brief because he wanted to talk to her about the next mission.

He concluded the tour by leading her into the house he and Deborah shared. "I would offer you something to eat, but I don't have anything you'd find edible." Mitch motioned to a chair near a table. "Please sit. Would you like some water?"

"Thank you, but I am sufficiently hydrated." Merelda sat, looking uncomfortable. She wasn't normally around so many humans, and some hadn't given her the warmest reception. It was nothing overt, but Mitch had hoped they would be more welcoming. "Your group has caused commotion. The Minister was furious after that latest attack."

Mitch nodded. "Good."

Merelda smiled. "Corey, Mitch told me that you led the attack. Very precise striking. I appreciate your skill."

Corey bowed his head. "I have well-trained pilots."

Merelda folded hands with long, slender fingers. "There are many unhappy citizens of Santanovia. Some have threatened to remove their operations if the situation doesn't change. Their threats are serious. The Minister taxes the commercial enterprises on this planet. They agree to these taxes because he allows them to operate freely."

"As in operate illegally," Mitch said.

"Precisely. Since this is a seldom used solar system, they can go unnoticed. However, if these disruptions cause them to lose revenue, they will discontinue their operations."

Mitch put his thumb beneath his chin and rubbed the stubble under his lower lip with his index finger. Normally he kept himself clean-shaven, but lately he could not find the time to shave. "So now is the time to really take it to them."

Merelda nodded, her face turning a light shade of green. This meant she was pleased. "It is as if you read my thoughts."

"We'll need time to mobilize," Deborah said.

"Not true."

All faces in the room stared at Merelda.

Mitch's eyes narrowed. "What's on your mind?"

Merelda settled back in her seat. "I have come across a shipment of explosive charges. They are tiny, easy to mask, and highly destructive. Although I have no need for such items, they suit your needs."

"You have these explosives with you?" Mitch asked.

"In my shuttle."

"That's great," Mitch said.

"I also have information you might find interesting."

Why was she sticking her neck out like this for them? She was risking her life. Since she didn't have any particular scorn against the Minister and those who ruled this planet, her source of motivation was obvious. Merelda's feelings for him ran deeper than he had thought.

"What's that?" Mitch asked.

"In two days, there will be a large conference involving intergalactic traders of rare elements. They are prospecting elements found on your planet like neptunium. Important business leaders are coming to this planet for the first time. It would be unfortunate if they experienced disruptions."

Mitch put his index finger to his lip. "Like if their meeting place was destroyed upon arrival."

Merelda nodded.

"Maybe using these new explosives," Mitch said.

"They could be used for such a thing."

Deborah's face tightened. "Enough dancing around. Where's this conference being held?"

Merelda gave her a cold stare. "In your old state of Texas. This would have to be done immediately."

Mitch frowned. "There's not enough time to prepare."

Merelda tilted her head back. Her thick-stranded hair reached her lower back. "That's why you must leave now with me."

"And you think this could collapse the Minister's society?"

"I do. What's that saying you have, the stalk of dead wheat that broke the camel's back?"

"It's straw," Deborah clarified.

Merelda shrugged. "Regardless, we must do this now. That is why I am here."

Mitch closed his eyes. He liked to employ thorough planning with contingencies, but he trusted Merelda's instincts. "We should go for it."

Without hesitation, Deborah said, "I'm coming with you." She stared at Merelda, as if expecting a rebuke.

Merelda smiled. "Fine, but we must keep the party to a minimum."

"No problem. The three of us will go. Anyone have any objections?" Mitch looked around the table.

"No, boss," Corey said. "It's a solid plan. I just wish I could join you."

Mitch waited for other comments. "Good. Let's fly out."

\*\*\*

As they entered Merelda's ship, Mitch whispered to Deborah. "Get ready for a bumpy ride. She's not the best flier."

Merelda turned her head. "I heard that."

"And this boat is fast," Mitch added.

When they entered the Spartan cabin, Merelda pointed at the wall. "Here is a map of the area."

"Wow. These are amazing." Deborah attempted to touch the map, but her fingers went right through it. "Hologram?"

Mitch nodded. "Very impressive."

Merelda stood in front of the hologram. "These are aerials that were taken a month ago. A colleague had performed a survey of the local area. I am still in waiting for discovery of when is the most opportune moment to lay our explosives." She pointed at a cluster of buildings. "This is the complex we will target, and these are underground passages burrowed by nalons."

"What are they?" Deborah asked.

Merelda's face turned orange and her eyes narrowed. "Imagine your caterpillars, but one hundred times as large. Some of the species living on this planet have a difficult ability to adjust to the planet's atmosphere, so they live beneath the surface. The nalons were brought to dig these underground sanctuaries. We will land nearby and travel on foot."

Mitch frowned. "I might get recognized."

"That's why you will be under the guise of my prisoners." Merelda opened a drawer containing shiny blue circular devices.

Mitch cringed.

"What do these things do?" Deborah asked.

Mitch picked up the blue ring. "They go around your neck and transmit a signal that binds you to your captor. Sudden movements will make it tighten around your neck like a noose."

Deborah looked incredulous. "And we're going to wear them?"

"No need to worry," Merelda assured her. "They won't be activated."

Deborah frowned. "I still don't like it."

"Without activation, it will be just like a dog collar." Mitch put his hands up. "Which isn't ideal, but it beats the alternative."

"You will be draped in these outfits." Merelda produced long, drab, brown oversized coats, common slave outfits some gladiators wore.

Deborah stared at him with apparent unease. Mitch squeezed her hand. He had been through worse.

"When we get to the destination, we can hide these outfits until we need them again. A black marketeer has deciphered the time we would least likely encounter anyone. It is important that we time it correctly, so the merchants arriving today are present to witness this."

"How will we ignite the charges?" Mitch asked.

Merelda unlatched a chest and picked up a shiny, black device that looked like a rock. It had buttons on it and could fit in Mitch's palm. "This is the timer. We will give ourselves a sufficient period of time to vacate before they ignite."

"But there might be collateral damage," Deborah said.

Merelda's face turned somber. "That is always possible. We must minimize risk. Any further questions?"

Mitch shook his head.

"Good. Prepare for departure."

Merelda took the pilot position, while Mitch helped Deborah into her chair. Since they were meant for larger beings, she struggled. Mitch made sure her harness was properly secured before he took care of his own harness.

Mitch braced himself for takeoff. The vessel wavered as it lifted off the ground, and for a second he thought they would crash. However, Merelda's blue-green face seemed calm, making him feel at ease.

Deborah's eyes were closed and her face pale. He had warned her in advance, but it was one of those things she had to experience for herself to know what it was like.

Once they were high in the air, it was smooth sailing with the bumpiness of a commercial flight in the pre-invasion era.

Mitch breathed easier. He reached out and held Deborah's hand. "That wasn't so bad."

Deborah took a big gulp. "That was awful."

"The takeoff could have been a little smoother." Mitch grinned. "Maybe we could request another pilot for the return trip. What do you think, Merelda?"

They flew through the sky faster than a fighter jet. Mitch settled back, trying to keep Deborah at ease. She still looked a little green from the takeoff. He was engaging Deborah in small talk and stopped suddenly at the near panicked look on Merelda's face.

Mitch's face tightened. "What's wrong? Is there a problem?"

Merelda nodded but said nothing.

Someone spoke in an alien tongue through the transmitter. Merelda still said nothing. The alien repeated its gibberish.

"What's going on, Merelda?" Mitch asked. "Talk to me."

"Damn." That was the closest to uttering a curse Mitch had ever heard from her. "They know who we are."

Deborah leaned forward, her eyes wide. "How's that possible? I thought nobody suspected anything?"

Merelda shouted something in her alien tongue, then turned to Mitch and Deborah. "Neither did I. There are too many links in the chain. Someone must have told the Minister to curry favor."

Mitch unstrapped his harness and went to the rear of the craft. His heart thundered at the sight of four ships following them.

Deborah screeched. "But you said they wouldn't find out."

Merelda glared at her. "Well, they did, and now we are toasted as you humans might say."

"What did they say to you?" Mitch asked.

"They said that they know I am transporting the Gladiator and must land immediately. Any other action would be treason, and they will be forced to fire on us."

"Just wonderful," Deborah said. "Just fucking wonderful. Now what do we do?"

Mitch ran up to Merelda. "You can't land. The Minister won't take me as a prisoner. He'll kill me. You too."

Merelda turned and stared at him. "I have no intention of landing."

"What do you plan on doing?" Mitch asked.

"The only option we have left. Fight."

## Chapter XXXII

Mitch swallowed hard. He had no idea how sharp Merelda's combat skills were or the ship's capabilities as a fighting vessel, making him wish he was back in the arena fighting aliens in hand-to-hand combat. At least he had more control over the situation.

"What kind of armament does your ship have?" Deborah asked.

Merelda didn't look back. "Sufficient for our purposes. Mitch, can you fly this?"

Mitch wiped the sweat off his forehead. The controls looked similar to those in the vessel Sarm had given him. "Yes. I think."

Merelda left the seat. "We have no time to think. Take the controls."

Mitch took a deep breath.

"I am taking you off autopilot." Merelda flicked a switch.

Mitch gazed at the rear viewfinder and spotted the four alien ships trailing them, closing in quickly. " What the hell are we going to do? We can't fight them all. Should I try to outrun them?"

Merelda took a seat on the other side of the cabin. "No. We may have the ability to fly faster, but they will get reinforcements. The Minister means to destroy you. There will be more than these to deal with."

Mitch frowned. They must have discovered that Merelda had been helping him and then trailed her. Now the only question was whether the aliens would try to blow them out of the sky or force them to land.

"What's our move?" Mitch asked.

"We will use the bomb that we were planning to use on the target. You are right. We have no ability to fight four vessels. Therefore, we will eliminate them all at once."

Mitch gritted his teeth. There went the one decisive strike against the Minister that could serve as the catalyst to having the aliens leave the planet. Then again, if the aliens shot them out of the sky, they wouldn't be able to deliver that strike anyway.

"Act as if you're going to land, then make a sharp reversal and fly toward them."

Wonderful. There was going to be no feeling out process for him. He punched a button and instead of lowering, the ship soared upward.

"I said act as if you are landing," Merelda shouted.

Mitch leveled the ship. "Got it."

On the transmitter, the aliens attempted to communicate. Mitch had no way of understanding what they were saying, nor did he care.

Mitch kept one eye on Merelda and one on the rear viewfinder.

Deborah had managed to release herself from her harness and stood next to Mitch. "Are you sure you can do this?"

He gave Deborah a sideways glance and a half shrug.

"Turn it around now," Merelda said.

Mitch flicked a few buttons, hoping they were the right ones, then pulled the steering column hard. Deborah fell forward, while Mitch held tightly onto the steering column to prevent the same from happening to him. The ship did a full reversal. He peered at the rear viewfinder and the enemy crafts were gone. He then looked at the panoramic screen that gave a near-perfect image of the area in front of the vessel. They were dead ahead, all four of them.

"Now," Merelda shouted. A shiny silver cylinder shot out of their vessel. "Fly full speed forward."

Mitch put on the rear jets at full speed, and their vessel roared across the sky at a frightening pace. He stared at the rearview finder and saw the cylinder Merelda had just sent latch onto one of the enemy vessels. Everything went black after that. The explosion that followed gave a deafening blast. The aftershocks tipped their vessel end over end. When he finally managed to right the ship after flipping over several times and losing serious altitude, he looked at the rear viewfinder and saw a massive mushroom cloud in the distance.

Deborah pumped her fist. "Great work, Merelda."

The alien left her position and stood next to Mitch. Her skin was dark purple, indicating she was fired up. "They are gone, but more will come."

Mitch nodded. "We have to get the hell out of here."

"Yes," Merelda said. "Plot a course west. I must find a place to hide."

Mitch entered coordinates to go toward California. He breathed easier. He didn't fly as fast as Merelda since he wasn't confident in his flying skills. Even so, the vessel screamed through the sky like a fighter plane.

"Where can we hide?" Deborah asked.

Merelda tapped her long fingers on the panel. "I am not sure. Your former Los Angeles is too populated. We would be found. We need somewhere remote."

"What about Hawaii?" Deborah asked.

Merelda shook her head. "That island chain doesn't exist anymore."

Deborah frowned. "It doesn't?"

"It was destroyed in the invasion and is now at the bottom of the ocean."

"Damn," Deborah muttered. "I can't believe those bastards destroyed Hawaii. What about Asia?"

"That may be possible," Merelda replied. "Great care must be taken since that region is controlled by a rogue group that does not care for Ruje. I would find little acceptance among them."

Mitch only passively listened, keeping his full attention on flying the ship, not sure where to go.

Deborah and Merelda continued to exchange ideas.

Mitch winced when three ships appeared on the rear viewfinder. "We've got company."

Merelda leaned down and stared at the screen. When the transmitter buzzed, she picked it up and spoke to the aliens.

Mitch's heart thumped as he listened to her short, curt phrases. He gazed at her. "What's going on?"

"We have been ordered to land, or they will shoot us down."

Just as he thought. This time, they didn't have the element of surprise.

"Can we outrun them?" Mitch asked.

"It is our only option. They will expect a counterattack."

Mitch activated the rear thrusters. He hadn't used them earlier because he feared he would lose control of the craft at such high speeds. "You still want me to pilot?"

Merelda nodded. Her skin had turned red, indicating she was in full fight mode. She had turned that color whenever he had stepped onto the arena floor to battle aliens. "I will fight them off with our limited ammunition."

*Limited ammunition.* That didn't sound good. Mitch neared Los Angeles, the biggest alien outpost, which was dense with infrastructure. Shiny, metallic buildings that dwarfed the tallest buildings of the old world filled the horizon.

Missiles shot at them. He took a deep breath and dodged them by tilting right. He had to remain in complete control. This wasn't his element, but gladiator fights had not been either.

More missiles fired. This time, Merelda intercepted them by shooting photon rays, exploding them in midair.

Approaching an alien skyscraper, Mitch activated the bottom thrusters, shooting the craft to the heavens. His stomach lurched. He snuck a glance at Deborah, whose face had turned white. The alien ships continued the chase. He dropped low after passing a skyscraper to avoid being a target in the open air.

They still followed. Damn. He had to try something trickier. He dove lower. They shot more ammunition, but not their missiles. They wouldn't risk using heavy armament this close to the alien population.

Mitch flipped the vessel to its side, but he wasn't quick enough, and they got hit. The ship rocked like they had encountered a big speed bump.

"What's the damage?" Mitch asked.

"Moderate," Merelda replied.

"That was moderate?" Deborah turned to Merelda. "What are you waiting for? Fire back at them."

Merelda's face was knitted in concentration. "I am waiting for the right moment."

Mitch hoped she wouldn't wait too long. If she didn't do something soon, his tumultuous journey would end in a blaze of melted shrapnel.

More shots came from behind. This time he avoided them, but he wasn't skilled enough to keep avoiding incoming artillery.

"Slow down and then swerve right," Merelda ordered.

It didn't sound like good strategy, but Mitch wasn't about to argue. She was far more experienced at this then him. He dropped speed and steered hard to the right. Merelda released a bomb. Mitch stared at the rear viewfinder as it hung in the air. As the enemy craft came near, it exploded, catching the ship in its crossfire. Two left.

"Great shot," Mitch said.

"Are the other two still on you?" Deborah asked.

Mitch nodded.

Out of nowhere, an enemy vessel hit them with something. This time, the ship shook. They careened out of control as Mitch attempted to keep them in the air.

Merelda howled.

"What do we do?" Mitch asked.

"We have caught fire. Deborah, I need you to contain the blaze at the rear of the ship. There is an orange cylinder by the rear hatch. Flip the switch to the top right of the cylinder and aim it at the fire."

Deborah wasted no time going to the back of the vessel. She operated at her best under pressure.

"Use the bottom thrusters," Merelda said.

"They're not working."

"Then punch in skyward coordinates. That should correct the descent."

Mitch's throat tightened. If this didn't work, they were cooked. Fortunately, after a few tense moments the ship stopped shooting downward.

"If Deborah can put out the blaze, that should restore power to the thrusters."

"She'll do it," Mitch said.

"If she has your mettle, then she should make a fine outcome."

Mitch's hands shook as he tried to keep the vessel under control, something that had become increasingly more difficult.

Merelda sprayed gunfire at the enemy vessels, but they remained on his path.

As they reached the densest part of the city, Mitch contemplated going skyward. It would make them an easier target, but he couldn't control the craft well enough to fly down low. Mitch regained control of the ship almost at the same time Deborah returned to the cabin.

"I put it out, but I think I used up all the stuff inside that cylinder."

Mitch's eyes went back and forth from the rear viewfinder to the panoramic screen. He soared near the surface. This gave him an advantage because Merelda's ship was smaller, quicker, and nimbler. "All right. Let's see what you're made of."

Sweat poured off his forehead, dripping onto the controls. He gritted his teeth and flew sideways between two buildings that had little clearance on either side.

A ship followed, and a harsh grinding sound reverberated as it scraped against the side of the building. The other one took a detour.

Merelda fired at the ship that had squeezed through the building. She hit the target but didn't disable the vessel.

Mitch set a path straight into a building. Before colliding, he made a hard left turn. Deborah, who had not been strapped into the seat with her harness, flew across the cabin. Merelda held onto a nearby column.

He missed the building, but the craft behind them crashed into it, causing a massive explosion to rip through the sky. From the rear viewfinder, Mitch spotted what he assumed was shrapnel flying in their direction. He activated the rear thrusters and accelerated past it.

"Where did you learn how to do that?" Merelda asked.

Mitch grinned. "On the job."

There was only one ship left, but the Minister seemed gung-ho on capturing or killing him, so he would likely send more after them.

Mitch flew so low that he could see aliens on the surface watching the battle.

The enemy ship stayed above him. This close to their infrastructure, it would not shoot at them. Still, he couldn't stay in the former Los Angeles and allow the Minister time to get reinforcements.

"Can we take this one head on?" Mitch asked.

"Perhaps with some trickery," Merelda replied.

"Tell me what I need to do."

Deborah returned to Mitch's side.

He glanced at her. "Strap yourself in. This is going to get dicey."

She didn't put up an argument and went to her chair.

Merelda pointed at the panoramic screen. "Fly in-between those two buildings. They will assume you are creating a trap. They will fly around the buildings, and then come after us. When you clear the building, fly straight at them, and I will shoot them down."

It was a sound plan. The only question was whether he could he execute it. He elevated so that he was at the same height as the enemy craft. He flew toward the opening between the skyscrapers. *Damn, this is even narrower than the last one.* He bit his upper lip so hard that it bled as he flipped the ship to its side. *Please God, just get me through this.*

He almost clipped the side of a building but corrected the ship in time. Upon reaching the end of the building, he scanned the viewfinder. The enemy ship had gone left. As they cleared the buildings, he turned hard at the other craft.

"Activate the bottom thrusters," Merelda shouted.

As he flicked the switch, she fired two missiles. Merelda's aim was true, and both missiles hit their target.

"Is that all of them?" Deborah asked.

Mitch stared at the viewfinder and found no ships on the horizon. "I think so."

"Thank God." Deborah unhooked herself from the harness and stood behind Mitch. "We need to get out of Dodge before they come after us. We've already taken significant damage."

"Tell me about it." Mitch glanced at Merelda. "Can we make it across the Pacific, or should we go to the southern part of the continent?"

Deborah stroked her chin. "We should go back in the direction we came from. They wouldn't expect that."

Mitch turned and stared at the panoramic viewfinder. Blood rushed out of his face. He blinked quickly, hoping he was looking at an apparition. "We're in trouble. Big trouble."

Merelda stared at the screen and covered her mouth.

"Is that a..." Deborah began.

Mitch nodded slowly. "Yeah. That's a salenko."

## Chapter XXXIII

The salenko loomed in front of them like a monstrous deity of a bygone era. It was three times the size of Merelda's ship. Its metallic skin was dark blue and served as body armor, shielding it from gunfire and the elements. It had dark, narrow eyes that looked like slits and bat-like wings that retracted into its body. The edges of its wings were so sharp, they could impale an aircraft. From its mouth, it could shoot enormous gusts of wind that created a hurricane effect. From its wide nostrils, it could shoot pulses of energy. It was the ultimate fighting machine in the air.

Deborah stared at the screen. "What are you waiting for? Shoot it."

Merelda shook her head. "Not a good idea. It will elude our missiles and destroy us."

"Then what are we going to do?" Deborah asked.

"Pray to your God that it will ignore us."

The Salenko flew at them. Mitch was certain the Minister had sent it as his backup plan.

Merelda's eyes grew wide. Her skin turned yellow, the color of fear. "Turn around, Mitch. We must find a way to elude it."

Mitch was a step ahead of her and had already begun turning the vessel. A kilometer behind, the salenko was closing quickly.

Mitch flew south away from the densely populated area, zooming through clear blue skies and flying overhead of wreckage from the alien invasion. Outside of the occupied areas, the aliens hadn't bothered cleaning the mess they had made when they took over the planet.

Mitch tried a few zigzag maneuvers, but the salenko continued to close the distance. Mitch still hadn't used the rear thrusters because he wanted to save them for a crucial moment since they could only be used briefly before requiring recharging. He flew close to the surface. The salenko glided behind, following Mitch's path.

"Merelda, do you want to take over?" Mitch asked.

"No. You are doing an admirable job."

Mitch frowned. He was hoping she would say yes.

Bolts of laser energy shot from the salenko. Mitch saw it on the viewfinder and dipped right, avoiding the beams. The salenko shot more beams, so Mitch soared higher.

"It's getting closer," Merelda said.

"I realize that, but what can I do?"

"Can't you fire missiles at it?" Deborah's face was a mask of worry. Mitch could tell she wanted a more active role in the fight.

"It would be ineffective. It would evade incoming missiles from this position. We must wait for an opportunity."

Mitch dodged more strikes. At the bottom of the panoramic screen, he spotted massive craters where the beams had hit the earth. The salenko was marking its target and zoning in on Mitch's flight pattern. To vary things, Mitch shot up in the air, then faded on a descending arc.

They flew for a few minutes without any more strikes from the salenko. Mitch kept anticipating more incoming blasts.

Without warning, his vessel flailed in the air and sunk toward the ground.

"What the hell's going on?" Mitch asked.

"It is altering the air by gusting wind," Merelda said.

The rear of the ship lifted, and for a moment they were vertical. Mitch couldn't straighten the vessel. They went side to side, and Mitch was certain they would crash. Just before they hit the surface, he shifted to an upward trajectory. He had avoided crashing, but now they were on a path to collide with the salenko.

"Hit the thrusters now," Merelda commanded.

Mitch hit the thrusters, and nothing happened. He looked at the panel in front of him, thinking he had hit the wrong switch. He tried again and still nothing. "It's not working."

Merelda leaned in and stared at the controls. "There is too much atmospheric disruption."

Mitch had to do something, or the salenko would crush the ship with its huge wings. He dropped the ship closer to the surface. The stationary trees on the panoramic screen indicated there was less turbulence down there.

His strategy paid off when he got the craft to fly straight. Before the salenko pounced on them, he activated the rear thrusters, and they took off as if they had been shot from a cannon. The salenko changed its course and tried to keep up with them, but for the moment they outpaced the alien. Once the energy source for the thrusters became depleted and they went at regular velocity, the salenko caught up with them once more.

Deborah slammed her fist against a side column. "We're sitting ducks. We have to do something."

They couldn't outrun it and they couldn't fight it head on. Mitch's SEAL training taught him to use all resources available. His one significant advantage was that he knew the geography better than his adversary. They were passing through the former San Diego, an area he was intimately familiar with from his SEAL days.

The salenko shot two blasts of its laser-like beams. Mitch swerved just in time to avoid them.

They were nearing Brown Field, which had been an airport for military and law enforcement aircraft. He had used it when he was in the SEALs. For a second, he was tempted to land the craft and escape from the salenko on foot, but the alien would squash them.

More blasts came from the salenko, but this time Mitch was ready and dodged them with ease.

Landing at the airport wouldn't work, but he had a better idea. Not far from Brown Field was a mountain range loaded with crevices and ravines large enough to shelter their craft, but too small for the salenko. He needed to create a diversion.

"Merelda, I need you to fire everything you have at the salenko."

"Why? I will not be able to create damage from this position."

"I don't need you to hurt it. I just need to buy time so I can hide in the mountains."

Deborah put her fist to her mouth. "Where?"

"I have a few spots in mind."

Merelda's face tightened. "Very well. I hope your plan works."

What option did they have? Before long, the salenko would turn them into hamburger.

He raced toward the highest mountain peak. "Get ready to bombard the salenko." He waited, waited. "Now."

The rear viewfinder lit up as Merelda sent missiles and photon blasts at the salenko. It stopped in mid-flight and turned, flying away from the incoming artillery. Merelda changed the trajectory of her shots and continued to fire at the alien.

Once he cleared the peak, Mitch sunk deep into the mountains, getting as close to the trees as possible. He had no time to waste because the salenko would be after them before long.

Mitch slowed the craft as he searched for a deep cave with a stream running through it. It had been a while, but he was certain it was nearby. While with the SEALs, they had done some caving in nearby areas during their R and R time. He was certain they had explored the caves in this area. When he spotted an opening in the thicket, there was still no sign of the salenko on the viewfinder.

He gently glided the ship in-between trees, clipping some in the process. Hopefully, the salenko wouldn't notice.

He flew in through the dark cave, not turning on the ship's high-powered lights. The illumination would be helpful, but it might alert the salenko to their location. Mitch grimaced. He had to land the ship blindly. Easing it downward, he thought he was close to the surface, so he released the landing spokes. Two touched rock, and the other two sunk into the surface, probably in the stream. When he felt confident that the vessel wouldn't tip over, he killed the power, surrounded by complete silence and total darkness.

The silence did not last long as the harsh shriek of the salenko reverberated in the cave. With the power off, Mitch couldn't use the viewfinder to determine its position. From its roar, it had to be close.

The wait was excruciating as the salenko flew outside. Mitch's body was tightly wound, but there was nothing he could do. If the salenko found their hiding spot, they were dead.

Deborah was the first to break the silence several minutes later. "I think it might be gone."

Mitch didn't want to say anything. Maybe it was playing possum.

"It must be," Merelda agreed.

Deborah leaned her head against her chair and sighed. "Damn, that was close. I felt so helpless not being able to do anything."

Mitch closed his eyes. "If I had to do that all over again, I doubt I could pull it off. It was all adrenaline."

"I am not surprised," Merelda said. "You are a true gladiator. Just like in the arena, you were at your finest in the most dire of circumstances."

"Well, if it's all the same with you, I'd rather not be tested like this again."

Merelda stood next to Mitch and powered up the vessel. "Even if the salenko has flown away, it would be foolish to think that the Minister has halted his efforts. We cannot stay here forever. We will have to find somewhere to keep ourselves hidden."

Mitch smiled. "I have just the place, and it's only a few miles away."

Merelda and Deborah stared at him.

"Well, Merelda, it so happens that you're not my only alien friend. It's about time the two of you meet Sarm, if he's still on the planet."

## Chapter XXXIV

Mitch's body tensed as they flew over Sarm's medical compound. He found no indication of the alien's presence. There were three buildings, but no activity. Mitch tried to keep calm, telling himself that Sarm could still be there.

Deborah pursed her lips. "What do you want to do?"

"Let's land and cross our fingers."

Mitch lowered the vessel. After leaving the cave, he had continually checked the viewfinder and three-dimensional panoramic screen looking for that damn salenko or enemy aircraft.

He landed the vessel, shut down the controls and led Merelda and Deborah out of the hatch.

"Should we make our presence known?" Merelda asked.

Mitch shook his head. In case Sarm had left, he didn't want to alert anyone else of their presence.

They turned the corner, and footsteps came in their direction. Merelda drew a gun and stepped forward, while Mitch and Deborah waited behind her. A limb as green as grass emerged.

Sarm shrieked when he stepped in front of Merelda. Mitch brought her gun hand down as Sarm tripped over his own legs and stumbled to the ground.

Mitch scurried past Merelda to held Sarm. He could tell the alien had been horribly frightened.

Sarm's narrow mouth opened wide. "Mitch Grace, the heavens come down, it is you. I never expected to see you again. It is a glorious day."

Mitch grinned, pulled the alien to his full eight feet of height, and hugged Sarm. "It's good to see you. I wish it were under better circumstances, but damn, it's good to see you."

Sarm rubbed his thin fingers together. "Your situation is not well."

"We're ten miles from well." He introduced Sarm to Merelda and Deborah.

Sarm's face lit up. "You are the Deborah who Mitch spoke of?"

Deborah nodded.

"It is a pleasure to have you met." Sarm extended his hand — a gesture Mitch had taught him — and Deborah shook it. "He spoke of you in grand terms. We thought that you were dead"

Deborah smiled. "I'm alive and I'm glad to finally meet you. You're living proof that not all aliens are bad, although I can't say I'm fond of the rest of your kind."

Mitch glanced at Merelda. If she took offense, she didn't show it.

Sarm scratched the back of his head. "I am understanding your feelings. It is not easy to have one's planet occupied. So, Mitch, what causes you to visit me after all this elapsed time?"

With all of the time apart, apparently Sarm was adopting his old speech patterns. Mitch took a deep breath. "Where do I start?"

Sarm gestured for the others to follow him inside. "Perhaps you can start with the time prior to your emergence as The Gladiator."

Mitch's eyes went wide. "You knew about that?"

"I followed you from afar. I could never bring myself to be witness your combative experiences. I had too much concern that a bad outcome would befall you. However, I made sure to view the telecasts only after learning that you emerged victorious. I abhor violence, but I had to see it. On more than one occasion I contemplated visiting you after your battle to attend to your wounds, but I knew you would be well attended."

Mitch crossed his arms. "Well, let me fill you in on what happened after I left this lap of luxury."

Sarm said nothing as Mitch told his tale. Meanwhile, Merelda moved the vessel inside the complex to conceal it.

Sarm gasped when Mitch told him they had been striking at alien targets, which led to his capture and subsequent career as The Gladiator. He had what looked like a frown. "I had heard of these attacks, but had no knowledge of your involvement. Do you not realize that such actions are futile? I have sympathy for your people, but humans lack the technological capacity to succeed in these endeavors."

Mitch shrugged, not wanting to justify his actions.

"Mitch Grace, I wish you would try to exist under the radar, as your humans would say."

Deborah smiled. "That's stay under the radar. I realize you're concerned, but it's worth the risk. It beats living in fear of being abducted as a slave. As long as that threat exists, we have to fight."

"Well, anyway, I guess I don't have to tell you about my gladiator days, since you seemed to have kept track of me. I'm a bit surprised you knew I was fighting. You don't strike me as a follower of the Games."

"I am not. I discovered your participation in an accidental manner. From that point forward, I was terrified every time you entered the arena to do battle. You proved to be most resourceful."

Mitch told Sarm about what he had done since gaining his freedom from Ruje.

Sarm lifted his arms, making him look like an oversized praying mantis. "Why would you resume the same activities that got you in trouble?" He turned to Merelda. "You should have advised him against this course."

Merelda crossed her arms. Her gestures and mannerisms were more human than Sarm's. "I am incapable of convincing him of anything. You spent time with him. You should know this."

Sarm tilted his head. "Most true."

Mitch rolled his eyes. "We're getting off track. We had a few big strikes and were ready for our biggest one yet."

"The precious element symposium?" Sarm asked.

Mitch nodded. No wonder the Minister of Science knew what they had planned. If Sarm could figure it out, then it must have been an obvious target. "The Minister sniffed out our plans. We dispatched a few fighter crafts he sent after us, but then he sent a salenko."

Sarm wiggled his long fingers. "And you escaped?"

"Barely. We're in deep shit. The Minister won't stop 'til I'm dead.

Sarm covered his eyes with his palms. "Oh, Mitch Grace, you are like a wayward child always finding trouble. Why have you engaged in a battle you cannot win?"

"We've already gone over that. Now we have to figure a way to make it out alive."

"You must evacuate this planet," Sarm said. "What you must have understanding of is that Santanovia, your former Earth, is the private kingdom of the Minister of Science. He will resort to any act of treachery to protect what he created."

"You are wasting your time," Merelda said. "He will not leave."

Mitch gritted his teeth. "It's not an option. I haven't accomplished all this and sacrificed so much just to give up. I'm going to see this through. If you don't want to help, I understand."

Sarm's mouth went wide. "Mitch, you know I will do everything in my capacity to assist you regardless of the risk."

Mitch sighed. "I'm sorry. I know. That's why I came here."

Sarm gazed at the gray afternoon through the lone window in his lab room. "We will discover a plan. I don't know what it is, but we have great intelligence among us. Why did your people ever let the Minister of Science onto this planet? That was your gravest mistake. It ensured the enslavement and mass death of your people."

Chills ran down Mitch's spine. He didn't know why, but this seemed like a huge revelation. "Hold up, Sarm. What are you talking about?"

"The worst thing your species could have done was to invite him onto the planet. That spelled your doom."

Mitch's face tightened. "That never happened. I was the only one who spoke to the Minister on the first day of the invasion."

Deborah grabbed Mitch's arm. "By the time I got outside, it was complete chaos, and the invasion had started."

Mitch clenched his fists. "I was the only person who spoke to the Minister of Science. I was the senior officer on the base. We had a brief conversation, and I distinctly remember him asking me to open the cage he was enclosed in so that we could talk further. I thought it a bizarre request, because if he had the capability to travel through space, then why couldn't he get out of a simple cage? So, I said no."

Merelda's skin turned off-white. He had never seen that particular shade before. "You didn't give him an invitation to enter the planet."

Mitch shook his head. "Absolutely not."

Sarm's body shook. "That scoundrel. He is in violation of intergalactic law. Once he has permission to enter an uncharted planet that contains intelligent life such as this one, then there is nothing to stop him from controlling it, but an official invitation must be made and recorded."

"It makes sense," Merelda said. "He made a swift and horrific strike, disabling all forms of government within days. Who would be able to tell that an official invitation had never been made? He probably falsified it."

Mitch narrowed his eyes. "Except I'm still alive. The one loose end he didn't tie up."

Merelda slammed her fist onto the shiny blue table. "If Zolmethier knew about this, he would place the Minister under arrest. He would never tolerate that predatory behavior."

Deborah's brow furrowed. "Who's Zolmethier?"

"The Emperor of the Twelve Circles. What is he, the president of the universe or something like that?" Mitch asked.

Merelda nodded.

"He was in attendance when I defeated Salandar to gain my freedom."

Deborah threw her hands in the air. "But there's no way we could prove the Minister gained entrance illegally."

Sarm picked up an alien plant and stared at it. "I have never told you this, Mitch, but I come from a wealthy and influential family. My father could gain an audience with Zolmethier. Perhaps we could plead your case."

"Even if we did, it would still be my word against the Minister's, and I'm sure he has more clout than I have. Unless…I have an idea that just might work."

Mitch went over his plan in great detail. When he was done, they all went to Merelda's vessel.

As they were exiting the laboratory, Deborah touched Sarm's hand. "I just wanted to thank you for keeping Mitch alive. I owe you so much. I could never begin to repay you."

Sarm said something to Deborah in reply, but Mitch tuned it out. He had one thought in his mind, and that was to get his planet back. For the first time, he thought he had a legitimate chance of pulling it off.

## Chapter XXXV

"Move, prisoner," Ruje shouted.

Mitch looked down as he trudged toward the massive skyscraper. He wore a slave collar around his neck. Once more, he was Ruje's prisoner.

Aliens gaped as Ruje led him up the smooth surface of the path leading to the building. Instead of concrete that humans typically used, the walkway's surface was made of some shiny, ruby-red acrylic material.

Earlier, Ruje had contacted the Minister of Science to inform him that he had once more captured the human who had caused so much consternation in Santanovia. When Mitch's people had started on their path of destruction after his release, the Minister had offered Ruje a sizeable bounty for Mitch's capture. Until now, Ruje had refused these overtures because he had been busy promoting the Games, having gained prestige due to Mitch's immense popularity as The Gladiator.

Ruje shouted something at aliens nearby, causing them to scatter. One of Ruje's faces had a mean scowl; the other remained fixed on his prisoner.

They stepped onto an open transpod. Within seconds a clear casing enclosed them. Ruje entered coordinates on the transpod, and it gave a slight purr before lifting off the ground and shooting toward the skyscraper. Inside, the Minister awaited their arrival.

Mitch thought the Minister would have made a public spectacle of his arrest, so all could see he was truly in control of

Santanovia. Making this private could only mean one thing — he was going to kill Mitch.

"Are you prepared for this, prisoner?" Ruje asked.

Mitch nodded.

"The Minister will be most pleased by your capture."

"I'm sure he will," Mitch said.

"I imagine the bounty will be quite substantial."

"It won't be nearly as much as the money I made for you."

Ruje's left face smiled. "How true. I have expanded my promotion of the Games in several different solar systems as a result of this new income."

He drove the transpod into a cylindrical hatch. The hatch shot upward. Mitch had no idea how far they ascended, but it seemed like the ride would never end. The Minister of Science had to be in the penthouse suite.

They did not speak on the ride. There was nothing left to say.

Mitch's heartbeat accelerated as they exited the shoot. This was the end of the line.

The transpod traveled through a winding corridor and made a sudden stop in front of the Minister's suite. He felt instant revulsion when he laid eyes on the short alien. His face was dark and furry, reminiscent of a raccoon. He had massive claws and spiked forearms. Physically, he didn't look impressive, but Mitch knew not to underestimate him.

The Minister of Science smiled, showing two rows of sharp teeth. He wiggled his fingers and shot forward. For a moment, Mitch thought the Minister was going to attack him, but he stopped short. "If it isn't the Gladiator. Mitch Grace, you have been a nuisance. I underestimated you. I never thought a species so worthless could produce someone who could create such trouble. Had I known, I never would have let you live on the first day we met."

Mitch's eyes narrowed. "So, you remembered me?"

The Minister stepped forward. "You were wary, with good reason."

He wanted to keep the Minister talking. "Do you know what happened to me during the attack?"

The Minister waved his hand. "Why would I care about one worthless human?"

"If I'm worthless, then why did you go through so much trouble to capture me?"

"I underestimated you. You turned out to be a worthy adversary, but I dispose of my adversaries."

Mitch nodded. "So, you're going kill me?"

The Minister smiled. "How very perceptive."

Ruje stepped forward. "What you do with the prisoner is not of my concern. I only care that you give to me what I have earned."

"I will transfer the amount we agreed upon. You have earned your fee."

"Thank you."

Sweat dripped down Mitch's brow. He tried to calm himself. He had been in pressure situations before, but none like this. The fate of his entire planet and the human race depended on what would happen in the next few minutes. He wouldn't let the Minister win. All of his years of training, both as a SEAL and as The Gladiator would have to serve him now. Losing was not an option.

Mitch lunged at Ruje, knocking over the large alien. He then elbowed him to the back of the head. He grabbed Ruje's blaster and turned in time to receive a backhand smash from the Minister. He wobbled and dropped the blaster. The blow was harder than he expected from such a small creature.

Mitch put up his hands to fend off another attack. To his left, Ruje lay motionless.

The Minister growled. "You will die. I should have killed you on the day you defeated Salandar. I only spared you because of the large audience present. You may be the great Gladiator, but I can crush you."

"Is that right?" Mitch would have thought that claim nonsense a few minutes ago, but after feeling the force of that backhand smash, he wasn't so sure. "Go ahead and try."

The Minister of Science shot past him like a blur. Mitch turned, but not fast enough. The Minister slashed him, his razor claws tearing into his arm. Mitch winced, then threw a punch that didn't connect as the Minister backed away.

He needed a weapon if he was going to beat this thing, so he grabbed a metal cylinder on a table. He threw it, but the Minister flew away.

"Is that the best you can do? I thought the human who defeated Salandar could devise something more creative."

The Minister flew at Mitch. He tried to swat the alien, but the Minister raked his face. Blood dripped into Mitch's eyes, and for a moment he couldn't see. He wiped the blood with his arm and searched for the Minister, who had raced across the room.

Blood streamed down his nose. He couldn't stop it from flowing. "Isn't it enough that you destroyed my people? Can't you leave me the hell alone?"

The Minister's posture relaxed. "You are the one who chose to make cowardly attacks."

Mitch glared at the alien. "Cowardly? You took over a planet whose people had no way of defending themselves."

Like a lightning bolt, the Minister shot at him. Mitch prepared himself to defend another attack from his razor-sharp claws, but at the last moment, the alien dived at his abdomen. He sunk his claws into Mitch's thighs and then bit his belly. Mitch clubbed the back of his head until the Minister backed off.

Mitch clutched his abdomen in agony. He looked down. Blood was everywhere. He had a terrible feeling that his entrails would spill out, but everything seemed to be intact. He felt weak and woozy. There was no way he could withstand much more.

"You son of a bitch," Mitch screamed. "Why did you come here? Nobody invited you. You should have stayed in that cage."

Mitch doubled over in agony. He was going to die. His luck had finally run out. He looked up to find the Minister hovering nearby.

"As your final lesson in life, learn this, Mitch Grace. Your species is inferior and unfit to survive. I did not need an invitation to come to this planet, just like I do not require one to kill you now."

Mitch's body trembled. He wanted to defend himself, but he was too weak.

The Minister of Science swooped down on him. Just a few feet away, Ruje sprung to his feet with surprising agility, and gave a backhanded smash that sent the alien reeling. He crashed hard against the wall, causing the entire room to shake. Ruje picked up his blaster and aimed it at the Minister. "Do not move, or I will shoot you." He then spoke something incomprehensible into his transmitter on his wrist.

Mitch grabbed a table and pulled himself up. Despite the pain, he grinned at the stunned disbelief on the Minister's face.

"What is the meaning of this?" the Minster asked.

Before anyone could answer, an entourage entered the alien's suite. Most of them were beings wearing shiny red, suits that gleamed and looked metallic. Mitch figured that they served as some type of armor. The beings inside of the suits all wore dark shields covering their faces. Their suits made them look like a cross between ninjas and Power Rangers. It was impossible to tell which species they belonged to but based on the way they walked and their upright stature, they were humanoid in nature.

In the middle of this group was Zolmethier, the Grand Emperor of the Twelve Circles. He wore a blue robe with various insignias. A little over seven feet in height, he was mostly bald with only patches of hair on the side of his head. His face resembled that of an eagle including a sharp, beak-like nose. His eyes were narrow and had yellow pupils. His exposed legs were thickly muscled.

"The meaning of this is plainly evident. You are knowingly in violation of the Olund Pact." Zolmethier glared at the Minister with open contempt. "How could you do this? Someone in your position should have a greater sense of justice. This is unforgivable."

The Minister's eyes shifted frantically around the room. "I can explain."

"And you will have your opportunity to do so in front of the intergalactic tribunal." Zolmethier turned to the massive contingent of guards he had brought with him. "Place him under arrest."

Before the Minister had a chance to escape, the guards closed in on him. One zapped him with an electric shocker, and another slapped him with a collar similar to the defective one Mitch wore.

Deborah, Sarm and Merelda fought through the crowd. Deborah rushed over and hugged Mitch. "Holy shit. You're bleeding all over the place. We need help."

Eyes turned from the Minister of Science to Mitch. He felt like hell. He could only imagine what he looked like.

In an unusual display of aggression, Sarm pushed his way to the front. His long fingers trembled. "Your wounds are most grave. I must attend to them immediately."

Merelda's skin had turned green as she stared at Sarm. There was some unspoken communication between them. "There is an infirmary on the eleventh floor. We must transport him there now."

*Definitely the right course of action. Just not quite yet.* Mitch edged toward the Minister. "Give me a sec. Please help me."

Carl Alves

Deborah supported one shoulder and Merelda took the other as they swerved through the guards.

"What are you doing, Mitch?" Deborah asked.

"You need healing," Sarm said.

Mitch grunted. "I know. Just one thing first."

The remaining guards parted, giving him a clear path to the Minister.

"What do you want?" the Minister screeched.

"Looks like I got the better of you." Mitch clutched his wounded abdomen. "Guess we're not so inferior after all." Mitch badly wanted to get in one last punch at the Minister, but instead he closed his eyes as darkness overcame him.

## Chapter XXXVI

Mitch took a deep breath and propped himself up on the cot. He was in the room Sarm had previously used to bring him back to health. Fortunately, Sarm had been able to treat him immediately following the attack by the Minister of Science. Still sore as hell, he was on the mend.

Mitch's mood brightened when Deborah walked into the room. After the hell they had been through, he would never take her presence for granted and would treasure every moment they spent together.

"You feeling up to this?" Deborah asked.

Mitch tried to get to his feet and then sat back down, groaning from the exertion. He could only walk gingerly, but Zolmethier, the Grand Emperor of the Twelve Circles, had requested his presence.

Mitch grimaced. "I wouldn't want to keep the big guy waiting."

She touched his face. "I'm sure he'd understand."

Mitch waved his hand. "Are you kidding? I've been looking forward to this for ten friggin' years. Well, I was in a coma for half that time, but that's beside the point."

"It could wait another day."

Mitch shook his head. "Not another day. Not another minute."

"I'll be by your side the whole time."

Sarm peeked his head into the room. "As will I."

"Don't you know it's rude to listen to other people's conversation?" Mitch asked.

Sarm looked down. "My apologies. I have greater hearing acuity than humans."

"I'm just joking, Sarm."

Sarm's face lightened. "Oh."

Mitch took a long breath. "All right, guys, help me up."

Deborah grabbed one arm and Sarm the other. Together, they lifted him.

Deborah frowned. "You have to go easy. Can you walk on your own?"

"Sure." Mitch took one step and nearly collapsed.

"I don't think so." Deborah put his arm over her shoulder.

Sarm supported Mitch on the other side, and they exited the alien's research complex to the vessel they had used in their getaway.

Merelda and Ruje stood outside. Her skin turned dark blue, the color that indicated she was worried. "You do not look well, Mitch."

"Thanks for the compliment."

Merelda's face tightened. "That is not what I mean. You need to heal."

Mitch shrugged. "There will be time enough for that later. I took worse beatings in the arena."

Ruje's left face laughed, while his right head bobbed up and down. "You speak the truth. Salandar crushed you."

Mitch braced himself as Ruje was about to pat him on the back, but the alien held back at the last moment.

"Is everything set?" Mitch asked.

Ruje nodded his left head. "Zolmethier eagerly awaits your arrival."

"Good. Let's get this show on the road."

The alien contingent did not react to his words. Then Deborah said, "He means we should leave now."

They boarded the vessel. Mitch cringed when Merelda took the pilot position.

Sarm put his green hand on hers. "Perhaps I can navigate today. If you would like to have the co-pilot seat, I can show you a few tricks."

Merelda smiled. "I would enjoy that."

Mitch breathed easier. In his condition, he wanted no part of her reckless flying.

Ruje sat next to Mitch. His face was dark and his tone solemn. "I would like to ensure an understanding between us that we are now even as you humans would say."

Mitch nodded. "Even Steven."

Ruje's left forehead furrowed.

"It's an expression. You owe me nothing. In fact, I want to thank you for taking that risk. I didn't think you would go for it. There was no financial incentive for you."

Ruje beamed. "I have always taken pride in my altruistic ways."

Mitch stopped himself from laughing. He didn't realize Ruje was a comedian.

Ruje continued, "You have made a great deal of wealth for me. I was quite prosperous before I came to this planet, but since you started fighting for me as The Gladiator, my fortune has tripled. I owed you, so when you proposed your plan, it was an easy decision. And we are friends. I am glad to help out a friend."

Mitch narrowed his eyes. "I wouldn't call us friends."

Undaunted, Ruje shook both of his heads. "You are mistaken. You are my human friend, Mitch Grace."

Ruje was a master manipulator. He doubted the alien had any true friends, only people that served his nefarious purposes. Perhaps in Ruje's twisted mind, their relationship constituted friendship. If pressed, Mitch would have to grudgingly admit that he liked his former slave master.

Mitch extended his hand, and the alien shook it. "Thank you, Ruje."

A few minutes later, Sarm said, "Prepare to land."

After they exited, Mitch pulled Merelda aside. "So, Ruje told me you might be working for him again."

Merelda smiled. "He made me a substantial offer to be the trainer of his fighters for the Games, but I rather enjoy this planet, and there is much work to be done in rebuilding. I can be of assistance in that area."

"I would love to have you stay. I wouldn't have survived without you."

They walked to a promenade with a large contingent of intergalactic press, who carried recording devices that looked nothing like human cameras. This was a big news event across the universe.

Zolmethier emerged from behind a throng of guards. He had requested to speak to him prior to the news conference. As Mitch and his party approached, the guards parted.

Zolmethier's pale eyes sunk toward his long chin. This time, he no longer wore a long robe. Instead, he wore what looked like a chest and shoulder harness that was sharp and metallic. Spikes jutted out from either side near the top of the harness. Now that he wasn't covered with robes, Mitch could see that he had a massive upper body that complemented his thick legs.

He bowed. "Mitch Grace, it is with great pleasure that I meet you again. How are you recovering from your injuries?"

"I'm getting better. I'll be back to my old self in no time."

"I am glad to hear." Zolmethier gave a long pause. "On behalf of the Twelve Circles ruling council, I would like to present to you an apology for the devastation incurred upon your planet and the injustices committed to your people. What occurred was unfortunate, and I have responsibility for it."

Mitch nodded. He didn't want to appear ungracious, but he was still bitter.

"I would like you to know that most species within the galaxy are law-abiding and peaceful."

"I can't say I have a high opinion of them at this point," Mitch said.

"I understand. However, I would like to convey an offer for Santanovia, or as you call it your planet Earth, to become part of the intergalactic community and have representation on the ruling council. Since your planet has no formal leadership, I would like to designate you as Earth's representative for what you have done in gaining your people's freedom."

Mitch folded his arms. Sarm had tipped him off that this was coming. After speaking with Deborah at length, they had come to a decision. "I choose to close off my planet to foreign species coming and going as they please."

"Please consider the offer. We will provide restitution in order to rebuild your planet."

"I appreciate your offer. That's certainly something that we can use, but I wasn't finished. I would like to open Earth or Santanovia as you call it, to foreign species who have had their home planet taken over just as mine was. I would like this to be a refuge for those people. We will set up a system where they can petition to be citizens of Santanovia and give them sanctuary. I would like this planet be a symbol where people of different species can live together in peace and unity."

Zolmethier nodded. "A wise decision."

"As for your offer to become part of the intergalactic community and take part in the ruling council as my planet's representative, I'm going to have to decline. I have too much work to do in rebuilding this planet. But I would like to offer somebody to take my place." Mitch nodded toward Deborah.

Deborah extended her hand. "I accept your offer to be on your council."

Mitch turned toward his alien friends. "And as a place of sanctuary and intergalactic peace, I would like to offer citizenship to the first non-native species — my friends Sarm and Merelda."

Sarm extended his long green fingers and touched Mitch's shoulders. "I still have much research to perform. I can be busy for years here. It will be very exciting."

Zolmethier wore no expression. "That is your decision?"

Mitch nodded.

"Then I will abide by it. Those who do not comply will face sanctions and imprisonment. I will order them to leave immediately."

"Thank you," Mitch said.

"I look forward to seeing what you can do with your planet Santanovia. It is in good hands, Mitch Grace." Zolmethier left to conduct his news conference.

Deborah held his hand. "I think Zolmethier really wanted you to be part of the ruling council."

Mitch shrugged. "I'm sure this whole intergalactic politics thing is interesting and all, but we're going to have our hands full putting the pieces back together. You'll be a much better representative than I can ever be."

Deborah squeezed his hand. "You know what this means. We fought so hard to be together, and now we're going to be apart again."

Mitch kissed her softly. "Not all the time."

Mitch looked at the large alien contingency, hoping it would be the last time he saw all these different life forms.

### Epilogue – three months later

Mitch opened his eyes after Deborah had knocked on the door. Still groggy from the couple hours of sleep he had since returning from Central Africa, Mitch tried to open his eyes, but they weren't cooperating.

Deborah sat on his bed. "They've arrived."

Mitch pulled himself up on his bed. He would kill for a couple of extra hours of sleep, but he would make an exception for his visitors. "Let me put on some pants. I'll be there in a minute."

After Deborah left the room, he struggled to get himself out of bed. He thought he had been busy while leading the revolution against the alien occupiers of the planet, but that was nothing compared to his new role. He was constantly on the move, traveling from one corner of the globe to another, visiting newly forming governments, or consulting on rebuilding infrastructure or law enforcement. His presence was in high demand, and he was stretching himself thin.

In the past three months, he had visited every continent except Antarctica. Everywhere he went, people hailed him as a conquering hero. He had been to more parades and receptions than he cared to remember, but if it meant something to the people, then he was willing to do it. He was certain it was more about what he represented rather than him as a person, so he did his best not to let the adulation get to his head.

Meanwhile, Deborah spent much of her time off-planet. She had been to three different solar systems just in the past month. They tried to coordinate their trips so that they would return home roughly around the same time. Their time together was fleeting and precious.

After getting dressed, he splashed cold water on his face. The bright morning sunlight assaulted his eyes. It was hard keeping track of the days and weeks. They all blended together.

He and Deborah drove a couple of miles to the landing pad. He had been so tired that he had not even heard the sleek black aircraft land.

Deborah glanced at him from the driver's side of the car, her face filled with worry. "You need to slow down. You're running yourself ragged."

Mitch closed his eyes. "I know. I'd like to, but these infant governments keep requesting my presence."

"Mitch, nobody elected you as the world's ambassador. It's not your job."

"I know. It's just that I want things to be different this go around. We have been given an opportunity for a fresh start, and I don't want us as a people to make the same mistakes we did before. I'll be damned if after all we went through that people are going to have the same disputes about religion and money and land and politics. There's no good reason why people should be fighting against each other, so if my presence can mediate disputes or unite people, then that's a good thing."

Deborah sighed in frustration. This wasn't the first time they were having this conversation. Of course, she hardly had room to speak since she was planet hopping half the time. Somehow, she seemed to manage far better than he did.

When Deborah stopped the car, Mitch smiled at the sight of the two aliens. He didn't get to see Merelda and Sarm as much as he would like, and he treasured any time he had together with them.

He paused at the sight of the two aliens in a passionate embrace.

When Mitch exited the car, they broke the embrace. He gave Sarm a bear hug and lifted the green alien off his feet, then planted a kiss on Merelda's cheek.

"Look who it is. My two favorite aliens. So how does it feel to be the first non-native Earth dwellers to be permanent residents on the planet?"

Sarm stood tall and practically radiated. "I feel like one of your Hollywood celebrities of yesteryear, at least as far as I have read on the subject. Whenever I venture out among the people, they all would like to converse with me and capture my likeness in a photograph."

"Who knew you would be a big star. So how is the lab going?"

"Very well. I have placed invitations to physicians in the Southern California area. I would like to teach some of your human healers my techniques. I have also invited several physicians from other planets to apply to the sanctuary program to become citizens of Santanovia. As of today, I only have three human pupils, but once the word has spread among the populace, I am sure that number will grow."

Mitch patted him on the back. "That's a great initiative. I think there's a lot you can teach them."

Deborah turned to Merelda. "I take it you're keeping busy."

Mitch had appointed Merelda the official liaison on the planet with all aliens who wished to trade with the people of

Earth. Mostly Mitch was interested in raw materials they would need to rebuild. In addition, he had tasked Merelda with obtaining alternate fuel technology that would virtually eliminate their need for fossil fuels.

"Right now, I am sourcing the marconium you had requested for your fuel cells. I am expecting to have several bids in the next few days. In addition, I recently met several individuals who would like to start a provisional government for new California, however I have rejected their efforts. Nothing more than gangsters, this group."

Mitch narrowed his eyes as he regarded the aliens. "Are you two...you know a couple?"

Sarm's green face blushed, turning a deep shade of blue.

Merelda put her arm around Sarm's waist. "Indeed we are. It can be awfully lonely being foreigners on this planet."

Mitch bit back his response. Since when had Merelda ever been lonely? He supposed that many of her lovers were now off-planet, so she could no longer see them. Slowly and gradually, more aliens were becoming residents of Earth. He smiled. "Well, I'm really happy for you. And I'm glad you're giving this female companionship thing a try, Sarm. It will suit you well."

Merelda gasped as she stared at Deborah. "You are with child."

Deborah's face turned white. "How could you know? We just found out a couple weeks ago. We still haven't told anyone."

"I apologize for startling you," Merelda said. "The females of my species have an intuition about this sort of thing. Congratulations. Congratulations to you both."

Sarm's face lit up like a Christmas tree. "This is such wonderful news. How joyous. I have never delivered a human baby before. You must let me deliver the child. I will read all about it and study the latest techniques."

Mitch glanced at Deborah, who had a startled look on her face. He put his hand on Sarm's arm. "We'll talk about that later. There's still a long ways to go before that."

Sarm nodded rapidly. "Ah yes, the forty-week gestational period. I understand fully."

Mitch looked out and found children at play, and people no longer in hiding. The work would be hard, the hours would be long, and there would be heartache along the way, but never again would they be slaves. Mother Earth was their planet, and nobody could take it away from them.

"Stuck is such a harsh word."

"It's not such a bad deal, you know. After years of being on my own, I have become quite the cook, and I keep my house nice and tidy."

"Go on," Kendra said.

Ron gave a sheepish grin. "And I have been told by others that I'm skilled in certain other areas as well."

"Now you have me intrigued, Detective."

Ron pulled her closer to him.

Kendra looked up at him. "Are we really going to be okay?"

Ron nodded. "You and Jared are both strong. And I'm a royal pain in the ass who is willing to stick by you."

As much as she and Jared needed him in their lives, Ron needed them as well. His partner's death had hit him hard. He tried not to show weakness and vulnerability, but she saw first-hand how broken up he was. She leaned her head in toward him and watched her son play.

Thank you for taking the time to read my novel, *Reconquest Mother Earth*. I hope you enjoyed it. As an indie author, book reviews are vital. I would sincerely appreciate it if you could take a few minutes to post a review of this novel on Amazon and/or Goodreads.

# Beyond the Shadow

## By Carl Alves

*Beyond the Shadow* is a terrifying journey into a world where reality and what lay beyond is blurred.

All around ten-year-old Jared, people are dying at the hands of a killer nobody can see. Only he is spared. No matter where he goes, people are massacred. Nobody is safe. There is no sanctuary. As the lines between our world and those beyond converge, Jared learns more about the father he has never known, who died before he was born. Jared's mom and Detective Chaney will do anything to protect him and stop the killer, but Jared knows that he is the only one that could stop this spectral murderer. Mirrors lead from our world to the next and are the key to ending this madness. But can anyone stop a psychotic fiend who doesn't obey the rules of the natural world?

## The Invocation
### By Carl Alves

*The Invocation* is a thrilling combination of Stranger Things and The Exorcist.

When Kenna Trigg plays with an Ouija board, little does she know that she is about to unleash a malevolent spirit upon the world, leaving her and her older brother, Jake, to stop the spirit as it leaves a trail of dead bodies in its wake.

In The Invocation, a supernatural thriller, Kenna Trigg and three of her friends from the fourth grade manage to befriend a spirit named Mia, who died in her late teens in a drowning accident, using of an Ouija board. Cotter, a malevolent spirit who had been a con-man and criminal in life, tricks Kenna and her friends into releasing him into our world by posing as Mia. Cotter has the ability to take control and possess people he comes across. With this new power, he begins a vicious crime spree. Kenna turns to her older brother, Jake, a professional mixed-martial artist who has recently been released from prison. Now, Kenna and Jake must stop Cotter from unleashing havoc in our world.

# Battle of the Soul

## By Carl Alves

Andy Lorenzo has no family, few friends, poor social skills, and drinks and gambles far too much. But in a time when demons are becoming increasingly more brazen and powerful, he has one skill that makes demons cower in fear from him—he is the greatest exorcist the world has ever known.

In *Battle of the Soul*, a supernatural thriller that is a combination of Constantin and The Exorcist, since graduating high school Andy has left a long trail of demons in his wake while priests are dying while performing traditional rites of exorcism. Andy is the Church and society's ultimate weapon in combating this growing epidemic. He needs no bibles, prayers, or rituals. Andy is capable of going inside the person's soul where he engages in hand-to-hand combat using his superhuman abilities that only reside when he is in a person's soul. When eight-year-old Kate becomes possessed, Andy finds an elaborate trap waiting for him. He will do whatever it takes to win the most important fight of his life—the battle for Kate's soul.

"Ready for a lighthearted Battle of the Soul? Andy Lorenzo's got the requisite exorcism skills, but he's no single-minded zealot nor cynical bleak arts practitioner. He gets the biz done with a deft touch and a wink and a nod to family values. It's not John Constantine here but try Cary Grant in Monkey Business. Battle of the Soul is a fine, fun supernatural read!—

Mort Castle, Bram Stoker Award Winning Author of The
Strangers

## About the Author

Carl is the author of seven published novels which span the horror, fantasy, and science fiction genres in no particular order. He lives in Central Pennsylvania with his wife and the two most awesome boys you have ever met. When not feverishly conjuring stories about monsters, aliens, and things that go bump in the night, he works as a quality manager for a medical device company. Find out more about him by visiting his website at www.carlalves.com.

Printed in Great Britain
by Amazon

86564489R00203